W9-BYU-161

HACKETTSTOWN FREE PUBLIC LIBRARY
110 CHURCH STREET
HACKETTSTOWN, NJ 07840

Tell the world what you think of this book		
Very Good	**Good**	**Forget It**

Also by Justin Hill

A Bend in the Yellow River
Ciao Asmara
The Drink and Dream Teahouse
Passing Under Heaven
Shieldwall

CROUCHING TIGER, HIDDEN DRAGON
SWORD OF DESTINY

Justin Hill

A NOVELIZATION OF THE SCREENPLAY BY JOHN FUSCO
BASED ON THE WRITINGS OF WANG DULU

WEINSTEIN
BOOKS

Copyright screenplay and underlying works:
© Hong Wang, Qin Wang and The Weinstein Company LLC 2015
Copyright novelization: © Little, Brown Book Group 2015

All rights reserved.
No part of this book may be used or reproduced in any manner whatsoever
without the written permission of the Publisher. For information address
Weinstein Books, 250 West 57th Street, 15th Floor, New York, NY 10107.

Printed in the United States of America.

US editorial production by *Marra*thon Production Services. www.marrathon.net
US book composition by Jane Raese

Cataloging-in-Publication Data for this book is available from the Library of Congress.

ISBN 978-1-60286-287-6 (print)
ISBN 978-1-60286-288-3 (e-book)

Published by Weinstein Books
A member of the Perseus Books Group
www.weinsteinbooks.com

Weinstein Books are available at special discounts for bulk purchases in the U.S.
by corporations, institutions and other organizations. For more information,
please contact the Special Markets Department at the Perseus Books Group,
2300 Chestnut Street, Suite 200, Philadelphia, PA 19103, call (800) 810-4145, ext. 5000,
or e-mail special.markets@perseusbooks.com.

FIRST U.S. EDITION

10 9 8 7 6 5 4 3 2 1

CROUCHING TIGER, HIDDEN DRAGON

SWORD OF DESTINY

PROLOGUE

Shulien stopped as she reached the top of the path, and looked down the mountain gorge. She had come to the hermitage on a day just like this, seventeen years before, heavy with grief.

She had been going in the other direction then. As she stood for a moment she thought she could see her younger self, dressed in a simple black padded jacket with a conical straw hat, plodding up the path, stick in hand, searching ever higher into the narrowing way.

She had come in winter, in the twelfth moon of the year. Snow was falling then too. Scarves of mist trailed from crag to crag. The air was still except for the sloppy gurgling of stream water as it tumbled over sharp rocks, frosted the leaning rushes in heavy coats of white ice, eddied in fat mountain pools, and then tumbled downhill again.

All she could hear was water and the light intake and exhalation of her own breath, just cold enough to catch at the back of the throat. She had thought she would end her days a hermit, here in the mountains; practicing her arts, preserving her *qi*, sallying out, if necessary, to fight injustice. But fate had been kind to her and despite the lines that life had worn into her face, she was very much still lean and strong, and handsome too, with hardly a single gray hair. Seventeen years of solitude, martial practice, learning to slowly conquer her feelings. She laughed. It had proved an impossible task. Solitude was too empty; the dragon could not hide even here; emotions could not be conquered.

And now she was leaving. News was an arrow to those for whom it was destined, and despite the distance and the inconvenience word had come, even to Shulien, that in the far-off capital her patron, Duke Te—a nobleman who had used his position as a nephew of the Qing Emperor to protect both her father and herself from persecution by corrupt officials—had finally died.

剑

Shulien had learned the tidings of Duke Te's death the day before in the local town of Wenxia. She came here once a month—for rice, for news, and, after so many years of isolation, she had started to come for company.

"Asking for a husband?"

She was standing with three sticks of incense before the statue of Guanyu, the gentleman god, the warrior, whose sandalwood effigy stood erect, dignified, unbroken. Shulien turned to the priest. He looked younger than he was: a smooth, intelligent face, long walrus moustaches, a fuzzy beard from his chin, his black hair beginning to be shot through with gray.

"It is a bit late for that."

Her initial reaction was that he was a little too self-assured. His eyes brightened at her words. It was as if she were a challenge.

"Is it ever too late?"

"Yes," she said. "I had one love, but he is dead."

"Ah," the priest said, stepping closer. He lingered. His small eyes had a gentle look. They seemed to draw Shulien out. Her thoughts spilled almost like a confession.

"His name was Mubai. He was a wushu warrior as well. We loved each other from the moment we first met. But I had been betrothed to his best friend. When his best friend died, I hoped that our moment had come. But the Heavens are not so kind to us, are they? Mubai blamed himself for his friend's death. He said he could not marry me for shame. 'People might say I let him die to marry you.' I understood his fears. He always tried to do what was right. It is a narrow and rocky path. And so we lived out our days, pining. When he changed his mind, it was too late . . ."

Most people shied away from revelation, but the priest drew closer, his small eyes intent. "How did he die, if he was a great warrior?"

"Did you ever hear of Jade Fox?"

The priest nodded and shivered at the same time. Jade Fox was a woman whose name had once been used to scare children.

"She and her disciple stole a great treasure from Mubai. He fought her and beat her, but in the battle he was poisoned. I came, but too late. All I could do was soothe his last hours." She smiled at the priest, but in her eyes was a far-off light, as she gazed back into the past.

"He told me then that he had been mistaken. He wished he had married me."

"What was the treasure?"

"A sword," Shulien said, and her gaze moved to his face. "Named Green Destiny."

"It's real?"

"Green Destiny? Oh yes. It still exists, though it is hidden."

The priest looked around. "Here?"

Shulien laughed. "No. Far away." Safe in the capital, she thought. With Duke Te.

The priest was about to ask another question when a young girl with a large head came around the corner. Her face was

3

almost as wide as her hips. She was an odd-looking child, self-important, bossy. "Da," she said, picking her nose as she waited for her father's attention. "Da! Ma's constipated."

A look on the priest's face seemed to say, not again, but he tried to hide his reaction as he bowed to Shulien. "Excuse me."

In the market Shulien looked for familiar faces and went to buy from them. The old woman with the sickly grandchild; the blood sausage saleswoman with the mole on her cheek; the rice salesman with the consumptive wife who smiled from her seat and waved.

"I tell her to stay inside but she said you would come today. Would you mind?" he said.

"Not at all." Shulien put her hands onto the woman's head, closed her eyes, used her energy, her *qi*, to feel for the blockage that was causing the woman's sickness, and slowly forced a way through or around it. "Sorry," she said afterwards, as the woman looked up, her face bright with hope as much as improvement. "I am not a healer. There is only so much I can do."

But the rice trader poured an extra scoop of rice into the paper bundle, neatly folded the end closed, and placed it into the bottom of her sack with elaborate care.

"Thank you," he said.

She found the crowds and people and voices and demands overwhelming, and she was glad when at last she took a side road toward the north gate. The late winter sky was clear, a pale, scrubbed blue, the mild sun was bright enough to cast dark shadows, and in the spots where it seldom shone the snow lay in melted lumps and angles. Solid-wheeled carts lurched from rut to rut—she pushed ahead of them, and their peasant drivers, bulbous in their wadded cotton jackets. Old women with bound feet hobbled around the puddles, hair smoothed back and glossy as beetles. Along the side of the road two men in thick felt shoes were winnowing last autumn's grain in rhythmic showers of golden seed. The sunlight caught in the drifting chaff, and slowly faded, and three shaven-headed children watched with wonder, and one of them rubbed his nose with the heel of his palm.

When they saw her, the children fell silent, gazing from under their eyebrows, their noses running clear in the cold. Her passing always had this effect. She stopped and searched in the depths of her padded black cotton jacket and found a sesame cracker, stuck to the wrapper of rice paper, and gave it to one of the children.

"Share it," she said, and smiled softly.

The children stared in open-mouthed silence, then, once she had passed, she heard the usual *Ya! Ha!* noises as they held their hands out, kung-fu style, and leaped about like kicking monkeys, and one of them said, 'What did she give you?"

The walls of the gateway were smooth adobe, long used for pasting handwritten bulletins from local magistrates, officials and scholars. They had been recently scraped clean of the leprous tatters of old news, and now there were just three sheets papered there. Before it an old Muslim sat on a three-legged stool behind a stall selling spices. He had a narrow hawk-face, held a brass pipe between his front teeth, and puffed gently on the thick bung of rolled tobacco. One booted foot was drawn up onto his knee. His parrot looked out from its black wooden cage.

"News!" the parrot said. "News!"

Shulien paused to read the one titled *Capital News*. She scanned quickly through the lists of scandal and rumor—the Emperor's concubines appeared to have slept with half the Empire—but it was at the bottom, almost lost amongst the minor news, that she read that Duke Te had died.

"News!" the parrot squawked. "No news!"

Duke Te was one of the last emperor's sons, by a minor wife, but he was old and old men died. There was little scandal. Hundreds had read of the duke's death. A few score even knew who he was. But the news of his death meant nothing to the townsfolk of far Wenxia. Most folk had no idea that he was Master of the Iron Way, the world of wushu fighters who traveled and drank and battled injustice wherever they found it. They just knew him as a member of the Imperial Family.

The news hit Shulien hard, though. She gasped for breath, even though she rarely thought of the old friend, or even of the treasure that he had hidden. But now it all came back like a torrent of dirty flood water that overtops the dike, despite the efforts of the farmers.

Once the first defense breaks there is no stopping it. She had to leave. She had to go to Beijing. She felt a stab of panic. The Green Destiny: who was protecting it now?

剑

Shulien's hut was too small to contain her frustrations as she searched for what she needed for this journey. Felt shoes, a rush jacket, silver coin, her swords.

As she searched she felt Mubai in the room with her. His ghost haunted her, and all the incense she had burned did nothing to quieten it.

The duke is dead, she imagined him telling her. His ghost stood over her. He was quiet, calm, impassive. She imagined him standing in his scholar's gown. He liked the casual air it gave him, even when fighting for his life. He had been nonchalant about his safety; his brilliance and talent got him killed. She had loved and admired him as a man, but his ghost had a detached and patronizing air. *I gave him the Green Destiny. It must be taken and hidden.*

You know the power of the sword. You know the power it has . . . She ignored him and his voice became reprimanding. *Shulien, you must protect the sword. How could you let the duke die without securing the sword? Shulien, you must go and protect the sword.*

"Yes!" she said suddenly. Her voice was short and impatient. The ghost hushed.

She was angry at the voice for nagging her, and angry at it for going silent now. Ghosts! she thought. She imagined the ghost was still with her. "I know. I was there. Remember? You died defending that sword."

We had to. I had to.

Yes, she thought. Whoever held Green Destiny could hold the martial world in their fist.

剑

The sun was setting as Shulien turned to take a last look at her mountain retreat.

A month or two, she thought. No more. Like a crouching tiger, the saying went, or a hidden dragon: she would slip silently back into the world of men and hide her true nature, unless imperative demanded.

"When I return, spring will be here, the first leaves will be unfolding, the birds will return." She spoke aloud, as if her thatched hut was an old friend, who would look out each sunset, and hope for a glimpse of her.

"I have to go. I have to protect Green Destiny. It and I will retire here. Then the kingdom will be safe at last."

Shulien turned her back; the hut was silent. It had a bedraggled air. Melting snow had soaked the roof thatch. A gray droplet fell from the end of a stray straw. It sparkled as it fell and disappeared into the winter mud.

She held that image in her mind, and turned and walked back into the world. She could not know it then, but every reassurance she had given her hut was wrong. She would never return. The sword would never remain hidden. The world, despite all her efforts, could not be safe.

1

It was more than seventeen years earlier, when Mubai was still freshly dead, and a grief-stricken Shulien was starting her search for a mountain retreat, when far off, in the west of the Middle Kingdom, a single rider bent forward into a Mongolian blizzard.

Her name was Jiaolong. She was young and proud and haughty: a noble's daughter, running from an arranged marriage to an ugly old man, running from a doomed love affair with a handsome young fighter, unable to hide the baby in her womb. Disowned by her family, she struggled west along the Silk Road, but winter came on so quickly here, and it had caught her three days from shelter and closed its claws tightly around her.

She felt the child kicking within and wrapped a hand around her middle. The traders she had met that morning had promised her the next city was not more than a day's ride along the Silk Road. Her fear was that she had missed the road in this vast and trackless country, that each step was taking her away from anywhere. She would end up alone, frozen and dead.

Her desperation grew. For a week Jiaolong had trudged west from the last great city of Lanzhou. The frozen dusty flats of the Gobi Desert on her right, the wall of snow-headed mountains to her left. Ahead of her, somewhere, was solitude. Peace. Escape. Somewhere she could give birth without the authorities asking after her, where she could live the wushu life she wanted: however short, or brief, or dangerous. A life away from the tight confines of the boudoir, gossip, the small lives of aristocratic women.

Her horse could go no further. It fell forward onto its knees, and rolled slowly to the side. Jiaolong struggled free just in time. The snowstorm howled in her ears: a mocking sound. She pulled her pack from the saddle and bent forward into the storm. Her long black lashes were rimed white with snow. The blizzard wailed over her. She did not know how far she went. It could have been a mile, it might have been ten. But each step was slower than the last, and when she slipped and fell she did not get up, but lay there in the molded snow. Warmth slowly spread through her frozen hands and feet. That was the sign that death was taking her, extremities first. She had no more fight within her. Death would be peace, she thought. Death would be nothing. But just as her eyes flickered closed the baby inside her gave a tough, hard kick.

The thought came slow to her brain. *Just the kind of kick you'd expect from Dark Cloud's bastard!* An image of her lover's face came to her as she told him that she had to leave him. He was at heart a hopeless romantic, a steppe bandit who waylaid rich officials and gave their money to the poor peasants. He had ambushed her party as she traveled to the capital in a covered silk sedan. "You have caught more than you bargained for," she told him as she leaped out and drew her sword, and his followers had formed a circle around them as they had fought each other to exhaustion. At last he dropped his sword and said, "Kill me, for I cannot kill you, your beauty is as fine as the whitest jade."

She had smiled and strode across the circle to him, put the edge of her sword to his neck.

"Strike true, and I will die gazing upon the light of your face, as the flowers turn to follow the sun," he had said.

She lifted the sword as if to strike his head off. He did not blink or flinch, and she stopped the blade a finger's breadth from his neck. All the while he kept his eyes on her and she—who had spent all her youth locked away in the private quarters of her father's mansion—felt a strange new power. It was not from training or practice or even luck.

"Your face has conquered where your sword could not," Dark Cloud said.

She liked the power over him. When her father had informed her that her wedding had been arranged to a gray-haired old minister, she had fled from that fate and sought out Dark Cloud. At the first sight of her face again, jade hairpins fixed into her high bun, he had dropped his reins and walked toward her. He had stopped and reached out, taken her hand and pressed it to his stubbled cheek.

"You're back," he said. He smelled of horses. One shoulder of his red Tibetan coat was thrown off; underneath he wore a simple white shirt.

He took her to his tent. Afterwards, her silk gown and his rough-spun red coat lay in a pile on the floor together, arms and necks all entwined. But this conquest had not brought her pleasure. It was too easy, his affection—like indulging in too many sweet lotus cakes—and it began to turn her stomach.

"I cannot stay with you," she told him. "For it is my destiny to be a great warrior, not a bandit's wife."

"I will be a great warrior's servant," he said.

"No," she told him. "You're a bandit. You will always smell of yak cheese and butter."

He had tried to take her hand but she had refused. She would not let love stand in the way of her destiny. As the storm grew stronger all this came back to her, and she laughed at her pride— an inhuman sound, like cracking ice. It was humor that saved her. She would not give up on her son. Jiaolong adjusted her pack over her shoulder and stumbled forward. Men said that when it is dark in the east, it is light in the west, but in her world it was dark north, south, east and west. Dark and cold and deadly.

剑

In the center of the border town stood the red-painted drum tower, its green-glazed roof tiles hidden under a large hat of snow. The wardens were struggling to stop the water clock within from freezing up. They ran back and forth with braziers of coal, kept the time running according to its nature. Each droplet was a success against the cold. Drop by drop sunset came closer and when the last bamboo *clok!* sounded, the clock warden called out, "Sunset!"

In the Chamber of Fortunate Drums, the drum master put his cup of green tea down and signaled to his mandarins that the end of this day had come, which was the twenty-eighth day of the twelfth month in the tenth year of the Guangxu Emperor, sixth Emperor of the Qing Dynasty, which was in the Year of the Snake.

The great padded knocker hung on two iron chains. A pair of shivering servants slowly pulled it back, swung it against the taut skin of the city drum.

Boom! The vast drum sounded. A note so low and deep that it made the dust on the windowsill dance for a moment. *Boom*, it sounded again. *Boom*, over the low huddled houses, onto the west gate where the sergeant pulled his fur hat down low over his bushy brows.

He cleared his throat and spat. He scuffed the spit with his toe and the gobbet froze as it touched the stone. "Shut the gates!" he shouted. One by one the heavy red gates were swung closed. As the second door was driven against the carved stone lintel, one of the soldiers stopped and pointed with a gloved hand. A dark shape staggered forward. They stood and watched it stumbling weakly, zigzagging toward them along the road, before falling. It did not move. The wind moaned as darkness thickened around them.

The two guards looked at one another. "Should I go?" one said.

The other shook his head. You never knew out here, there were so many bandits, so many ruses to trick a soldier into making the wrong decision.

剑

Old Wife Du was boiling noodles in the kitchen of the Happy Lucky Inn when she heard the insistent banging on her gate. It was too late for guests. It was the night before New Year: everyone with sense was home and safe and warm.

All she had were a few strangers marooned in the middle of their journeys by the inclement weather: a camel trader who insisted on sleeping with his five pack-camels in the stables; a poor scholar, who sat up late burning the oil and writing desperate petitions to the local officials, begging for work; and then, of course, Concubine Fang and Maid Wang, who kept a constant vigil over the concubine's month-old daughter: a pretty, snub-nosed child, with white skin and a tuft of silky black hair on the crown of her head.

The banging kept going. Old Wife Du wiped her nose. It was dripping from the heat. "I'll get it!" she shouted to Husband Du, who was pretending not to hear. "Don't you move!"

Husband Du had his knees under a thick blanket and his feet on a warm clay pot of coals. He waved a hand. Yes, you go, it seemed to say.

Old Wife Du stomped across the yard in her padded cotton shoes. They left large duck-flapping prints across the snow. "I'm coming!" she shouted as the banging started again. She opened one door and peered out. Four soldiers at Old Wife Du's gates. They were lean and thin and shivering, their dark coats freckled with snow, one of them thrusting his bare hands, blue with cold, deep into his pockets.

One pushed a wheelbarrow. On it lay a heap of dark clothes. They pulled back the blanket and Old Wife Du saw that the rags had a face. The face was that of a girl with black hair and white skin, blue lips. Her eyes were closed, her teeth were rattling like a Tibetan drum.

"She is pregnant," the soldier said, and pulled back an arm. "We found her by the gate."

"*Aiya!*" Old Wife Du said. "Bring her in!"

Each soldier took a limb and she murmured as they carried the girl into the hostel courtyard. Old Wife Du ran back and forth, from door to door, all in a fluster. Another baby to be born! What a month! Her fluster turned to panicked shouts and her husband looked up in wonder. "There is a girl," she shouted, "and she is in labor!"

The commotion roused the interest of the other guests and they all came to stop and stand and stare. The camel herder rubbed the scabs on the back of his hands and scratched his head. The poor scholar saw the girl's face and sighed, and for a moment the thoughts of official posts were banished, and he thought of warm rice wine and a little cold meat, chanting poems with this beauty late into a summer's night.

"Brazier!" Old Wife Du shouted. "Blankets!"

It was only the concubine's maid who helped. Her mistress had given birth only weeks before, so she knew what a woman in labor needed: pretty or not, young or old. She elbowed the men out of the way; stoked the fire, boiled water, fanned the charcoal outside until the smoke had been driven off, then set it near the bed, licked a scrap of paper and stuck it over the hole in the papered windows.

Across the courtyard Concubine Fang sat silent at the side of her daughter's cot. The gray of her silk sleeve caught the thin winter light, illuminating a simple pattern of tiny twigs. Within the wooden rocking cot, wrapped tighter than a dumpling in padded silk, a fat face showed, with pink cheeks and almond eyes.

She looked up when her maid came in. "The girl is giving birth?" she said.

Her maid nodded.

Her baby had one of the concubine's fingers clamped tightly within her fist. "You look after her. I will be fine." The concubine shooed her maid away, tugged gently, but her daughter would not let go. "You look after her."

"Yes, ma'am," her maid said and grabbed a bag of herbs she had used before, and hurried back across the yard. As the moans came more and more regularly, Concubine Fang picked her daughter up, unbuttoned her top, and helped the child to find the milk.

Her daughter was thirsty. She sucked greedily at life. The concubine rocked back and forth.

The darkness had a strange brightness to it, with all the snow filling the yard. From across the courtyard another moan came. Low and pained and strangled.

Concubine Fang knew that sound.

The birth would be soon, she thought. Another life spilling into the world, taking a sudden first breath.

剑

The storm had stopped by the time Maid Wang knocked gently on the door and slipped inside. Her hair had come undone, hanging untidily around her ears in uncombed strands.

Concubine Fang sat before a silver mirror, plucking her forehead so that her hairline was straight and gave her face a pleasing, high, square brow. "It is a boy," the maid said.

Concubine Fang rubbed where she had just plucked a hair, peered close to the mirror to isolate another hair. She caught an odd note in her maid's voice. "She's just a child. Alone and lost and wandering. What can she do for a son?"

Concubine Fang bit her lip. She knew what the maid was thinking. She felt tears inside her, joy and horror boiling together, building like a thunderstorm.

"Does the boy look healthy?" she said at last.

"He is the fattest, healthiest little boy you have ever seen. Such pink cheeks. Soft dark hair. And his nose. A Manchu nose, I should say."

Concubine Fang glanced up. She caught the look in her maid's eyes.

"There would be no harm in going to see him," she said at last.

Birth was exhausting for both mother and child. Both of them slept, the girl had a hand held out to her boy, it rested gently on his tightly swaddled body. A blue cloth bundle lay untied, and all the contents, lovingly stitched garments, were laid out in a line: split trousers of red silk lined with cotton, a jacket of soft washed cotton, soft blue nappies, tiger-head red shoes, red tiger cap with ears decorated with silver bells, a bright red quilt for swaddling. The spread of long-prepared clothes spoke powerfully of love and care and expectation. Concubine Fang put her hand to her heart as she drew near to the bed. She spoke in a whisper. "Poor child. She is sick, you say?" she said.

The maid nodded. She had been almost half dead when they brought her in, nose bitten black with frost, the fingertips of her right hand already blistering.

As if to reinforce the fact, the mother coughed, a dry racking cough, but did not wake.

"Will she live?"

"I do not know."

They turned away from the sleeping mother to the baby. His face was bruised from birth and he had the odd look of the newborn, where the head was still taking its normal shape.

The old wife had dressed him in some old baby clothes: a red cap, red blanket, with a worn old yellow lion propped up against the bed head to ward off evil spirits.

Concubine Fang stared for a long time. At last she put out a hand and touched his cheek. He smelled like her child. She stroked his head.

"Isn't he a fine child?" the maid said.

Her mistress nodded sadly. "He will make a fine son."

"He will," the maid said. "Can you picture it?"

"Oh yes," Concubine Fang said. She thought of herself, her daughter and this poor girl who slept and coughed again. It is hard, Concubine Fang thought, to be born into this world as a woman.

2

Jiaolong did not want to wake but someone was crying and that sound was like a chain dragging her from dreams of warmth and weight, very slowly, like coming up from a deep cave back to the light. The noise grew louder and more insistent, until she could no longer ignore it.

Something was missing, she thought, and the absence of the life within her, which had been so strange for so long, so pressing, so uncomfortable, so heavy, startled her. Memories rushed back. Pain, yes, but then utter relief as the baby slipped through at last.

Jiaolong blinked awake. It was not snow that pressed down on her but thick heavy mattresses. They smelled cheap and dusty and old. Above her were papered rafters, torn and rippling in unseen drafts of air. She swallowed back distaste. She was used to fine rooms, palaces and silk-hung beds. Her father's stables were finer than this room.

She put a hand to her belly, and it was no longer taut and stretched but fat and saggy and sore. Fragments of memory came back to her like shards of a smashed porcelain cup: a city gateway, snow like cherry blossom, hands and warmth and her empty womb. It took a long moment before she understood where she was, and she turned and saw her child lying next to her, toothless mouth open, gums wailing loud.

She felt the warmth in her breasts as the milk began to rise like spring sap. She gathered the child in. She kissed his forehead. His eyes were high and narrow and noble-looking. He was fat and heavy. She could barely believe she had carried him inside her.

"Hush," she whispered. "Hush!" and fumbled at the clasps on her top, pulled away her undershirt so that her left breast came free, the dark nipple already beaded with white. "Here," she whispered, and pressed milk out, and the baby opened wide and took hold. A powerful, hungry movement and he began to suck nosily.

Jiaolong let her son drink, and when she was done she laid him on his back and opened his cloths. He wore slit-bottomed trousers so that he did not soil himself. The cloth there was wet. She pulled it away, to clean and dry him, but she paused.

Her son was not a son.

Her son was a girl.

She pushed the hair from her face. Her voice had command within it. "Old woman!" she shouted. The world seemed empty and quiet as the snow covered them all. "Old woman," she shouted three more times before she heard the door across the courtyard open and footsteps crunch across the snow.

Old Wife Du had a belly full of this morning's dumplings. She had cooked extra for the girl as well, and when she heard her calling she took the lid off the steamer and tipped them into a bowl, drizzled on some dark vinegar and flakes of chili and set out into the cold.

"Old woman!" The words came again, impatient, threatening.

She paused at the door, chopsticks in one hand, dumplings in the other, and pushed the door open. "I made some dumplings,"

19

she said, but the girl sat straight up, her top unbuttoned, her black hair hanging unkempt around her face. She seemed very white against the red of her top. The baby lay on the bed before her. It was naked from the bottom down, legs kicking as it started to fuss. "Explain to me, old woman," the girl said, her hand shaking as she pointed at the child. "I gave birth to a boy last night—or a girl?"

Old Wife Du stomped forward and stopped, confused. She frowned as she held the bowl of steaming dumplings. She looked down at the baby that was no longer a boy, but a girl, and she had to put a hand to the wall. "Well," she said, "he was a boy last night!"

Jiaolong was only eighteen years old but she seemed to rear up over the poor, simple old woman, her voice harsh with authority. "You have sold him!"

"I have not!" the old woman said, and fell to her knees and lifted her hands in supplication.

"Liar!"

剑

The commotion brought Old Wife Du's husband. "A disaster!" she said. "Look—he's turned into a girl." Her husband stumped forward to look. True enough, he thought. The baby was a girl. "Oh heavens!" he said. "How did that happen? I thought the concubine had a girl, and this one had a boy?"

Jiaolong pushed past the old fools. She was already at the door and crossing the yard.

The beauty of her almond-shaped face turned harsh as she spoke to them. "She's taken my son," she said.

They ran back and forth, crisscrossing the courtyard with footprints. All they could find in the concubine's room was a silver vase, engraved with a scene of winter snow, and a silver boat-shaped ingot, stamped with a Shanxi banker's mark. Jiaolong flung it into the corner of the room.

The burst of energy had exhausted her. She pulled her sword free from her baggage, and drew it so fast it flashed in the cold air. She looked wild and deadly.

"Find her!" Jiaolong said as she clung to the doorpost. She waved the sword, and the old couple wailed so loudly that the camel herder stumbled out of the stables, his head groggy with last night's wine.

"She has stolen my child!" Jiaolong hissed, holding herself up. She held out a bag of silver at the end of a trembling hand. "Find them," she said. "Please."

剑

The camel herder took the money and hurried off, but the weather was so bleak and the silver so heavy he could not stop himself from going to a house where he paid for a pretty singsong girl to light his opium pipe, and she sang to him as he dreamt simple dreams of palaces and warmth and food and wine.

How long he lay there he had no idea. Whenever the dreams wore off he waved to the bag of silver he had, and a girl with a white-powdered face and small red lips bent over him again and cooed softly like a dove.

It was a trip to heaven. But then came a woman whose voice was not soft. He tried to roll away, and reached for his pipe, but a hand gripped the front of his padded jacket and lifted him from the bed. A hand slapped his face. "Where is my money?" a voice shouted at him. "Where is the coin?"

There were screams and shouts that made no sense to him. He distinctly heard the sound of a sword being drawn, then the screams grew louder and more insistent and he did not know anymore.

剑

Before she was fit enough, Jiaolong set off in pursuit of the concubine. She took the girl babe with her. It was a simple decision. She would not leave the child, but wrapped her up, fixed her into the basket on her back, and set off with pack and babe and staff. The cold and the winds meant nothing to her. It was her son, her blood, the night with her lover, Dark Cloud.

Everywhere she went, east and west, she asked for news of a woman with a maid and a child. Innkeepers shrugged, soldiers had seen nothing. The baby in the bamboo basket cried, and she had wide unbound feet, like a peasant. When she arrived at an inn in the Silk Road town of Zhangye, she put the bamboo baby basket down on the table and asked the innkeeper, "I am looking for a concubine named Fang, who has a baby boy. She belongs to a magistrate named Han. She took my child. I want it back."

She drew the characters of the names on her open palm as she spoke, but the baby in the basket started crying.

The man was peeling garlic cloves with the square end of a chopstick. He looked the girl up and down, saw unbound feet, and mistook her for the lowest form of peasant, spoke to her as if she were stupid.

"If she took your child then what is that?" he said.

"It's *her* child. She gave me a girl. I bore a boy."

The man gave her a look that said fate was an arrow that was hard to dodge. "If I was a beggar and my son was taken in by a magistrate's wife, I would consider the Heavens had been good to me. Clear off. They'll give him a better home than you.

Sell the daughter when she's old enough, and save yourself the pain."

His eyes widened as she threw her cloak aside and put her hand to the pommel of her sword. "I am no beggar!" she said, and he ran in terror from the room. Jiaolong looked for one who would meet her gaze. The others all kept their heads down. "My name is the Wronged One," Jiaolong said. "The Mother-with-no-Child. Once when a swordsman saw injustice, he would draw his weapon to assist," she said, and glared about the room looking for an antagonist. None offered to take up the fight. She picked the crying baby and its basket up from the table, slung it back over her shoulder and turned on her heel.

剑

Jiaolong strode out of town as a crowd of children gathered behind her, jeering and calling.

She cursed the baby. When she was out of sight of the town gates she set the child on the ground, next to a mile marker.

"You are not my child," she told it. "I cannot take you if you keep on crying. You are her child and she is a thief. I cannot take you." The baby was silent as she explained why she had to leave it. In the end Jiaolong turned and marched away, alone.

The setting sun was in her eyes. After dark there would be tigers and snow leopards. She felt like a cuckoo had come and left her with its child, whilst stealing her own. Why should she raise this child? It was not hers. It was the daughter of a thief. Dragons begat dragons, the saying went, snakes begat snakes. She stood still as the arguments went back and forth. The baby started to cry, and Jiaolong could feel her milk rising. She is a girl, she told herself. How can you abandon her to a cruel fate?

Jiaolong turned and started walking, her long embroidered red silk gown fretting with the breeze. Ten steps away from the girl she stopped, took in a deep breath. I will feed her one last time, she thought, and crouched down to let the child feed. She pressed the girl to her chest, and rocked back and forth.

The baby had a fierce nature. She sucked so hard it hurt. Jiaolong understood that she was a mother to this baby, even if not by blood. What else could she do but raise this child as her own?

She put out a hand to touch the baby's cheek. Jiaolong, for the first time in many years, had been defeated. She could not do what she had intended to do. But defeat did not feel bitter. She lifted the child to her shoulder and held it there, and inhaled its scent deep.

After a long time she sniffed away the tears and wiped her nose on the back of her hand. "You shall be my child now," she said. "And being my child you should have a name." Jiaolong took a deep breath.

"I will call you Snow Vase," Jiaolong said. "I will teach you all that I have been taught. You shall be a daughter to me."

剑

Jiaolong was good to her word.

Snow Vase's early years were spent wandering from border town to fortress. But when she was five her mother settled in the oasis town of Dunhuang. Golden sand surrounded them, and north and west stretched the endless tracts of the Gobi Desert, but along the southern horizon reared the snow-bright mountains of Tibet.

Her mother was still young and beautiful. She had many admirers and benefactors, and the spice and silk merchants gave her many gifts, for she spent her days keeping the caravan routes clear of bandits.

Jiaolong set up a great household in Dunhuang, and men said she was their little Empress. She lived up to the gossip, dressed in the finest gowns of dyed Suzhou silk, elaborate sleeveless jackets richly embroidered with dragons, chrysanthemums and wind-blown willow trees. In the autumn she held late-night parties where men drank wine and watched the moon rise through the branches of the apricot trees.

She had a dazzling collection of fine hairpins, all gold and silver, jade and turquoise. Some had the shape of butterflies and dragonflies, one was a carved jade comb, and her favorite was a cricket of silver wire and lapis lazuli. After combing her hair she would lay them all out, set her silver mirror before her, and position each hairpin with care.

Snow Vase could not resist them.

"Don't touch!" her mother said sharply and slapped the girl's hand, but otherwise Jiaolong treated her adopted daughter as her own: raised her, trained her, and in her own way, loved and cared for her. Snow Vase grew wild and determined: not a dragon like her mother, more a phoenix, Jiaolong thought as she saw her daughter bloom.

3

As the blazing hot summer faded far too slowly into the cool clear days of autumn, Snow Vase was counting the weeks until her seventeenth birthday. Late in the afternoon she sat on her horse on the high crags above the oasis and looked down to her home. Fields of rattling maize and golden wheat stretched toward the town, and along the lines of irrigation ditches the green-striped watermelons sat waiting for the mule carts to take them to market. She loved this time of year, loved the smell of evening bonfires, the sadness of change, the end of summer and the quiet thoughtfulness of autumn.

The desert was a dangerous place. There were tigers and thieves and worse. Snow Vase was calm, but no girl should be out here after dark.

"We should return home," she said, and her horse picked a safe way down the cupped curves of the great dunes. Warm golden sand tumbled down around White Swallow's hooves, slipping and sliding ahead of them. Through the snorts of her horse Snow Vase could hear the gentle drumming of the sand. On nights like these, as the sun—a red ball of fire—slid low to the west and the full moon rose and the evening breeze blew over them, the dunes would hum to themselves.

The words were hard to make out, but Snow Vase was sure

that one day she would be the first to listen to the earth singing and understand.

When the song was over, and the sands' golden hues faded to many shades of gray, then the wind was almost chill.

剑

White Swallow galloped through the city gates as they were closing for evening.

"Hoi!" the guards called out. They liked Snow Vase, liked it more when she stopped to talk, or even when she turned their way and smiled at them. But now she was lost to the joy of riding. She crouched in her stirrups, one hand raised for balance, the other loosely holding the plaited leather reins, her unbound black hair streaming behind her like a silk banner.

"Hoi!" they shouted, as the gates banged shut behind her. "Careful next time!"

Snow Vase laughed as she clattered down the streets, weaving through the peasants and rickshaw pullers, the night tradesmen with kebab stalls of hot coals and noodles.

Lao Bai, their steward, was waiting on the steps with his hands tucked into his sleeves.

His eyes were not as good as they had once been, but he had a sense regarding Snow Vase. He could always find her when others thought her lost. He was like an uncle to her, and even as she returned his eager wave, she felt a little sadness seeing him old and shrunken as she grew tall.

He is in the autumn of his years, a voice said to her. *Time to change. Winter will come soon enough.*

"I knew that was your horse!" he called out, and waved her in. "Hurry. Your mother is back. She wanted to see you. I said that you were studying."

Snow Vase swung her leg over the head of White Swallow and dropped into the yard. "What was I studying?" she said.

"I believe it was Ban Zhao's *Admonitions for Women*."

Snow Vase stopped. She looked imploring. "Oh no. You didn't, did you?"

Steward Bai winced as he half bowed. His old tanned face was expressive with apology.

Snow Vase took in a deep breath and sighed. "Remind me," she said.

"The girl and the pot shard," he said.

Snow Vase drew a long breath in through her nose. "Right," she said. "Pot shards . . ."

He smiled and nodded and gave her the thumbs up. Pride radiated from him. She wished sometimes she knew exactly why. "Dinner is in the second courtyard," he said.

剑

Snow Vase threw off her riding clothes. There was just time to splash the dust from her face and loosely pin her hair before the gong for dinner sounded.

Her mother hated to be kept waiting by anyone, and Snow Vase saw with relief that her maid had left out the gown she had been wearing that morning: the light blue one with the white collar. The echoes of the gong had barely faded by the time she was hurrying through the fourth and third courtyard. At the moment she reached the round moon gate into the second courtyard she paused, breathed a long slow breath, and entered demurely, bowing toward her mother.

"You are back," she said. "I was just reading . . ."

Jiaolong looked up. "*Admonitions for Women*," she said.

"Ah, Steward Bai told you."

"Yes. What did you learn?"

"Well, you must know the story."

"Of course," her mother said. "When a girl is born she should be taught that she is lowly and weak, and if she asks for a toy to play with she should be given a pot shard so that she might understand the meaning of household items and hard work."

Snow Vase nodded. "I learned nothing," she said, "except that when fighting a man, he will come at me thinking that I am weak and feeble and lowly, and that will be his last mistake."

Jiaolong nodded. "Good," she said. "I fought a man named Li Mubai once . . ."

"You fought Li Mubai!" Snow Vase said.

Jiaolong nodded. "I was willful in my youth," she said. Snow Vase thought her mother willful still. "I wanted a great treasure that he held. The finest of blades. The Green Destiny. I stole it, and we fought."

"And who won?"

"He did."

Snow Vase didn't know which question to ask first. "Was he as good as men say?"

"Yes," her mother said.

"How did he beat you?"

"I was young. He was faster than me. He was as calm as a deep pool, but when he moved he was faster than lightning. He took Green Destiny from me."

"The Green Destiny!"

Jiaolong was like a closed door sometimes. She nodded and picked out a piece of lotus root, dabbed off the slivers of ginger, and placed it into her mouth.

"You fought with the Green Destiny?"

Her mother crunched the lotus root but gave no other reaction. The cricket hairpin moved slightly as she chewed. She folded her silk sleeves back. Her arm had once been pale as jade, but the long desert rides had tanned it to the color of yellow clay. "I fought with it and against it."

"How?" Snow Vase said. "When?"

Her eyes widened and her mother clearly decided it would be easier to tell all rather than have it dragged out of her, like a criminal whose guts are drawn, foot by foot, out of his belly. She paused. "When my father was made Governor of Beijing, he arranged a marriage for me to the Emperor's favorite minister. He was fat and dull and ugly. I could not bear it. The wife of my tutor helped me escape. Her name was Jade Fox. I loved her at first. She spoke kindly to me. She cared for me, and when I swore that I would die rather than marry this man she promised to help me. I thought she loved me, but I was mistaken. She only wanted to use me.

"My family were guests of Duke Te. The duke was also patron to Shulien and her father. On the morning of my wedding I heard that there was a lady named Shulien who had arrived. 'The great warrior Shulien?' I asked.

"Jade Fox nodded. 'And she has brought Green Destiny.'

"'What is Green Destiny?' I asked her.

"'Not just Green Destiny. *The* Green Destiny. A mighty sword,' she told me. She pursed her lips. She wooed me with soft words. Bewitched me. She told me that I should have that sword. 'The Green Destiny is the finest sword ever forged. It can cut through steel as if it were pine.' Jade Fox filled me with longing. 'Why does Shulien bring this sword here? She has common blood. You are a noblewoman. If anyone should bear this sword it should be you.'

"'You're right,' I told her, and on the night of my wedding I stole the sword from Duke Te's study. I took it and fought Yu Shulien. I beat her!"

30

It was like saying, "I kissed the Buddha."

Snow Vase spoke in a whisper. "You beat her. Then why didn't you keep it?"

Her mother paused. "I escaped, but Mubai came after me. He saw talent in me. He saw that I had been led badly, by an evil teacher. He had a good heart. He promised he would be my master. I resisted but he disarmed me and promised to be my teacher. But eventually Jade Fox caught up with us," she said. Jiaolong's face had opened for a moment but now it was closed again. "And they fought over me. Mubai ran her through, but he was stuck by a poison dart, and there was no cure for the evil Jade Fox had put into his blood. Both of them died. I was flattered then. Such are the vanities of youth. Now I think, what a loss. Mubai. I don't think I've met his like since. He was the finest of all the warriors of the House of Te." She paused and shook her head, and fell silent for a moment. "Now tell me what you were really doing today."

Snow Vase paused and tried to read her mother's expression. It was like looking into the depths of black pearls. "I went riding," she said.

"How far did you go?"

"To the Singing Sands."

"And?"

"Nothing," Snow Vase said.

Her mother's eyes narrowed, but at that moment servants came in bringing their dishes and Snow Vase preempted her.

"What was it like?"

"What?"

"Green Destiny."

Her mother's face softened. She had a distant look in her eye. She so rarely looked like this that Snow Vase could not help but drink the moment in: the lanterns, the painting of willows on the wall, and her mother, chopsticks in hand, smiling fondly on her past.

"Green Destiny," she said, and savored the name, as if it were the name of a cherished lover. "The sword that Guanyu wore in the time of the Three Kingdoms. The finest sword ever forged. Light, harder than steel, too perfect a blade for any common man to wield. You have not held a sword until you have handled Green Destiny. There is no finer sword. And whoever masters that sword, they shall rule the martial kingdom."

"Did Mubai master it?"

Her mother thought for a moment. "Yes, I think he did."

"Then why didn't he keep it?"

"He gave the sword to Duke Te. He had mastered all the arts of fighting, but he had lost joy in his ability. He was tired of killing. I don't think he wanted mastery."

"What did he want?"

Jiaolong gave a short laugh. "He wanted Yu Shulien," she said. "But she had been betrothed to a warrior called Silent Wolf. He and Mubai were oath brothers, but Silent Wolf was killed in a fight on Vulture Peak. She wanted to marry Mubai, but he was filled with grief for his friend and did not want to dishonor his memory by marrying his betrothed. So she went away full of grief. Slowly he changed his mind, but by the time he went to find Shulien again, she had grown distant from him. Both of them were filled with longing. Neither of them could find satisfaction."

Snow Vase shook her head. "So Mubai died . . . but whatever happened to Shulien?"

Her mother drew in a long breath. There was much she didn't tell her daughter. "She left the sword with Duke Te as Mubai had wished, and determined to go into the mountains and meditate. She had loved Mubai. She had lost the man she loved. The Iron

Way is paved with grief. I never heard of her again. Nothing certain, anyway. Maybe she has passed on. Maybe she and Mubai are united at last."

Snow Vase bit her lip. Mubai. Shulien. She envied her mother for the people she had met, was irritated by the walls she put up about her past.

As she ate she thought of the Green Destiny. Such tales she had heard! Even in the marketplace tonight there would be men telling the tale of Guanyu and his sworn brothers, and their battle against Cao Cao. The finest sword ever forged.

If her mother had handled it, then Snow Vase made a resolution that she would master it.

That night before she went to sleep she squeezed her eyes shut and imagined the sword, lying on the table before her, and she reached out and touched it.

There! she thought, as she lay listening to the last cicadas calling out in the warm darkness. I have seen it. It shall come true.

Snow Vase had lived all her life here in Dunhuang. The warrior-mistress Jiaolong was mother and father and teacher: a strange and solitary woman; half beauty, half dragon, an unlikely parent to any child.

"I follow the Iron Way," her mother told her once, when Snow Vase had asked why she trained each day with spear and sword and fist. She had taken in a slow breath. "The Iron Way. It is the world of wushu. Of martial arts. In this world men are not masters by birth or rank or patronage; they are masters because they have great skill and power. The wushu warrior steps outside society. Their lord is their teacher, their master. Their brothers are those they fight beside. Some of them group themselves into

Houses, each with their own laws and customs. Others wander alone, fighting injustice wherever they find it. Their law is not the Emperor's or the administrator's, but their own code of justice. The best of them keep to the narrow path. They right wrongs, challenge unjust rulers, remove oppressors, bring retribution to the corrupt. The worst of them are seduced by power. It corrupts them; they rot from within like the old tree that is slowly hollowed out. You must not be like them. You must be loyal, fearless, just, benevolent. And you must forgo wealth and glory. And often much more . . ."

Her mother trailed off.

"What else?"

"Enough questions," her mother said.

剑

Snow Vase had gleaned fragments of her mother's history by listening to what men said, and most importantly to the gaps where they did not speak. Her mother could not disguise her clipped aristocratic accent, nor her skill at all the arts a young lady was supposed to know. She had taught Snow Vase all of these, and Snow Vase combined this Confucian education with a wild border spirit. But there was a sadness within her mother that she could not place.

"Did you ever love anyone?" she asked.

"Yes," her mother said.

"Who?"

Her mother looked at her. She had small hard eyes, beautiful when she smiled, but hard as a rock wall now. She ignored the question. "You rode out today to the Singing Sands." It was not a question. "It is not safe."

"But you go there," Snow Vase said.

"I am trained," her mother said. She had a withering stare. She turned it onto Snow Vase but she refused to yield, tossed back her hair and returned the stare with interest.

"I am trained too," Snow Vase said.

"You are too young," Jiaolong snapped. "Trust me. I was young once, and made too many mistakes."

Snow Vase looked down. On the table before them was a platter of five-spice cold beef, pickled peanuts and sweet and sour cucumber. The servants had set out two bowls and two cups painted with wild dark horses on a vast green land. Yellow lanterns lit the room. There was a pot of rice wine on the table.

Her mother let out a sigh. She set down her chopsticks. "I have something to tell you," she said. Snow Vase stopped and waited.

Jiaolong drew in a deep breath. She sighed and looked at her daughter. "When I was your age my father was Governor of Gansu Province. He raised me as any girl: to be pretty and obedient and strong enough to bear a husband as many sons as he could plant inside me. I could not stand it. I was a wild horse. I would not bow to such a fate. I could not.

"I was a terrible child. I endured a stifling succession of tutors who wished to teach me nothing more than needlework, singing, playing the *erhu* and entertaining men. It was the life of a songbird. I was this close to hanging myself, or dashing my brains out against the wall. All my governess ever wanted me to do was learn the tales of eminent widows and hard-working mothers. You could not imagine a duller bunch of women in the whole wide world. Who wants to be remembered for raising good sons? What am I—a brood mare? I wanted to leave my mark. I trained secretly. I was the hidden dragon," she laughed. "Alone, after dark, when all the household was asleep. And I became good."

She paused. "It is a long story, but I became pregnant."

Snow Vase looked away. This felt too close to home. Her mother coughed to clear her throat. "He was a warrior," she said. "I felt such desire for him. It tormented me. I ran from it but it pursued me. Whenever I hid it was there in the morning. It tormented my dreams. I knew that I could not defeat my feelings, so I decided to master them.

"I gave birth in a hostel, weak, alone, in the middle of a snowstorm." Jiaolong took a sip of wine, and looked directly at her daughter. She did not want to tell this tale, and almost shied away, like a skittish horse. But the memory of that blood on her fingers came back to her, and Snow Vase was the closest person to her. "My child was lost," she said. "You were a foundling. I took you in. Cared for you. You were a comfort for me who had lost my own child."

"Why are you telling me this?" Snow Vase said, the temper in her voice rising. Her mother was a difficult woman, and Snow Vase was angry at her for not telling her before, but at the same time she felt a surge of joy: she had never thought she had much in common with her mother, and now she had the proof. They were not related. She was not her mother really, somewhere her real mother was out there, beautiful, kind, gentle, loving. Everything her own mother was not.

"I am telling you this . . ." Jiaolong paused for breath. "I am telling you this because I am sick."

Snow Vase looked at the woman who was not her mother. "Sick?"

"Dying," Jiaolong said.

"What do you mean, dying?" Snow Vase didn't know if this was another tale she should believe, or not. She loved her mother, but sometimes she was impossible. The two of them looked at each other. Neither spoke.

"I'm dying," her mother said again. She put a hand to her chest. "It is my chest," she said simply. She saw her daughter's expression, and held out the cloth she held scrunched up in her fist. The white cloth was spattered with dark, arterial red. The pattern clearly stated Jiaolong's coming death.

"I summoned the local doctor. 'Drink this twice a day,' he said. 'Will it help?' I asked him. He nodded. 'Will it cure me?' I said, and he paused and sighed through his nose, and gently shook his head. 'Nothing can cure the sickness you have.'"

Jiaolong laughed at the end of her story. There was no greater disaster in life than one's own death. "It is ironic. I have fought so many battles, and learned a hundred ways of turning an opponent's blow, of preserving my life from violence. And death comes, not in a sword or club or fist, but cloaked, unseen. Inside me! Like a maggot within the rotting carcass."

Snow Vase didn't know how to take this news in. Mothers did not die. Not so soon. Not when they appeared so . . . she looked for the word . . . *unvanquished.*

It began to rain. Tiny drops, so rare this deep in the desert. They were almost refreshing in the warmth. It was a good enough excuse. "Bring more wine!" her mother called, and Steward Bai came back with a warm pot that he set in the middle of the table.

Snow Vase felt somehow her mother's equal now. It was as if the years of deception had dwindled her mother's moral standing and elevated her own. She was like the lotus flower that rises from the mud of the lake: clean, white, perfect.

"Will you drink with me?" her mother said.

"Yes," Snow Vase said. She deliberately did not say "Mother." It felt like a little victory to her that night.

They drank three cups together, but three cups was not enough for Jiaolong, and too much for her daughter. That was how tragedy was made, she thought, and when her mother went to fill her cup a fourth time she put her hand over it.

"It is late," she said at last.

Jiaolong nodded. Her daughter was right. She let her go, refilled her own cup to the brim and held it up with two hands in a gesture of gratitude. With a cup of wine all troubles diminish, the saying went, but wine only deepened her melancholy.

剑

The next morning the rain had passed but there was a pleasant damp to the air, and a scent of earth. In the south, mist wreathed the mountains, and the waning moon still hung in the western sky.

Snow Vase sat to meditate in the yard.

A host of conflicting thoughts had gathered in the night like a mob of voices. They had woken her early, insistent and loud: clamoring at her door. She took them out, one by one, and addressed them as a wushu master takes on a crowd of fighters and leaves each in the dust. Her breathing was slow and deep and regular as the night faded around her, the world fading from black and white moon shades to the rich colors of day: the green roof tiles, the blue of sky, the yellow earth, sprinkled with the drowned cherry blossom.

剑

Her maid had laid out her clothes but Snow Vase put them aside, opened her chest and picked out thin black trousers, leather boots and a short black jacket lined with blue silk.

She took the long way around to the front courtyard. Her mother had always welcomed fellow wushu fighters. There had been many of them when she was young.

The eastern courtyards had once been full of young men pitting their skills against each other, or training their muscles to leap harder, faster, more explosively. But now the paper windows were brown with dust, holes flapped in the wind, and there was a carpet of moss on the doorsteps. Snow Vase paused. She could remember the day Bald Wu had taught her Flying Crane Fist; the first day she showed her mother.

Jiaolong's face had been impassive as she watched her daughter: a slender girl, hair plaited to the sides of her head, in black trousers and top, suddenly assuming the stance of a striking crane. She was grace and elegance and then she struck and she was speed and power and penetration, then soft and flowing and graceful again, as the dancing bird.

"Who dared teach my daughter this?" she said at the end.

Bald Wu fell to his knees and touched his forehead to the dirt.

"Forgive me!" he said. "She taught herself at first. Following the men in the yard. I never saw such a fighter! Talent should not go untrained."

"It seems you have the heart of a boy, and the talent of a warrior," her mother had said. The words were spoken solemnly. Seriously. "Do you understand what that means?" she had asked.

Snow Vase had nodded. "Yes, Mother," she said.

When she reached her mother's courtyard, Steward Bai stood waiting for her.

Snow Vase sat silent as the servants brought in her breakfast of steamed pork buns. She took the buns and walked out into the yard. The sky was clear and early summer blue, but the heat had not yet got up, and the air was cool still with just the hint of dew that occurred in these dry regions.

She paced across to the well and sat down on the stone lip. One of the women had been washing this morning. There were large wet stains on the ground, but the parched earth had sucked the water in and left no mud: just a dark brown bruise.

Snow Vase chewed slowly. She watched the round moon gate that led to her mother's courtyard, but the sun rose over the roof of the gateway and still she had not come.

"Where is my mother?" she asked one of the maids as she came to sweep the yard.

"I do not know," the girl said.

"Can you ask Steward Bai to come?" Snow Vase said.

The girl bowed, and hurried off with little steps.

A few minutes later Steward Bai arrived.

"I'm waiting for my mother," Snow Vase said.

Steward Bai bowed slightly. "She went out this morning," he said.

"Where?"

"A messenger came. Before the sun rose."

"From the magistrate?" It was common for the local authorities to turn to Jiaolong when there were bandits on the road.

Steward Bai shook his head. "No. I do not know who he was. Your mother went out early. With her sword and two horses."

"Did she say where she was going?"

He shook his head.

"Did she say when she would be back?"

He shook his head. There was a pause. "That is all," Snow Vase said. She looked down at her bowl, where her pork bun lay half eaten.

剑

Snow Vase waited all day, pacing the courtyards, practicing her swordplay, reciting old scraps of poems she had learned as a child—her ears always eager for the sound of a horse returning to her home.

A number of times she felt the distant thunder of hooves and stood still and paused, but the horses passed by or turned onto another path some way off, and they did not trouble her gate.

It was typical, she thought, for her mother to tell her she was adopted, and then disappear. It was infuriating. It was also concerning, and as the day went on she began to fear for her mother.

She summoned Steward Bai back. "Mother is sick. Did she take any medicine with her?"

Steward Bai did not know. He didn't know much, Snow Vase thought.

剑

When the sun began to turn the world to gold and shadows Snow Vase walked to the compound gateway and looked out. She looked north and south and east and west, but there was no sign of a rider. No sign of the woman she had thought her mother.

One day passed, and another. Snow Vase's emotions rose and fell like the tide. At last she summoned Steward Bai.

"I'm worried about my mother," she said. "I'm going to take two horses."

Steward Bai bowed low. "I will see it is all arranged," he said.

剑

Snow Vase was gone for a week. When she came back, thirsty, exhausted, the guards on the gates of Dunhuang looked up expectantly. "Miss?" they said as they saw her walking from the desert. "Is that you, miss?"

Her eyes were downcast, her spirit defeated, her horses had a weary, lethargic air. She had found the messenger, and learned his message; and now she knew that her mother was not coming back. Her confused feelings exhausted her.

Steward Bai watched her from the doorstep of the house.

Snow Vase let her horse drink before she did so herself. She washed the rims of dust from her eyes, she sat back on the wooden trough. "She has gone," she said. "She has gone away. I do not think she means to come back."

Steward Bai looked at her. "Why?" he asked.

Snow Vase splashed more water over her face. "She has one last thing she wants to do before she dies. She is looking for someone very special to her. A young man. I do not think we will see her again."

"None of us?"

Snow Vase looked at the old man and saw the sadness in his eyes. She put her hand to his shoulder. "None," she said.

Snow Vase paused. *She has left us. She's gone to meet her fate. I cannot stay here, without a master. I will have to go too, my destiny awaits.*

4

"What is this?"

Wei-fang's mother held up his training manual, *Shaolin Monastery: 108 Styles*. Wei-fang had known that this was not going to go well from the moment he had been summoned that morning, in a hushed whisper, to come and speak to his mother in the family shrine. "She's not eaten all morning," the maid whispered to him. "She's been asking for you since dawn. We've been trying to put her off, but she says we must wake you now or she will come herself."

"I'll come," Wei-fang had said, and quickly ruffled his hair to make it look as though he had just woken.

Now he was standing in his family shrine, and his mother had dressed in her formal red jacket, eyebrows freshly plucked and hair rigidly combed into place. She was waving his wushu manual at him, and from under the high forehead she was fixing him with her hard black eyes.

"Well?" she said.

He wondered how much he should tell her.

"Imagine I know everything," she said, "and for once tell me everything."

He opened his mouth but no sound came out. She was a dramatic woman, and if he told her the truth she would

43

make a scene. Or a worse scene than she was going to make anyway.

"Speak!" she said, her voice shrill. She had always treated him, indulged him, loved him—overloved him, some said, if such a thing were possible. He had never seen her this angry. "Tell me what this is!"

"A book."

"I can see that."

The book was ancient and well-thumbed, and as she held it up some of the papers fell out onto the floor. As he bent to pick them up her voice became shrill. "Leave them alone! Tell me, what is this?" She took a step toward him.

The skin of her face was so tight her face was a snarl, her teeth small, stained needles of fury. She screamed at him. "Just because you are nearly seventeen years old you think that means you can do what you wish! That is not so. You have lied to us! You have lied to me!"

He saw her gold-plated fingernails raised above him like the claws of a bird and realized that she was actually going to hit him. Both of them paused for a moment and then, deliberately, intentionally, she slapped him across the face.

The blow did not smart, except for where her nails had raised a red welt. But she had never struck her son before, and from that moment, when he fell to his knees in apology, and she saw his face and what she had done to him, and she fell to the floor next to him, and wept for his forgiveness, then Wei-fang knew that something he and his mother had shared, a deep, secret thing that bound them together, had finally broken and could never be repaired.

"This is all his fault," she wept.

"Whose?"

"You know whose! Master Zhang! I wish he had never lived!"

Wei-fang could not bear to hear the old man spoken of in this way. He stood over his mother. "It's not his fault," he said gently. "And anyway he's been dead for two years."

"His ghost refuses to let go. I will summon the priests and have his spirit banished." He laughed at her and she threw him off. "He corrupted you. I warned your father. He told you all those silly tales and now look at you. You want to study these *fighting* skills. What karma will you earn? You'll come back as a dog or a rat. Our souls will never reach the Pure Land," she said, and pulled her hair and wailed.

剑

Master Zhang had run a medicine shop in the southern quarters of Luoyang. He was old and wrinkled; his skin as brown and polished as old copper. He had no sons that anyone knew of. No wife either. But Wei-fang's father liked him, and went to buy medicines from there, and when he turned eight years old Wei-fang had started accompanying his father to the shop.

Master Zhang had taken a liking to the eight-year-old boy. He smiled kindly, beckoned him over. "Come!" he would say. Wei-fang was a trusting child, and he would climb up next to the old man and take a licorice root, and chew it as the old man told him tales of Monkey King and Pigsy, and how they fought demons across the Western Deserts. Sometimes Master Zhang would act out the fights, leaping into the air, kicking his upraised palm, balancing on one toe while he slow-kicked the other leg up to his nose.

Wei-fang dropped the licorice root. "*Wa!*" he said. "Again!"

Eventually Wei-fang said, "Master. Can you teach me how to do that?" And Master Zhang had looked toward his father, a genial man, now retired from office, who was enjoying life as a retired scholar by indulging in his penchant for Buddhism.

His father had always said that he did not think his son would become a fighter, but at the time he had not really been paying attention, and he liked to say "yes" to his son. It was a habit. He was an only and beloved child.

Wei-fang had tugged his sleeve and jumped up and down and his father had said, "Yes. Why not?"

剑

Wei-fang started to go daily, not weekly, and then twice a day and stay for hours. He learned quickly and was not afraid of hard work. It was refreshing to be with an adult so unlike either of his parents. Neither his mother's fussy adoration, nor his father's vacant smiles. Here was a man who watched him so closely he could lift his fingers a little higher, or change the angle of his bent elbow a fraction, or the bend in his knee. "Good," he would say when Wei-fang did well. And when he was lazy, or tired, or sick of taking up the same stance over and over, Master Zhang would tut and shake his head and look at him with disappointment. "No," he would say. "Not good."

At first Wei-fang sulked. But sulking got him nowhere with the old man, so he tried something new: pushing himself, being as strict as the old man, stricter sometimes. In those months he flourished. He took on an adult air. He was calm, focused, managed his feelings, spoke his mind.

Wei-fang was proud of all of the changes with Master Zhang, but they disturbed his mother, and as she privately fretted at his father, they disturbed him too.

Wei-fang did not know what to do. Returning home each night became a more and more difficult experience. It was like the kite that flies high in the air, soaring as free as a bird, being wound unwillingly back to the ground, where it sat clumsy and awkward.

At dinner with his parents, Wei-fang learned to keep his silence.

His mother tried to charm him with the treats she had charmed him with as a child. "Sesame crackers," she would say. "Sugared plums!"

"I'm not a child," he said.

"Don't speak to your mother like that," his father said, and the silence returned.

The next morning Wei-fang was up before dawn, and the old man was waiting for him. "Good!" he would say. "Have you practiced?"

"Yes, master."

"Show me."

The old man sniffed and spat as he watched.

"Faster," Master Zhang would say. "Quicker. Harder, with more conviction. You're a warrior, not a baby!"

Wei-fang trained until the sweat ran down his face in streams. He squatted in the horse stance until his thigh muscles burned and his whole body trembled like a bamboo leaf.

One day Master Zhang seemed sad. "Wei-fang, you are good. Very good. I have not seen one so committed. You have something special, I think. Something more than I can teach."

"What are you saying?"

"I am saying," the old man said sadly, "you need another master. A better master."

"But I have you."

"Yes, but I will not be here for long."

"You look so well."

"I am old."

Wei-fang didn't know what to say.

The old man looked at him. "If you are serious about your skill you should go to the Twelve-Sided Pagoda. There are great masters there. They can teach you."

"Where is this place?"

"South," the old man said, "and east. In the mountains there is a great valley, near the temple of the Shaolin monks. There are many temples there. Many schools of learning. Many great masters . . ."

That night his parents sat Wei-fang down.

"No," his father said. "Listen. Your mother is worried."

His mother sat forward. She spoke kindly at first. "All this training," she said. "It is time you put such childish things aside, and think about your future."

"It is not childish," Wei-fang said.

"Listen, you are our only child. We are not young, your father is already retired. If you go to the mountains to study, who will look after us? We cannot let you go to some mountain master, to train to be a fighting man. It is not right. It is not how a gentle-man should live," she said. "You have all a man could desire. Wealth, education, learning. Stay home. Be a good son. Study hard. Your father will help you pass the civil service exams. He will help you find a good job."

Wei-fang felt her words like a cage that was being built around him. "But I don't want that," he said.

His mother looked at him. "Wei-fang," she said, "you are still a child. You do not know anything about the world. We will choose for you. We know what is best."

He felt his stomach ache. "But I want to be a warrior. Master Zhang says it is all about self-discipline. Honor, fighting evil. That is why I learn. He says I am good."

His mother looked at him. She had based all her fortunes within her husband's family on him, a male child. His birth raised her from the common position of a concubine, easily dropped and discarded, to a proper wife, with all the status and respect that brought. And when First Wife died childless, his mother had been promoted and now she acted as if she had always been First Wife. It was a matter of pride to her, and now her eyes brimmed with tears as she slowly raised her sleeve to cover her face. "I see it all now. You do not love us. What have we done to raise such an ungrateful child? I carried you into this world and this is how you repay our love and care." She lifted her sleeves to hide her face from him, and Wei-fang felt humbled and selfish for following what would make him happy at the expense of all around him.

The worst sins for Buddhists were injuring a Buddha, killing a holy man, then matricide, then patricide; for Confucians the worst was unfilial behavior. But in this household, nothing was more heinous than the sin of making his mother cry.

She sobbed like an opera singer and Wei-fang felt such guilt. He was an ungrateful child. He wanted to do what she wanted. How could he be so ungrateful? he thought. "I'm sorry. I did not know that this would cause you so much pain. I swear I will stop this. I will study hard. I will be a good son."

Next day Master Zhang nodded sadly as Wei-fang stood before him and told him what his mother had decided. He folded back his sleeves and half smiled. "I cannot stop you if you mean to go but I shall miss you. You have talent. Not many can say that. With teaching you could become very fine!"

In the years that followed, Wei-fang always remembered how his master had said those words. Always thought about what might have been, if his fate had been different. But he wanted to please his parents more than anything, even though it made him miserable. He would wear the clothes they set out for him, even though they fitted him less and less.

For two years Wei-fang kept his word. He had folded up his wushu clothes, put away his martial training, stopped dreaming of a life of adventure and challenge. He focused on his Confucian texts, read all the Imperial Edicts, made his parents proud. And he became more and more miserable, until he felt he would explode like a New Year firecracker, where powder is packed into a paper cylinder, and remains quiet until the fuse is lit and it tears itself apart in the explosion.

One day Wei-fang was returning from his tutor's house. There was a funeral procession blocking his usual road home, so he took a detour and after half an hour's walking found himself on a street he knew, passing Master Zhang's medicine shop. "Honor your teacher as if he is jade," Confucius had written. And armed with those words he knocked on the door, and called out Master Zhang's name.

He did not think anything bad would come from going in to visit his old master, to pay his respects. He pushed in, and a young woman came out from behind the counter. He did not know her. She had a pleasant face, wide at the eyes with a small, delicate mouth and a curious lopsided smile.

His dress, as a young scholar, with writing brush under one arm and a set of books under the other, always impressed. He smiled back, and saw she had a limp, and as she came out from behind the counter, he saw that one of her legs was shorter than the other.

"Can I help?" she said.

"Yes. I was looking for Master Zhang."

"Oh," she said. "He's dead."

Wei-fang felt his heart sink. He was still new to death: its suddenness, its permanence, its finality.

The girl nodded. "Six months since."

Wei-fang felt as though he were standing before a locked door, searching for a crack or hole he might peep through. "Was he sick?"

"He was old. It is the same, I think. And he was sad." She pointed to her leg. There were the ruffled scars of healed sores. "He took me in and healed me, and I stayed on. His old assistant left to get married and there was no one else to take over the shop. He taught me a little. I tried to keep him going, but he had already given up hope."

Wei-fang felt as though these words were aimed at him. They were like a needle that lances the boil and brings the inflammation to the surface. He thanked her and apologized. He seemed a little confused as he bumbled back out of the door. She seemed almost sad that he was leaving, and he stopped. "I'm sorry, I didn't ask your name."

"Plum Blossom," she said.

"Thank you, Plum Blossom. I should like to pay my respects. Where is he buried?"

She described the place, and then seemed unwilling to let him go, and asked, "Were you his student?"

Wei-fang made a face. "Well. I learned a little." She was standing looking up at him in a way that made him shy. "You know, I really should go."

That night he was sad when he told his parents that the old man was dead.

"You should not have gone there," his mother said.

He looked at her, and did not know how she could be so self-centered at this moment, when he was sharing his sorrow with her. It was typical, he thought, that she was concerned only with herself. "I could not pass by and not pay my respects."

"Hmm!" she said.

Wei-fang kept his mouth shut. "I thought you would be pleased. A student must respect his master, Confucius said. Didn't he, Father?"

His father looked up from an illuminated version of the *Diamond Sutra* he liked to read. "Hmm, what? Yes. You did right."

It was only later, when his mother had gone to bed, that Wei-fang got his father's full attention.

"Master Zhang is dead, you say?"

"Yes, Father. There is a girl running the shop now. She was taken in and healed. He adopted her. Maybe we can buy our medicine from there again. I do not think she has many customers. It would be a good deed."

"Yes," his father said. "Right. Yes. There are so many ways to earn good karma in this world. You are a good-hearted boy. I'm proud of you."

Wei-fang felt lighter hearing these words. It was rare for his father to say anything affectionate like this. He usually looked up from a book or scroll and made noncommittal grunts.

"Father, I am sad that Master Zhang died. I feel I should have kept going to see him. I feel it is my fault."

"What? No. Surely not. He was old. Old age kills us all in the end. Then it is our time to come back again, in another life. He is already back in the world. Don't grieve. He might be living in the next street. There was a baby born there. Or he might be a young chick in the nest." His father laughed. "Life is a blessing indeed!"

Wei-fang smiled. He found his father's religious beliefs slightly disconcerting. He had been so serious and solemn when he was a civil servant, but since he had retired he had started to seem more and more like a child.

He sat quietly, keeping his father company, and then he stood up. "Good night, Father," he said.

"Oh," his father replied, "are you still here? I quite forgot. Good night, my child."

Wei-fang bowed and made his way to the door. His father stopped him. "Wei-fang," he said, "I am sorry that Master Zhang is dead. He was a kind man. Yes, I think it is fitting that you go to his tomb and pay your respects. His ghost would like that."

"Thank you, Father. I will."

"Just don't tell your mother."

"No, Father, I won't."

"She would make a scene. Good deeds done in private are still seen by the Buddha."

"I'm sure he sees us all."

"Indeed he does. I can feel him like a shadow. He comes with me all day. It is humbling that he should lavish such attention on our family. I am sure we don't deserve it."

Wei-fang's smile faded a little. "Yes. I'm sure. Good night, Father."

剑

The tomb was on a hillside a mile from the west gate. It was simple, with a carved headstone with his master's name. Wei-fang took out dumplings and meatballs, burned incense and said a prayer.

He wore a simple dark blue scholar's gown, and started to pay his respects on every seventh day, four times each moon, and on the day of the new moon Plum Blossom came with him. She waited for him by the gate, and when he appeared she was shining and eager.

"Let me take the basket," he said, and when her foot was too sore, he would carry her on his back. "You're light as a willow wand," he said, and when he put her down she blushed.

"You know Master Zhang talked about you."

"Really?"

"He said, 'I had a student who had such natural skill, such talent, but his mother would not let him study. Now they have made him into a scholar. It is like turning the mighty mountain pine tree into chopsticks. It is a waste. It is against the nature of the world.'"

"He must have been talking about someone else," Wei-fang replied, but he thought about the words as the long cedar needles combed the slight breeze. It was a soft sound, like a gently foaming stream, or the roar of the wind heard when lying snug in bed.

It had a sad note to it, and made him think of the mountains, the high hermit temples where wushu masters lived. Chopsticks were used and washed and then thrown away. It was not what he wanted from this life.

5

The day before Wei-fang's seventeenth birthday his mother came to him, a fox-fur muff in one hand. He could still feel the welt on his cheek. His mother drew herself up, as if speaking to him were a great effort, but then she forced a smile, and there was a desperate look in her eyes.

"Tomorrow is your birthday. I have a special lunch."

He sighed. "Long-life noodles?" It was *always* long-life noodles.

She nodded, and came into his room to sit next to him.

"I am sorry I struck you," she said.

He nodded.

"Can it be the same between us?"

"I don't know what you mean."

"I just want you to be my little boy again."

"I'm not a boy," he said.

She sighed and looked at him and nodded. "No, you're not." She sighed again and said, almost to herself, "You've grown so quickly!"

剑

Next day he joined his mother in the Red Chamber. A couple of her lady friends were with her. He had dressed in a simple scholar's gown and the new jacket she had embroidered. He felt uncomfortable, but it pleased her, and when they were all sitting down she waved her chopsticks at the bowl of noodles and soon all the ladies were doing the same. "Eat!" they shouted. "Eat! Eat!"

The forced jollity weighed heavily on him as one lady seized his bowl and another filled it to spilling with long white noodles, bright with mutton sauce. Wei-fang nodded politely as his mother and all her friends watched expectantly as the bowl was set before him.

"It will be so good when he is married," one of them said.

"Yes," his mother said, and there was an odd note in her voice.

"Married?" Wei-fang said.

His mother put out a hand to shush him. "Don't listen!" she said. "People have asked," she added. "Nothing more. But I thought I would ask Aunt Ma to be your matchmaker."

The smile Aunt Ma gave was purely perfunctory, and went no further than the strained corners of her mouth, which was black with tobacco-stained teeth. She was a dreadful old skeleton with white hair pulled back from her head, bony prodding fingers, enormous eyes and a smile as black as crow's teeth.

The skeleton turned and assessed the young man, and he felt like a market goose being prodded and squeezed to see how much meat he had on him.

He smiled politely at her, but she frowned. "Are you arguing with your mother, who knows best for you?" she said.

Wei-fang shook his head.

The skeleton stared at him for a dreadfully long time, then turned to his mother. "Is he filial?" the matchmaker said.

"Very," his mother said definitively.

The matchmaker squinted at her.

"Does he listen to his elders?"

"Always."

"Gamble?"

"No."

"Smoke opium?"

"Never."

"Does he visit the sing-song girls on Pipa Alley?"

Wei-fang watched his mother closely as she answered this particular question.

She did not pause for a moment. "Certainly not," she said.

"Hmm." The matchmaker looked at him now, and sipped her tea. "On what day was he born?"

Concubine Fang paused, and the matchmaker sensed something in the delay and looked at her.

"You do not remember?" she said. "The horoscopes are important. If I cannot draw up his horoscope how can I find a girl whose fortunes will combine with his? It is very unlucky to put two people together whose fortunes are not alike. It is like feeding bananas to the sheep."

Wei-fang's mother paused. "Of course I remember," she said. "I was there, of course! It was winter. Seventeen years ago. The twenty-eighth day of the twelfth month, the Year of the Snake that was the tenth year of the Emperor Guangxu. It was evening. After sunset. I cannot tell you the exact hour."

Concubine Fang grew more confident as she summoned the details back to mind. Across the room her maid Fai kept her head bowed as she sewed mating ducks into the bridal quilt, but Wei-fang knew that there was something wrong.

The two ladies talked and Wei-fang could barely bring himself to eat, and they watched him as he sucked up long-life noodle after noodle, careful not to break any of them lest that brought him bad luck.

The matchmaker watched his every slurp, her small black

teeth giving her face a sinister appearance, and then at last she smiled. "I know the perfect kind of girl."

剑

That evening of his seventeenth birthday, Plum Blossom and Wei-fang stood at Master Zhang's grave. She knew why they were there, and she was almost managing to maintain a happy air as Wei-fang lit the three sticks of incense and bowed three times, burned paper money, paper gold ingots, food, and a string of paper coins he had asked the funeral shop to make for him.

At the end he knelt and prayed aloud to the four winds. "Old master," he said, "I am, like you, an unfilial son. It is too late perhaps, but I am going to do what you told me. I am going to find a new teacher, and I will right some wrongs in the world and leave it a better place than when I was born."

He bowed again, and lit the incense sticks and stuck them in the ground where Master Zhang lay. The wind in the cedars sang gently as he rose slowly and bowed to the earth, and sky and heavens.

剑

"Please don't," she said, but her foot always hurt her on the long walk, so when she was biting back the pain, he lifted her.

"You're no weight," he said.

By the time they got back to the shop the shadows were lengthening. "Come inside. I have something for you," she said, and she smiled quickly.

She pulled out a stool and stood a little unsteadily to bring an old chest down from a top shelf. It came down in a flurry of dust. She puffed on it, took a damp cloth and wiped the lacquered wood clean. "If he had lived I am sure he would have given you this. This was his old weapon."

She took out a bundle and set it on the table, next to the medicine scales, and fold by fold he opened up the cloth. Inside were three lengths of wood, dark and smooth with use, the middle length joined at both ends by three links of iron.

It was a nunchaku, a three-sectioned staff, the "coiling dragon staff."

Wei-fang's face lit up. "Thank you," he said. "Many many thanks!"

He picked it up reverently. "I remember he showed me this once. He said it was first used by Chao Hong Yin, the first Emperor of the Song Dynasty. Look, it is made of red maple. It is heavy but not stiff. Yielding but not soft. Each length of wood is matched to the other."

He took up a stance and spun the staff around his head, and it whirred in the air despite its age and frailty. He remembered the old man telling him about this weapon. "You can strike far," he had said, and the staff whistled through the air. "Medium, and close! Strike! Trap a weapon and pull it free, entangle horse's hooves, encumber an enemy and allow you to close," he had said, suddenly stepping forward and placing his foot on Wei-fang's, holding him in place, "and strike!"

Plum Blossom stood back and Wei-fang moved with growing confidence. Each night he remembered the words of Master Zhang: "Go to the Twelve-Sided Pagoda. There are great masters there. They can teach you."

The drum tower was sounding sunset when he finally said his goodbyes. Plum Blossom lingered at the door. Her old jacket was fading at the collar. Part of him wished that he could be satisfied with the simple home life. She might have made him a loyal and honest spouse.

But his spirit yearned for something more. A grander life. Less sure, less steady.

"Goodbye Wei-fang," she said. She put out a hand. She did not want to let go.

"I'll send word," he said. "I'll come back when I'm a great warrior!"

"Good," she said, and wondered how long she would wait, and very suddenly she stepped up and kissed his cheek.

He blushed to his navel, but she pushed him away. "Go. I will miss you. But do not come back until Master Zhang's ghost would be proud of you!"

Wei-fang was sadder than he could imagine as he walked home that night for the last time.

6

It was past midnight. The moon was rising. Wei-fang's pack was light. What else did a young man need when facing the unknown but food, a warm padded jacket, a spare pair of cotton shoes, his fighting manuals, and a pot of rice wine?

He moved silently from his own courtyard, past his parents' yard, the kitchens, the stables, and right to the back, where his father's chrysanthemum garden was cleared of pots and ready for winter.

Duung! From the drum tower the low throbbing note vibrated over the city. *Clok-clok!* came an answering sound. *Clok-clok!* as the night watchman struck his wooden block as he made his rounds. Wei-fang knew the man. He was a pleasant enough fellow, when not given power.

"All is well!" the man called out.

Wei-fang waited until the watchman had passed, and then waited a little longer. For a moment he felt regret and fear. There was a moment's clarity as he realized how the household would wake. In the morning, when the maids found his chamber empty, he knew what would happen. They would run back and forth, searching for him, and one of them would run to Pipa Alley to see if he'd spent the night there.

No one would dare to tell his mother. They would draw lots

as they always did, and at last when it could be hidden no longer, one of them would walk trembling into her room and fall to her knees and kowtow, and, trembling more, tell her that her only son had fled.

He pictured the maids in his mind. They had been like aunts to him: spoiling him, laughing at him, slipping him treats.

It's a fine way to reward them, Wei-fang thought, and steeled himself. With a sudden resolve he leaped up, and caught the top of the wall. He lay on the top of the tile roof and lingered for one last look.

Your last view of home is always the most beautiful, a poet had once written. So it seemed, he thought, as the moon rose over the gray tiled roofs with their curving eaves.

剑

As Wei-fang dropped down into the street, he felt a hand on his arm. He could tell from the instant it touched him that it was not the lazy night watchman. One finger pressed on the lines of his *qi* that ran up the inside of his arm, the thumb pressing hard onto the *lu* pressure point on his elbow. The application of force was hard, precise, and his hand curled uselessly. He tried to twist it away, but the hand held him tight. He fought harder, but he could not shake the hand off. Panic rose within him and through panic came fear. With his other hand and knee he pulled and shoved, kicked and tripped, but however much he used his strength the dark figure held onto him. "What is your name?" he said as he tried another shove.

The figure was shorter than him. It stepped into his attack. There was something familiar in the shape and movements of the man who had him. No, he thought, not man.

"You are a woman!" he said in surprise.

There was a low laugh that sounded familiar. "Am I?" a woman said.

He blocked the openhanded punch at his throat a moment before it choked him.

In an instant he knew who the fighter was. "You cannot stop me leaving," he said. The pressure on his arm increased and sweat started to form on his head.

"No?" the voice said. "Why should I find a bride for you, young warrior, if you are going to flee your home?" The figure stepped forward and in the shadows he saw the black smile and tried desperately to wrench his hand free. How could an old lady grip him so tightly? She laughed at his efforts. "You have much to learn," she told him. "There is no power in strength. The soft overcomes the strong. Weakness consumes the stiff. The man who fights will always lose. Struggle is weakness."

All this time her finger and thumb pressed into his *qi* lines. He tried a punch to her chest, and the blow was diverted. He kicked and the kick was blocked. He threw his pack at her and she was not there, and then suddenly he was on his back with steel fingernails prodding deep into his throat.

He felt them nick his skin.

"I said," the matchmaker purred, "that you have much to learn. Patience is one. You have skill. Just like your mother."

"My mother?"

"Not the one you call mother," the woman laughed. "But you are too old and willful and stupid! You should have left when Master Zhang told you."

"You knew Master Zhang?"

"Of course," she said. "I know much that is hidden."

"Do you know where the Twelve-Sided Pagoda is? He said his master might teach me."

"You want to go to the Twelve-Sided Pagoda? The old masters are dead. Hades Dai is master there now!" she said. "But you are too old to learn! He will not take you—go back to your mother!"

She let go of his wrist and pain flooded into his hand and fingertips. She put a hand to his chest—it was an almost gentle movement—but the force was such that he slammed against the wall. He grunted and slid slowly down, shaking his head to clear his vision.

At that moment came the *clok!* of the returning night watchman. In a single leap she landed on the opposite roof with a flap of robes.

Wei-fang saw the swinging paper lantern and grabbed his backpack. His hand throbbed uselessly as he tried to scramble up the wall after her, but she disappeared from view. He winced as he pursued her—a shadow running from rooftop to rooftop—lithe, animal almost. He hurtled after her. His legs pounded as he leaped from roof to roof, his pack flailing wildly in his hand.

He ran across the top of the Temple of Bounteous Truth and saw the matchmaker below him. She was crouched on all fours like a bat that has just landed. Her face turned up toward him in an inhuman movement and he understood that this was no human but a devil in human form sent to torment the weak.

Her lips peeled back in a snarl and her teeth were not stained black, but sharp and pointed white fangs. A red tongue hissed at him, and she suddenly leaped forward. He fell back in his terror, tumbled down head over heels, and landed with a heavy thud on his back in the middle of the temple yard.

A hiss made him jump once more in fright. He leaped up and grabbed for his sword, and saw a black mottled cat, back arched sideways like a moon bridge, hissing at him.

"Is that you?" he said and the cat hissed again.

"Where is the Twelve-Sided Pagoda?"

The cat teetered like a girl in high platform shoes. He wasn't sure it was the matchmaker. He had heard of shape-shifters and demons, but a temple did not seem the place to find them. "Ya!" he said and clapped his hands. It worked, the cat skittered off, and Wei-fang just had time to grab his pack and his staff before a sleepy monk thrust his head from the door of his sleeping chamber and looked out into the empty courtyard.

Wei-fang walked through the night, past sleeping villages where only dogs barked, and empty fields where bullfrogs bellowed. At the end of the first day he paused and leaned on his staff and looked back when he heard the faint ring of a bell carry over the fields. It struck three times. Miles of carefully tended wheat and cabbage fields, and the loess mud-brick houses with their bamboo groves that sprouted up like untidy clumps of mushrooms separated him from home.

Before him mountains rose, forbidding as temple guards on either side of the entrance hall, tumbling torrents of white water, and thick bamboo forest ahead. To the Twelve-Sided Pagoda, he thought, wherever that might be.

Wei-fang traveled from village to village. The peasants were wary when they saw the lone wanderer. The women hurried back to their homes. The men stood on the narrow walkways between the diligently planted fields and held their hoes and watched him until he had passed along the road.

At night he stretched and closed his eyes and slowed his breathing, until the world turned dark around him and he heard the creatures of the day replaced by the watching silence of the night, and he felt fear creep slowly over him, like rising water, and he breathed deeper and more calmly, kept his mouth free.

Each day after a breakfast of yesterday's bread or wild roots and hardy winter herbs, he pulled his pack onto his back and set off into the miles ahead. "I am looking for the Twelve-Sided Pagoda," he said when he met locals. Some were inbred and stupid people. Others refused to understand. But when he met fellow wanderers, or scholars, or crazed poets, then they would stop and listen, and perhaps share their wine and food with him.

"The Twelve-Sided Pagoda?" one man said. "I do not know, but if you are to study wushu, then Mount Song is the place to go. Shaolin Temple is there. I have heard that there is no better place to study the martial arts."

"No, my master said I must go to the Twelve-Sided Pagoda."

One day the sun was shining and the air was still and watchful, and Wei-fang opened up his padded jacket as he began to sweat. He came to a village. A fat man with a shaved scalp was sitting by the side of the road with a pot of wine, a bowl of rice half eaten by his side, his cotton padded coat open to let his belly air, his blue cotton trousers pulled up to his knees. He was chewing a dry rice stalk. He spat it out, looked Wei-fang up and down, pushed himself up, and waded toward him, belly first.

"Welcome," the man said. "It is a hot day for walking."

Bullies attracted cronies like flies around shit: noisy little men who needed a bully to make themselves feel important. Wei-fang took them all in, assessing their strengths, postures, weaknesses. His senses were suddenly sharp.

"Where are you going?" the bully said.

"Along the road."

The bully hitched up his trousers, sniffed and stuck out his gut. "There's a fee for this road."

"Is there?"

The bully nodded, belly out.

Wei-fang leaned on his staff. "And what is the fee?"

The bully laughed. "Cash, coin, work? You have a sister, perhaps, you could send her to pour our wine?"

Wei-fang laughed and the fat man's face turned unfriendly. He looked to his jackals and they all came forward. Wei-fang did not move. The first came at him from the right. Wei-fang dropped into fighting stance, the staff twirling around so fast it whistled through the air and knocked the man flat.

Two more came from the right, and Wei-fang gut-kicked one and felt the connection solid and true, the grunt of shock as the air was driven out of his lungs. The other tried to jump on Wei-fang's back and hold his arms. But as he leaped Wei-fang stepped in and met him with the end of the staff: a quick jab to the sternum. He landed next to the first, a sprawling mess of pain.

Wei-fang swung the staff and dropped into position, his fore-fingers together, pointing at the fat bully, his mouth closed, his nostrils flaring as he breathed. His confidence made most of them skittish. He lowered his chin and breathing, and the rest turned and ran, while the fat bully fell to his knees.

"Do not punish us!" he said.

Wei-fang scowled. "You shall let travelers pass on their way without worry or hindrance."

"Yes!" the fat man nodded.

"And if I hear otherwise, I shall return and take my revenge on you and all your family!"

剑

Wei-fang took the pot of wine as he left. He had a pleasant night that night, drinking to his own success.

Next morning, early, when the peasants were still walking out into their fields, poles balanced across their shoulders, Wei-fang reached a great crossroads. North was Luoyang, west Xian, south Nanyang, and east the Thirty-Six Peaks of Mount Song rose up straight from the plains: the chiseled valleys reaching up to high crags, thick with thorny bushes and low trees.

He turned that way. The mountain seemed to lure him forward. The villages fell away as the land rose and the fields were replaced by wild forest. The path was sometimes so overgrown that it was a green tunnel through trees and grasses and bamboo. The soil was dry and light; the scattered rocks turned underfoot, or slid away down the slope. It was tough climbing. Wei-fang set his staff in the ground and pushed himself up. The last pot of wine was long gone and he missed the taste and energy it gave him.

This was a strange wild land. The only huts here were those of woodsmen and hermits. As he reached the top of the mountain, he saw that what he had climbed were just foothills, mere essays, and before him rose the majestic peaks of Mount Song. Paths clung terrified to the edges of sheer drops. Looking up he could see the dark shapes of high temples, clinging like swallows' nests to high crags. As he stood a gibbon howled high up—the noise almost lost on the breeze—a strange and wondrous sound that echoed back from the sheer cliff faces.

Wei-fang sat and shook his head. He had thought of many challenges ahead but the heights before him were dumbfounding. Before him he could see no path, and without a path there was no way through.

He sat down almost in tears. He felt defeated. He would have begged for a pot of wine then, he thought. And racked by lonesome thoughts, he lay down, alone under the stars, and slept.

7

On the second day of searching Wei-fang came across a little track, such as goats made, and followed it through the dappled green shadows of bamboo and cedar trees. The wind whistled a light and mournful note in the long-hanging cedar needles. The bamboos rustled and swayed all as one.

The path led down through sharp craggy rocks to a torrent of white water. He clambered down over mighty fallen rocks, wet with moss and spray, and stood at the brink and felt the cold damp on his face.

The torrent made him tremble. How could he cross such a deluge?

He looked up and down and saw that it would be death to try and pass: one false footing would send him tumbling into the writhing snakes of water.

He squatted down and splashed his face. The water had a clean fresh taste. He refilled his wine pot, and let the white noise wash over him.

He was about to go back when he saw a deer come down to the stream on the far bank. It did not notice him. It was a young female with lean brown flanks and nervous ears. She stepped delicately as she came down the rocks and bent to sip the water.

If he had a bow, he thought, and at that moment the deer

looked up and saw him, and in a flash the dappled forest was empty. In the shadows he saw a simple bamboo bridge, and he clambered toward it over rocks that were twice his height or more. All the time the roar of water filled his hearing. But when he got to the top he saw the bridge, if three lengths of bamboo lashed together with reed ropes could be called such a thing.

Muttering a prayer of blessing he balanced his way across and leaped up the rocks on the other side, finding the path again, which after an hour or so brought him to a level space and a little clearing where stood a shaggy little hut of bamboo with reeds as a roof.

A little monk sat cross-legged on the bare earth outside his house, a copper begging bowl on the ground before him. Over his shoulders was thrown a raincoat of leaves. His eyes were closed. His face was as wrinkled and brown and glossy as a polished walnut.

Wei-fang stopped and looked around. The clearing was empty. Birds were calling. It seemed like a trap. He walked warily forward.

"Hello," he called.

The man did not move or open his eyes. Wei-fang came forward again. He held onto his staff and crouched down a few feet before the man. In the bowl he saw no money, but a few green leaves, a twig with two chestnuts, and a wrinkled old peach.

Under his raincoat the monk appeared to be naked. The skin of his chest and belly was slack and empty and sagging, like old women's breasts.

Suddenly his eyes opened. "Welcome," the man said, and smiled.

Wei-fang hesitated before moving any closer. He held his hands open. "I have nothing to give."

"I find that hard to believe," the old monk said. "It is a poor

71

man who cannot give another anything. You do not seem so impoverished. Not to me, at least."

"You are right," Wei-fang said as he sat down on the other side of the copper bowl and pulled open the top of his sack. "I have this." He took out half a steamed bun he had saved. "It is all the food I have left. I've been thinking all day of eating it. But it is said that a man can find good friends with half a piece of bread and a cup of wine."

"A cup of wine. Did you bring wine?"

Wei-fang took out his wine pot, removed the porcelain stopper and tipped it on end, and let the last few drops of water fall.

The old man shut his eyes and said, "Even in the water I smell wine. It sings to me. Does it sing to you?"

"Yes," Wei-fang said and tore the piece of stale bread in half, dropping one half into the monk's bowl. The monk took the bread and tore off a small piece.

They sat silently and ate. Wei-fang swallowed his piece in two mouthfuls. The monk nibbled slowly at his, like a mouse. Wei-fang watched each crumb with the yawning hole of his stomach wishing he had kept the whole piece for himself. At the end the monk looked into his bowl, took the twig with the chestnuts and broke them both off, handing one to Wei-fang and cracking the other open with his back teeth. He shared the leaves also, and then he lifted out the peach, dusted away a few scraps of dirt from the fur-matted skin, and after a moment's consideration he presented it to Wei-fang with both hands.

"Eat," he said, and when Wei-fang tried to hand it back he shut his eyes and shook his head.

The peach was soft and sweet, and Wei-fang was so hungry he ate it all, even where the wasps had scarred it.

At the end the monk reached behind him and brought out a bamboo dipper filled with rainwater. He lifted it to his mouth and slurped loudly. After he had drunk he offered it to Wei-fang. He took a long draft, and handed it back.

"It is better than wine, is it not?"

Wei-fang laughed. He was not so sure.

The monk drank again. They sat in silence for a little while, paused to listen to the forest.

"It is so quiet here in winter. No one sings, except the gibbons. But in summer the cicadas fill the forest with song, until one by one, their song lessens, and when autumn comes, the last cicada sings a solitary song, and there are none left to answer. I think it is sad to hear the call of the last cicada. Does it know its season is almost over, I wonder? Is that why they sing so loud in summer? What do you think?"

"I do not think so much of cicadas, to be honest."

"No? Why? Tell me you are not one of those who thinks only of himself. That way lies madness." He held out his arms. "I think little of myself, but much of the world. All the world, from the black cicada to the mountain leopard. I think of them all. They are all my concern, all living beings."

"Cicadas sing in the spring as well as the autumn."

"Yes, but not so long or so intensely."

They sat and listened to the forest's deep silence for a while. There was a rustle of wind through bamboo thickets.

"What is your name?" the monk said.

"Wei-fang. You?"

"Me? Do I need a name? Wild Old Man, some call me. The Mount Song Hermit, say others. You can call me whatever you like. It does not change what I am. Names do not have such power."

"I will call you Mount Song Hermit."

The Mount Song Hermit bowed. "Did you come looking for me? No, I see not. So you must be looking for something else.

73

Tell me, if this is not your destination, then where are you going?"

"I am looking for the Twelve-Sided Pagoda."

Mount Song Hermit looked at him and shook his head. "Why?"

"I am looking for a master."

"A master of what?"

"A teacher. Of wushu."

"Ah! You are a warrior. I see. That is a dangerous path."

"I am not afraid," Wei-fang said quickly.

"No? You should be." Wei-fang felt foolish. The old man sighed and nodded to himself. "There are demons and sorcerers and fox spirits and worse."

Wei-fang nodded. He would not show his fear.

The day was drawing on. The sun set early here and the mountains blocked out the light. As it touched the high western crags and lit the edge with gold the Mount Song Hermit suddenly stood up. "It is time to sleep," he said. "Would you like to share my poor hut?" He went inside without waiting for an answer and lay down on a bed of old brown bamboo leaves. Wei-fang noticed that there was no door on the hut. He was going to ask about it but the Mount Song Hermit was already snoring gently.

Wei-fang used his pack as a pillow, and soon he slept too: a deep and gentle sleep.

剑

In the morning the Mount Song Hermit had already risen. Wei-fang could hear him rustling outside. He yawned. He felt strangely refreshed and when he went out he saw the Mount Song Hermit putting the last touches to a feast of roots and herbs.

"Come," he said. "Eat!"

Wei-fang had never seen such curious dishes. The Mount Song Hermit introduced each to him. He held up a worm. "This is good for the spleen," he said. A knobbly thin root was good for the liver. "This is for fat women. It will help them lose weight." He took a nibble from each and Wei-fang hungrily crunched through them all.

At the end the Mount Song Hermit, who had hardly eaten anything, patted his stomach as if he had consumed a great feast. "So," he said. "You are taking the narrow road up into the mountain interior?" They stood and lifted their faces to gaze the mountain in the face. "I am going down, it is an easier path. If you go up it will not be easy."

"Sometimes the hard path is a better one to tread."

The Mount Song Hermit did not look at him, but he nodded slowly as if weighing the young man's words. At the end he smiled. "You may be right," he said. "If you go I do not think we shall meet again."

The words seemed ominous.

"Perhaps we shall meet in another life," the Mount Song Hermit said as farewell. There was no sadness there, simply fact.

The Mount Song Hermit led Wei-fang to the base of the path. The cliff rose ahead like an enormous wall. "There are steps carved into the rock. It is steep sometimes. You will need to hold the chain to make your way across."

Wei-fang wanted to embrace the man, but he waved his hand and turned and left with a rustle of his reed cloak.

Wei-fang walked to the cliff face. The steps were little more than chiseled hand- and foot-holes. He put his hand to the rock.

It was cool but not cold, hard and gritty to the palm. It did not crumble. He looked up. The cliff face was a little off vertical, but now as he stood at the bottom the height seemed to have grown, but there was only one way up, he thought, and put his right foot into one hole and his right hand into another, and then he began to climb.

It took him half an hour to reach the chain, and there the cliff was less steep and the path slanted left and then right, before an overhang where the chain hung down.

Wei-fang looked behind him. Space yawned at his back. He swayed for a moment as the space seemed to suck at him. It was almost sentient, as if it willed him to jump.

He closed his eyes. When he opened them he found that he was clinging to the rock, his face pressed against it, his breathing wild. He did not look down. He looked up to where the chain hung. It was old and iron, and even though it was mottled with rust, the links seemed strong and uncorroded.

He tugged at it. It was solid. He let out a breath, tugged once more and then pushed himself up. The higher he got the more pronounced the overhang became, until his legs were swinging wildly, looking for purchase. There is no foothold, he told himself, and calmed himself. Panic here would be death. He would not panic. He would keep climbing. The chain creaked. The iron links ground against each other. They were stiff with the weight. He kept climbing. He felt the muscles in his arms strain and for a wild moment he imagined letting go and tumbling back to the earth's rough kiss.

And then he was at the top. It was hard getting purchase over the lip of the cliff. He scrabbled for the chain, but it was pulled so tight he could not get his fingers underneath. He pulled at grass and it came away in his hand. He found a stem of bamboo and his hand clamped around it and it seemed firm. He shut his eyes and pulled, and inch by inch he made it, crawling like a worm, not daring to lift his weight in case he lost his footing and tumbled down to his death.

剑

Wei-fang lay on the top and shook with delayed fear, then rose and dusted himself down, and looked around him. He pushed through bracken and found a narrow trail that met the path, which was lined with gray pebbles, and led off through the thick forest. He picked up his pack and started walking.

Wei-fang climbed for two days toward the peaks of Song Mountain.

There were thirty-six peaks, men said, and as many temples. There was the Shaolin Temple, where the finest wushu masters were trained. Fawang Temple, the Temple of the Bounteous Fist, the Forest of Pagodas.

The ways were deserted, except for old Taoist masters, who stood like stones, exposing themselves to wind and rain and lichen. Above—always above him—gibbons called out: long and strange and melancholy. Or old monks who sat with their sutras and mumbled through them, waiting for passing birds to fill their begging bowls with nuts or fruit, whatever was in season.

"I am looking for the Twelve-Sided Pagoda," he told them, but none of them knew.

As the day darkened the air grew chill, and mist rose up from the valleys below, until he stood in evening gloom with a wall of pale mist all around him. He was lost and he was alone, and he was going to starve if he did not turn back. Then he stumbled forward; a great chasm opened up before him, but fifty feet below he saw a man dressed in simple black trousers, stripped to the waist despite the cold, practicing Eagle Style Fists: clawed fingers gripping, catching and locking an arm or leg to their maximum, striking pressure points.

The style reminded him of the old woman who fought him the night he left home.

"Hoi!" he shouted.

The man kept fighting, but once this move was done, he stopped, performed the last moves, and then turned and looked up.

"I am looking for Hades Dai and the Twelve-Sided Pagoda!" Wei-fang shouted, then waved and scrambled down the slope.

The man turned. He was lean and fit but his hair was shot through with gray. He gestured for Wei-fang to approach, and stood silent and still as he waited.

"You are looking for Hades Dai? Are you sure you want to find him? He is not a gentle man. Many fear him. Even I fear him."

"You?"

The lean man nodded. Wei-fang drew in a deep breath and nodded. "Yes," he said. "My first master told me to come to study at the Twelve-Sided Pagoda. I am Wei-fang."

The man took Wei-fang in. "My name is Iron Crow. Hades Dai only takes the best fighters. If you wish to join his band you must defeat one of his men."

"I can do it."

"Can you?"

Wei-fang jutted out his chin. "Yes," he said.

The man named Iron Crow made a sudden movement, and Wei-fang found himself slammed flat on his back. He groaned and pushed himself up.

"Why did you do that?" he said.

"Wrong question," Iron Crow said.

"How did you do that?"

Iron Crow put out a hand and pulled Wei-fang up. The old man's smile was as sudden as monsoon rain. "Good," he said. "There is hope. If you really want to join Hades Dai then I will teach you."

Wei-fang nodded seriously.

"Only when I think you are ready will I take you to meet Hades Dai. And the rest is up to you."

8

"Is it far?" Wei-fang asked as they tramped along, but the warrior named Iron Crow did not answer. As they climbed, the trees and bushes and bamboo fell away, and at the top of a rocky outcrop Iron Crow stopped. There was a black pagoda, stabbing up into the evening blue sky, closer. "We are going there?"

Iron Crow nodded. Each step they took toward the pagoda increased Wei-fang's sense of foreboding. Iron Crow had spent many days training him, and this morning he had decided. He was a man of few words but, after he had finished the rice that Wei-fang had cooked, he had said, "You are ready."

"I am?"

Iron Crow nodded. "We shall go today."

"Is it far?"

"Far enough," Iron Crow had said.

They had spent a long day winding deeper into the hills. A bat flew overhead. Wei-fang flinched as if it were a missile aimed at him. He cursed himself and bumped into Iron Crow, who had abruptly stopped.

"You are come to the Camp of the West Lotus warriors," he said. "And the master, Hades Dai . . ."

Wei-fang stopped and looked up at the pagoda and the ringing mountain crags. Two great stone guardian statues leered down at him, their enormous sabers and halberds ready to fend off evil spirits.

He faltered. This was not what he had expected. He had imagined Hades Dai to be an older, wiser version of Master Zhang: jutting white eyebrows, smooth baby skin, riddling speech. Instead he saw grisly totems, scalps and worse, nailed to the trees, and before, at the foot of a great black tree, was a pyramid of skulls: the empty sockets staring out at him in silent warning.

Wei-fang stopped.

"What is wrong?" Iron Crow said, and then saw where his student was looking. "I told you this was dangerous. Those are the ones who tried to oppose Hades Dai," he explained, "and those who have tried to join the West Lotus Temple and failed. Are you sure you still want to continue?"

Wei-fang opened his mouth, but before he could answer a voice boomed out.

"Who approaches the camp of the West Lotus warriors?"

"It is Iron Crow. I bring one who wishes to join the camp."

"What is his name?"

Iron Crow stood aside. Wei-fang told himself that this was his moment. It was the trial he would have to pass through. His voice betrayed his fear. "I am Wei-fang. The Iron Knight."

"That is a grand name."

"And I am a grand fighter."

There was low laughter. Wei-fang's eyes were drawn to a giant who moved through them like a grown man through children. Stripped to the waist, he had a broad belly, thick leather girdle, and coal-hard eyes. His hair was white, but there was no infirmity about the man. He was broad and tall, moved like a tiger, heavy and lithe and deadly.

"Greetings, Iron Knight," he said, and with a casual move swept his blade, a broad saber, calmly through the air. "You like my sheath?" he said, and held it up in an absent-minded manner. "I had it stitched from the skin of the last man who tried to kill me. His name was Ox Neck Lo. He accused me of sleeping with his wife." As he spoke he put the edge of his sword to a spinning whetstone. Sparks flew off, he lifted it clear, tested it, and put it back to grind once more. The second time blood started from his thumb. Hades Dai slid the blade back into the scabbard. "In that he was not wrong . . ." he said, "but is it a crime to love a beautiful and easy woman?"

He licked the blood and took a step toward Wei-fang. "What do you think, child?"

Wei-fang shook his head. "No crime," he stammered.

Hades Dai strode toward him, and Wei-fang wasn't sure if the ground was shaking, or if his own legs were quivering. "I killed her too," Hades Dai said, and patted the sheath of his knife. "Because she could not keep a secret. Can you keep secrets, child?"

Wei-fang nodded. He willed Hades Dai to believe him, for he was sure that the only other future for him was death.

"Really?" Hades Dai said, and stretched out a hand. Iron Crow stepped between them. "His name is Wei-fang. He has come to seek a master."

Hades Dai gave a short, almost sad, sigh. "Another for the pyramid of skulls," he said. "Where do you come from, child?"

"Luoyang," Wei-fang said.

"Who was your master?"

"Master Zhang of the Three-Sectioned Staff."

Hades Dai looked at Wei-fang as if calculating how much his dead body would weigh. "Can you fight?"

Wei-fang nodded and scrambled to pull the three-sectioned staff from his pack. "I have this," he said.

Hades Dai plucked it from his hands and regarded it for a long time. He looked up, and his eyes were black pits, into which the last dregs of Wei-fang's courage flowed.

Hades Dai returned the weapon to Wei-fang, then faced his guards, deliberately leaving his back exposed.

"You." At last he picked out one of the masked warriors, a fat man with a face mask of red and white swirls. It was an evil-looking face. The man stepped forward smartly.

"Put this child to the test. See if he is worthy."

The man did not speak and there was no warning as he leaped into the attack. Wei-fang leaped aside as the halberd point whistled over his head. There was barely time to react. He jumped up, and the backhanded swing swished under his feet. The red-masked warrior was like a tireless puppet, stepping forward, swinging, thrusting, dancing from one posture to the next.

His halberd was six feet long, tasseled red, and with a great saber blade on top. Wei-fang watched it. His life depended on its every move and movement, the angle of the next attack, the set of the warrior's shoulders. Any mistake meant death.

He caught the shaft and tried to pull it out of the foe's hands, but through the mouthpiece the enemy smiled, and wrenched the three-sectioned staff out of Wei-fang's hands instead.

Now he was weaponless.

"Kill him," Hades Dai laughed, and the fat warrior strode forward to do his master's bidding.

Wei-fang leaped and jumped and fought for every second of life, and as he bent back to avoid another swipe that shaved the cloth clasps from his jacket, he heard a gasp from the spectators. The red-faced opera-masked man was grunting now, his breath coming in slow gasps.

Wei-fang saw his moment and knew that if he did not strike now he would die here. He caught the halberd shaft, broke it on his knee and took the blade from the end. He brandished it as a sword.

There was a thud, of a butcher's cleaver chopping through pork. The red-masked man fell heavily onto his face. Blood covered his back, and ran onto the floor in a thick, dark puddle.

"A halberd against an unarmed man. Fat, pathetic fool," Hades Dai said, and held out his sword for one of his guard to wipe.

The ring was tight around Wei-fang. All the camp denizens, who had been sitting at open fires boiling medicine or cooking dinner, had gathered to watch this duel. Some wore their hair long and unbound, others had their hair in a long queue, hanging by the side of their head, or bound up like a snake. A few were also monks, with clean-shaven scalps. There were women also. Some of them were clearly warriors from the way they stood, others cooks, and a few had the painted faces and red lips of concubines. Their eyes were keen now, as bright as cats who smell blood.

"You!" Hades Dai said, and a girl came sliding sideways. She too wore an opera mask: painted white face, pink cheeks and elaborately painted eyes. There was something sinisterly beautiful about her, long limbed, lithe and graceful as a crane, but then she came for his throat with the speed and violence of a mantis. Hands, knees, elbows, fists, heel-kicks, bow-leg kicks, fingers stabbing for his vital points. Death blow after death blow

84

whirling at him until her limbs were a blur and his arms were giving up, his forearms sore from the constant blocking and turning.

She came forward at him, and he stepped back, once, twice, three times, and then suddenly a blow connected and he grunted as the wind was knocked out of him. He tried to inhale but the woman had him over her knee. The soft and gentle face of the female opera singer stared down at him, and behind it he saw the eyes: large, dark and deadly. And at his neck he felt her fingers, ready to stop the flow of blood to his brain.

"Shall I kill him?"

There was a long pause. Wei-fang looked for pity in her black eyes, but there was none. They were hard and set and they were the last thing he would ever see.

"Yes," Hades Dai said.

Wei-fang did not struggle. He had failed, he told himself. But this death was better than a common life, growing old, wishing for things he might have done. Her fingers pressed and he felt the world going dark.

"Stop!" a voice shouted. "Do not kill him. Give him to me. He is mine."

Wei-fang shook himself as he sat up. A skinny hag came toward him, measuring each step with her staff. She reached out for him with one hand, bony and skeletal, and touched his face. It was then he saw that she was blind, and he shivered with revulsion. There was something witchlike about this woman.

"Fools! I have not lost my sight," the Blind Enchantress said. "Nor skill of scent. This one should not be killed. Hear me, swordsman."

A shadow fell over them as Hades Dai approached. His saber was pointed at her chest. Wei-fang could see a curling red dragon on the blade. It was still smoking from the whetstone.

"This one smells of fear," she said. "And you smell of pride and lust and longing. Don't point your sword at me, warrior. It was sharp enough for your thumb. If you want to kill me how can I resist?"

"So tell me, witch. Why should I not have this one killed?"

"Because he is the one I foretold."

The Blind Enchantress reached out. As she touched the broadsword she flinched for a moment, as if stung, then she ran her fingers along the blade. She pressed just hard enough to open up her skin. She sighed at the cut, and tenderly caressed the flat of the blade, leaving a smear of fresh blood.

The timber of her voice changed. It became rhythmic. Intoning, like a wild shaman. "The blind see better than the sighted. I see a blade forged in deepest mountain fire. Nine hundred times was its metal turned. Steeped in its iron is the blood of kings and priests. To hold such a sword is to lay a claim on greatness."

Her forefingers walked along the blade until they found the hilt, then she reached a bloody palm up toward Hades Dai's face.

A hand seized her wrist.

"Let go of me, Iron Crow," she said. "This is between me and your master."

Iron Crow looked to Hades Dai. He nodded slowly, and did not flinch as the blind witch peered up at him with hollow sockets. She put her bleeding hand onto his face, smeared it with her own blood.

"He is dying," she said. "I feel it. His spirit is getting ready to leave the world."

Hades Dai's voice was deep, like gravel. "Who?"

"A great lord has passed away. He was the only prince who took an interest in the Iron Way. Now he is gone there will be chaos in the martial world. One warrior must rise. To rule. To do that he needs a weapon that all will obey."

Wei-fang saw the light in Hades Dai's eyes change. He saw lust for power. Lust to dominate all others. To be obeyed.

"Who is this 'great lord'?" he asked.

"You ask the wrong questions, priest!" the Blind Enchantress hissed. "I see a straight sword. A sword from the mists of history. From the hands of the greatest of warriors. That sword has always marked the ruler of the martial world from the others. If you wish to command, then that sword must be seized and held. It is the Green Destiny."

A hush fell over them. In the silence one man laughed, and clapped.

"The Green Destiny, the magical sword. That's a tale for children." Iron Crow looked at the hag with clear distaste. She hissed at him and reached out, fingers gripping the air like claws. Those who were there thought they saw the image of a sword, a green sword, slowly turning as if it were proffering its hilt to any who would take it. One by one they stepped back, but Iron Crow reached out, and there was a sudden flash of green light, and when Wei-fang opened his eyes again he saw that Hades Dai had swatted Iron Crow to the ground.

"Do not speak of that of which you know little," the Blind Enchantress hissed as Iron Crow blinked away the green stars, but he could see them even when his eyes were closed.

"How do we know it is real?" he said. "How do we believe this fox spirit!"

The hag shuffled toward Hades Dai and he drew back as she did a little circular dance at his feet. "I am offering you the Green Destiny. Do you know what powers it possesses? It was forged by masters in the time of the Three Kingdoms. Guanyu himself carried it. No one has seen that sword for years. Imagine the sword of Guanyu at your side. What could you not achieve? Do not question me, Crow." The hag dismissed him with a flick of her hand and laughed. "It is a waste of time to speak to the man who lacks wisdom. The sword is not lost. It is hidden, hidden by the House of Te. Its keeper is no more. It seeks a master. It looks for power . . ."

Hades Dai's voice became distant. "What power?"

"The sword gives power of command," the Blind Enchantress hissed. "Who would not obey you, if you wielded the sword at your side?"

"Where is this sword?"

"It is in the House of Te."

"Then how can we hope to storm the place? The House of Te lies within the heart of the capital. How can we get it?"

"Sow chaos across the Empire. You should draw out Duke Te's warriors. The spirits are gathering. Now the old man is dead, and the nest is empty and the eagle can strike." The witch stood behind Wei-fang. He flinched as she put a hand on his head. The hand was cool and hard and leathery. He felt uncomfortable at the touch. More uncomfortable as she pushed him forward. "Not legions, priest. Not armies. Shadows. Shadows on the wall shall seek the Green Destiny. A shadow can pass where a cat cannot go."

"Speak plain, witch, before I make you a head's length shorter."

"Glory is not won with words," she said. "But by action. Your time is now. But you must act soon. I have seen it, but your chance is short. It will not outlast this moon."

"And who should be our shadow?"

The witch put both hands onto Wei-fang's head. "This one," she said. "I have seen it."

Hades Dai and Iron Crow exchanged looks.

Wei-fang stood up. Hades Dai was a head and more taller than him. He faced the naked chest, bull neck and jutting head. Intelligence as well as power was there. A cunning, evil look.

"You have been chosen," he said. "Can you do this? Swear to me that you will bring this thing to me!"

"No!" a voice shouted. A woman's voice, clear and stern. They turned, and a black-clad figure came down the slope, a straight sword sheathed over her back.

She came down without drawing her weapon, calmly walked into the circle. She stopped before Hades Dai.

"You cannot take this one," she said.

"Why not?"

"Because I say so. I have crossed the Empire looking for this boy. Now, at last, I have found him."

"And who are you?"

She lifted her chin and spoke without fear in a voice that was both loud and clear. "My family name is Jade, my given name is Jiaolong," she said.

Wei-fang looked from one to the other. As Hades Dai's attention shifted from him to this woman, he felt a wave of relief. He was out of his depth. These were real warriors. Deadlier than any snake.

As Wei-fang stood, Hades Dai put his head back and laughed. "I know you," he said, and as he pulled his great broadsword from its leather sheath the blade erupted in blue flames. "I knew your teacher, Jade Fox. Think you can fight better than her?"

"Of course!"

He laughed. "But not well enough to beat me."

"Let the Heavens decide that."

He glowered at her. "I killed your friend, Dark Cloud. His skull sits on my trophy pile. Yours shall join it."

The great warrior leaped forward and the Hellfire Blade flared yellow as it descended, but Jiaolong was not there. She drew her sword faster than Wei-fang could see and opened a long red gash across the giant's ribs.

"You're tickling me," he said and laughed, and came forward again, his sword roaring with flames, as if he were waving a torch before him. Wei-fang had never seen a woman fight so well. She was small, stern, handsome and utterly fearless. It was like watching a dog stand before a buffalo and refuse to yield—and start, impossibly, to win.

Silently the West Lotus warriors formed a ring around the two fighters. The law of their fraternity meant that one of the warriors had to die. There was no escape here. It seemed to Wei-fang that Hades had met his match and would soon have his head displayed on his own trophy pile. The woman's breath came in ragged gasps, but she was turning the battle. Hades Dai was bleeding from a dozen cuts. He was starting to slow, his sweeps becoming more and more frantic. Wei-fang cheered Hades Dai with all the others, but he secretly willed the female warrior to be victorious.

"Faster!" Wei-fang willed Jiaolong. She was twisting and turning like a snake, always an inch ahead of Hades Dai's blade. But at that moment the hag threw something onto the fire and a thick acrid smoke began to curl up into the air. It made them all cough, but as Jiaolong coughed, her breaths came harder and more strangled, and each cough slowed her and seemed to seize her ribs in their fist.

She put her hand to her lip, and the hand was smeared with blood. She stopped suddenly, held her sword up in salute, and caught Wei-fang's eye.

"I have found you at last," she said under her breath. Then spoke louder and with growing confidence, "Do not fear. Take your destiny. Take the Green Destiny!"

Hades Dai roared as he swung the Hellfire Blade. Wei-fang blinked and turned away as her neck was cut clean through.

There was a thud as the head hit the ground, and another as the body fell the other way. There was a great roar from all the West Lotus warriors. Only Wei-fang and Iron Crow made no noise.

Wei-fang opened his eyes and saw Hades Dai laughing as he gathered the woman's head up by the long black hair.

"Jiaolong!" he laughed as he threw her head to the ground. "Dark Cloud has been waiting for you!"

The woman's eyes had rolled up into her head. Her mouth was open and blood trickled from the stump of her neck. Next to the head a white skull sat. Bigger, broader, with fine white teeth still rooted into the jaws.

Wei-fang swore. "Who was she?" he asked.

"You have not heard of Jiaolong?"

He shook his head. "She was a great warrior. Very great, but she disappeared nearly twenty years ago. I thought she was dead. Dark Cloud certainly thought so," said Iron Crow.

"And who was he?"

"A bandit. Charming, but a bandit."

Wei-fang paused to look at the two heads.

"Were they lovers?"

"So Dark Cloud claimed. But he was a braggart."

Wei-fang turned away.

"Come," Iron Crow said. "It is time to train."

剑

A fortnight later, Hades Dai summoned Wei-fang to him.

"It is time," he said. He pointed to the full moon, rising above the mountain ridges. "The hag has seen it. She says you must seize this sword before the moon is full again."

Wei-fang packed his sack. He stood aside from the rest of the West Lotus warriors. They had never accepted him. He had not beaten their sister in combat. He should not be one of them. Wei-fang did not feel safe turning his back on them. He did not feel safe around any of them, least of all Hades Dai.

Only Iron Crow came to say farewell. He walked with him to the waiting horse and spoke confidentially. "Do not fail," he said.

"And if I do?"

"Do not. There is no escape from Hades Dai. Wherever you run, he will track you down, and he will make you pay."

Wei-fang met his teacher's gaze and solemnly nodded.

"I understand."

剑

The night Wei-fang left, Hades Dai stood with the blind hag over a brazier of hot coals. "The chosen one leaves," she chanted, "the ones who might obstruct us must die."

She threw herbs into the fire and breathed the acrid white smoke.

One by one she named warriors who had to be killed to help her master.

Black Mountain Bear. Gold Phoenix. Eagle Hu. Mantis Li. After each name, Hades Dai looked at his warriors: "Find him and kill him."

And they nodded and ran for their weapons and horses.

The air grew cold as the list went on.

And at the end of the list the blind hag said, "Wait, spirit, wait! I am saving her for last." She turned away from the spirit world and seemed to be addressing them now. "Oh, how she has called to me."

"Who?" Hades Dai said, but the hag went on without answering.

"On clear nights her ghost calls out for vengeance. Always vengeance." She shivered with pleasure. "And Hades Dai, greatest of warriors," she said with a low moan that was half grief, half pleasure, "you must kill the swordsman, Yu Shulien. She will come to the capital via the Vulture Peak Pass. Find her and kill her."

Hades Dai looked and picked out five of his finest warriors. They came forward smartly and looked up at their leader, whose gaze lingered on the trophies he had collected. "Bring her to me alive, if you can. I should like to add her skull to my collection. Her hair would make a fine sash for my sword, do you not think?"

9

Shulien had the odd feeling that she was being watched as she stepped up into the carriage. But the street was empty except for three Mongol horsemen, the six bearers of a Shanxi banker's palanquin as they lifted him up, and an old Tibetan beggar woman, swinging her prayer wheel around and around.

Shulien paused for a moment. But there was nothing unusual, and no one looking her way. The Tibetan lady shuffled toward her, a wooden bowl thrust out from her heavy woolen coat.

Shulien put a copper coin into the bowl, and the old lady slipped it into the folds of her sash and shuffled on. Shulien's gaze followed her.

"Something wrong?" Mule Wang, her driver, said as he hitched the pony to the front of the two-wheeled carriage. He was skinny and talkative and she was happy to let him talk. It took the pressure from her. "Sure you don't want to wait for the caravan to be assembled?"

"No. They will be too slow. I have to be there before the next full moon. It's urgent."

"Really?"

"It is. Life and death, really."

"Whose?"

Shulien laughed. "A friend of mine died. Well, my patron. Duke Te."

"Duke Te?" Mule Wang said. "*The* Duke Te?"

Shulien nodded. It was odd to hear of Duke Te being spoken about with such reverence. She had known him since she was a child. Her father had worked for him as a guard, and they had visited the duke's hall many times when he was the governor of their province. She remembered him as a kind and gentle man, who turned a little to fat in his middle years, and sported long, slender moustaches, and a simple round black cap. One day, when Shulien was five or six, she was allowed in to see the duke and he had slipped her a sesame cracker, turned to her father and said, "Your daughter is very pretty. Will you teach her the Iron Way?"

Her father had smiled wanly. "Her mother wants her to marry."

But the young Shulien had leaped up and down at the chance. "Yes, please, Father! Please! Teach me, teach me, teach me!"

"Let us see," her father had said.

Her father, who had worked as a guard for traveling merchants and scholars, had served the duke faithfully, and when he had fallen foul of corrupt local magistrates, it was Duke Te who had saved him from being beaten with the bamboo pole. Since then faithfulness and loyalty had deepened between the families, until Shulien had come to think of the duke as a second father. He had spoken up for her many times, in particular when the day came for her feet to be bound.

"Please don't let them break my toes," Shulien had said. "I want to be a warrior, not a housewife. Will you speak to my parents for me, please?"

"I think you would be wise to teach her," Duke Te had said, and when her mother had protested, the duke had spoken to her as well and won her around.

"Do not bind this girl's feet," he said. "Her future is finer than that of a wife and mother. She could be a warrior."

"My fear is that the Iron Way is not one for a woman. She will die alone and lonely," her mother had said.

It was only to Duke Te that Shulien had admitted that she wished she had married Mubai when she'd had the chance. "You were faithful to Silent Wolf's memory," he told her.

"But I did not know him," she had answered.

"He was the man your father chose for you. And he chose well. I knew Silent Wolf before his death. He was a hard and determined fighter. But he was lost, as are many who travel the Iron Way."

Shulien sat for a while, letting the past rise around her and fill her thoughts. "Yes, *the* Duke Te. And I want to be there at his funeral."

Mule Wang hurried to strap the pony into place. "Well, let me get the pony hitched and we shall be off!" he said.

剑

Shulien had hired Mule Wang two days before to take her the last stage of the way to Beijing. "I started with mules," he had explained as she agreed a price. "But I saved money. Now I buy ponies. I have ponies, my son has ponies, my brothers have ponies, even the brothers of my wife have ponies! But still men call me Mule Wang! Ha!"

The cart was a simple construction: two large wheels and a small lattice-covered carriage on the back. As Shulien stepped up she saw that it was almost filled with sacks of wheat and fresh cotton mattresses and embroidered shoes of the type that village girls made for other women's marriages. She turned and looked at him. "Where do I sit?"

"I bought those this morning." Mule Wang frowned as he slapped the cotton sacks aside. "These will make you more comfortable," he said. "The last stretch of the road is not so good these days."

Shulien squeezed herself between the wheat sacks and bags of raw cotton and then he handed her pack back to her. It sat on her lap like a fat child. She could not move left or right or forward. She felt like a pig in a wicker basket being carried to market.

Mule Wang grinned. "Good?"

Shulien made a non-committal movement of her head.

Mule Wang grinned as he jumped up onto the lip of the carriage and pulled out his whip. "Ya!" he shouted and the cart lurched forward. Shulien let out a weary sigh. However far you travel, the saying went, the road will lead you back home.

It was not the same for her, she thought. Travel always took her away from home. It took her back to the past as well, a place she did not want to go.

剑

It was the end of winter. The wind was cold, but the fields were busy with peasants ploughing the yellow soil, while the women followed behind, beating drums to frighten off the crows.

When the sun shone it was a pleasant time to travel. The air grew warm, neither too hot nor dry, the scent of wood fires on the breeze. The winds were gentle and women were sweeping out their houses, hanging their thick cotton mattresses in the sun to air. Spring was nearly here, and then it would be summer. Shulien's mind rested on the thought of warmth and light and plenty. She was startled when Mule Wang spoke.

"Duke Te was the son of the Emperor?"

"Yes," Shulien said. "The third son. He cared deeply for the kingdom. Heaven is high, and the Emperor is far away, men say, but Duke Te saw there was injustice and was determined to fight it. He brought the best warriors to his household, and sent them out into the world, to right wrongs."

"*Wa!*" Mule Wang said. He seemed speechless for a moment. "A good man!" There was a pause. "To think I am carrying a friend of the son of the Emperor in my lowly horse cart," he said. "I will tell my sons and brothers when I get home and they will want to know all about you!"

Shulien smiled. It was not so exciting, she thought. She knew. She had lived every minute of it. Much of her life seemed a little dull.

"What is his house like? How many pigs does he keep? How many chickens?"

"His house is a palace. He has fifty courtyards, three whole gardens, and more than a hundred servants. He has whole farms to feed his household. More chickens than a village could eat in a year! And more treasures besides . . ."

"*Wa!*" Mule Wang said. "What does he do with all those houses? Does he have fifty wives?"

"No," she said. "One wife, four concubines. No more than is fitting. The courtyards are for his sons and their sons, and their wives and concubines as well."

"Sounds like a city," he said.

Shulien nodded. It was: and there were other things hidden there. Secret and deadly things that needed an Imperial duke to hold and protect.

On the second day they reached the top of the White Cloud Pass. Behind them the flats were striped with the last ragged crop of winter cabbages. Before them the Beijing plain was dark and brown and dusty. The Great Canal gleamed with sunlight. An eagle soared above their heads, wings outstretched, gliding effortlessly on the rising currents.

"So how do you know Duke Te?" Mule Wang said.

"Through a friend . . ." Shulien trailed off. Mule Wang nodded sadly but said nothing.

The wind was harsh so high in the mountains. Shulien could smell incense on the breeze. It was the Grave-Sweeping Festival, a pleasant day when families carried picnics up into the mountains and left offerings for their ancestors. Who would sweep her grave when she was gone, Shulien wondered. She had no family. No children to carry out the sacrifices for her ghost. Her father was gone, her fiancé was killed long ago, and even Mubai had fallen to Jade Fox. She alone had survived, lingering uncertainly into the autumn of her days.

Mubai's death had hurt the most. Perhaps it was not her destiny to be happy in this world. The wind moaned through the lattice screens of the carriage. Outside she saw high crags and lone trees, clinging by their roots to the overhanging rocks. Beneath them the cliff was crumbling. How long until they fell? she thought.

Shulien leaned against the rough sack of cotton and tried to sleep, but the jolts of the carriage kept throwing her from side to side. The conversation seemed to hang, unresolved. "I must go and pay my respects," she said finally. "And there are other things I must concern myself with. Serious matters," she sighed, for which she felt too old.

剑

That evening they camped under Vulture Peak. The pony chomped on its nosebag of grain, and Mule Wang got a fire going despite the wind that blew the flames sideways against the night dark; sparks, like fireflies, tumbling back up the pass before fading from view.

Shulien used the last of the daylight to climb up the rocky slope to Vulture Peak itself: a great hunk of hard granite that stuck out of the cliff like a beak. It used to be famous as a place for warriors to meet. When men fought on Vulture Peak only one ever came down alive.

She reached the spot just as the sun was turning red and hung low on the horizon, the bottom lost in mist and dust.

She had never been up here before. She stood here now, and imagined fighting. The way was narrow, the edges were sheer. She paused on the lip and looked down and the wind clawed at her, blew her robes tight against her legs. It was a long way down. Any man who fell would surely die.

When she came back down to the fire it was fully dark, the stars were gleaming overhead, and the nearly full moon rose in the east: yellow at first, then clean and white as it ascended from the clutches of the earth and into the sky.

Mule Wang had a small wok he used to heat oil. She had smelled the garlic as she came down, heard the hiss of the fat as he threw in noodles.

They were cooked now and sitting in a chipped white porcelain bowl, the noodles rising like an island of snakes, a generous spoonful of tofu, black beans and red chili flakes sitting on top.

"Eat!" Mule Wang said. He offered her a bowl of picked garlic, and she took one and bit into it: it was soft and sweet and sharp, but it did not shift her melancholy.

Shulien ate slowly. She had little appetite. When she put the bowl down he looked at it hungrily.

"You're finished?" he said.

She nodded.

"Can I?"

"Of course," she said.

Mule Wang took her bowl and started shoveling the noodles.

"My wife says she does not know where the food goes," he said. "You eat like a pig but you are as skinny as a rabbit! Look at me—I am!"

Shulien smiled. "I had a friend who died here. His name was Silent Wolf. Did you ever hear of him?"

Mule Wang shook his head. He continued shoveling in his noodles, laughing and chewing as he talked. "Men say that a scholar's name will last five years, an artist's for ten, and a swordsman's for twenty years of men. But how long do they remember a mule driver's? Not at all. But do I care? Not with a full belly, no!"

Shulien gave another brief smile and looked away, toward the mountains, thinking of the man her father had chosen to be her husband.

Silent Wolf was lean and hard as his name suggested: a sharp face with narrow eyes, his long hair pulled into a knot at the back of his head. He had a brooding air, an intense stare, and an odd habit of breaking into laughter like sunlight suddenly emerging over a winter landscape. He had been a fine warrior, but she had not wanted to marry. Marrying would have meant giving up the Iron Way. As long as she was a wushu warrior she was a man in all but name. More than a man, indeed.

She had refused marriage until she had seen him fight. Then she had gone to her father and bowed before him. "Thank you, Father. I know you are thinking of my happiness. I refused to marry him at first, but now I have seen him I understand that you have chosen a man who will be good to me, and treat me fairly, and that is more than most of us can hope for in this world."

Her father had smiled. "I want nothing more than your happiness. I hope for nothing greater than that you should live safely, and prosperously, and be blessed with many years and many children."

She smiled. "Thank you, Father."

But before the date could be set for the wedding, Silent Wolf had fallen foul of a corrupt official and fled into hiding, and in the months that followed she had met Mubai. Young hearts heal soonest, old women said, and Shulien had seen Mubai and she had been unable to speak in his presence, such were her feelings for him. She feared love then and turned to leave. But she could not help herself, risking one last glimpse, and then she saw that his gaze had followed her. Their eyes met, and she looked quickly away, cheeks coloring.

Fate had played tricks on her, it seemed. Her father would not let her marry another man. Mubai could not bear to see her and not touch her, and Shulien did not know where Silent Wolf had gone.

Mubai had come for one last meeting, and they had sat together, holding hands, as chaste as Buddhist nuns and monks. "I cannot be here and not hold you," he said.

She bowed her head. She understood. Love was not a joy when it was a barrier between them, when their affections remained secret.

"You will go then?"

He had nodded. She had let him walk from her courtyard. It was autumn. It was the time that the cicadas were falling from the trees, their summer song ended. She sat alone, listening to the last cicada singing, and understood what it meant to be alone in the world.

Mubai had journeyed far in search of consolation, and found a friend in his travels, a stern, silent man, much his own age, and they had fallen in together and become oath brothers. It was only then that they opened their hearts to one another, and he discovered that lean warrior was Silent Wolf.

"What fate is this!" Mubai had said. "That I have fallen in love with your betrothed. I will leave you both. I will travel to the end of the Empire and find death in the pursuit of some great adventure."

Silent Wolf had said nothing. But he saw that he was the thing that stood between Mubai and the woman he loved most and his eyes had narrowed. "If she loves you, then I should be the one to leave."

"No," Mubai said. "You were chosen by her father to be her betrothed."

"The father picked me. The girl picked you. I know who I would want, if I were Shulien. If I died you could marry her," he said.

"Do not even speak of such a thing," Mubai had said. "You are as dear to me as she is. I could not bear to lose you, just as I have lost her. She is betrothed to you. You should marry her. She is a girl with a great heart. She will make you a fine wife."

Silent Wolf had nodded slowly and poured them both wine. "To the beauty, Shulien," they had toasted, and then each had gone on their way.

All this Shulien had learned much later, from Mubai. "Not long after, Silent Wolf sought to defeat a mad priest named Hades Dai," Mubai had told her. "He was terrorizing the locals and even the city magistrate feared him so much that they did what he said. The law of the Emperor was overturned. This man was the Emperor in all but name. Silent Wolf saw that this could not be allowed to continue. Where justice fails, then the sword must intervene. He took his sword and bow and met Hades Dai on Vulture Peak. But the priest tricked him, and he had hidden warriors there to help him."

It was here, on Vulture Peak, that Hades Dai had killed Silent Wolf.

As Shulien watched Mule Wang fill his belly she remembered the time Mubai brought Silent Wolf's broken sword to her.

"I could not save him," he'd said. Mubai had knelt before her and her soul had been torn in two.

Even as he had said this, hope had leaped inside her. But he had shaken his head.

"I said I could not marry you, and I must keep to my word."

"It was not your decision to make," she had told him. "I am not chattel to be bought and sold at the market for a string of coins." But he had refused her touch, though he could not resist coming in from his wandering, and sitting by her side, and bathing in her presence, as the old are brought out on a sunny day to soak up the warmth.

So the years passed. Shulien took over her father's business escorting men through the wilds. She grew prosperous. Well respected. Loved by many for her honesty and steadfastness in the face of corrupt government officials.

"Shulien," Mubai had said one day, "I have something to say."

She gave him a look. "Speak."

He had stammered then, and his cheeks had colored, just like that first time they had seen each other, and she knew immediately what he was going to say, and she found herself feeling deeply sad.

"I wander through the world, alone, fighting dishonest men. I meditate in the mountains, and yet something keeps calling me back to the world. Well, someone ..." His eyes looked to her for help, but she resented the years alone, and as he spoke, she had refused to help him. Her eyes were hard and set, and she looked at him and did not give him a hint of her feelings.

"Do you feel this way?" he asked.

She shook her head. The thought of accepting his love had frightened her. "What can we offer each other?" she had said. "We are two warriors, next week we could both be dead."

"More reason to accept our fate," Mubai had said.

"I wish I could," she said and put a hand to his arm. "But please don't ask me again."

Mubai had nodded and obeyed her request, even when she wished—yearned—for him to break his word. And by the time he died it was too late for her to change her mind.

All these thoughts came back to her as she sat with Mule Wang, under Vulture Peak, and the wind blew sparks off toward the stars. She remembered holding the shards of Silent Wolf's sword in her hand.

She had shown her father the broken sword. "He is dead," she said.

Silent Wolf had been like a son to her father. He had taken the shards of Silent Wolf's sword and held them tight. There was a long silence before he spoke. When he did his voice was thick with emotion. "His father did not live to see this. Who killed him?"

"Hades Dai," Shulien said.

Her father shook his head. He had never heard of this man.

"He was a monk at the Shaolin Temple," Shulien said. "But he was banished for witchcraft."

Her father nodded. He was too old for anger. He took the shards and walked away.

It is what we have lost that drives us on, she thought. She shivered, and looked around. It was as if she felt the eyes of Silent Wolf's ghost, staring down at her from the cliffs above. She put her hands to the fire. Mule Wang was oblivious. He tipped the last of the sauce into his mouth and belched quietly.

"It will be a cold night. I'll get the cotton sacks down. They'll keep us both warm."

剑

Next day they were up early. The pony went easily, trotting along the winding road that led down to the plains of Beijing. Shulien peered ahead, seeing the walls of the capital rise from the plain, and one by one the towers and palaces became distinct from one another.

As they dropped down to the level of the plain Beijing disappeared behind the trees. They started to see milestones marking the distance to the city; and the closer they came the more ornamental archways marked the miles, with ancient steles commemorating famous scholars or virtuous widows, or sons who were filial.

They came to a turning in the road. One led straight to the capital, the other led into a birch wood that skirted the foothills.

"I always go this way," Mule Wang said. He turned and smiled. "There are no tolls this way. It is pretty too, this time of year."

Shulien sat forward. The copper birch leaves littered the floor. The forest was filled with a pale misty light, the webs were white with dew.

"Only a few of us know this road. There's a village up ahead. We will sleep there tonight, and you will be in Duke Te's palace in the morning. The food there will be much better, the beds much more comfortable. But the village is good. No lice. And the woman there. She has a big pond full of catfish. You pick the one you want and they scoop it up, flapping and kicking, and five minutes later it is on your tray." Mule Wang seemed strangely keen to spend the night there, and Shulien began to wonder what this woman was like, and what else she offered to weary carters.

But the day was drawing on, and Mule Wang started singing bawdy village songs, so Shulien sat back into the hollow she had made for herself, and shut her eyes and tried to sleep.

They stopped by a stream to let the pony drink, and then they were going again. The dark had become darker, and the wind was up. They could hear it in the treetops, which swayed back and forth, but in the green depths of the forest the air was still and cool and silent.

Too silent, Shulien thought, and sat up. At that moment there was a shout and the cart lurched suddenly to the side and toppled over, throwing Mule Wang.

Shulien struggled to shove the sacks and cotton off and jumped out. Black-robed men were leaping from the ferns. They had clubs and knives and they were already upon her. Too many, she thought as she punched the first in the throat, caught the next by his wrist and broke it with her knee. But it seemed they were not too well versed in the arts of a warrior.

She found the hilt of her sword and she pulled it free of its scabbard. It felt good to have it to hand. Now this wouldn't be too hard, she thought, and the men hung back, like jackals waiting for one to take the lead.

She stood with her back to the cart. "Come on!" she said, and one of them looked up and smiled.

"We're coming," he said.

A net had been strung over the road. Shulien looked up too late as it fell on her. The rope smelled of fish. It was thick and coarse and too tough. She swung her sword, but the links were too thick. It was useless but she kicked and struggled. She heard Mule Wang shout out as the men seized him, and one of the men bent over her and struck her with a club.

Darkness came. And she knew no more.

10

Burial was much more complicated than birth, Sir Te thought as he watched his father's corpse being dressed in his funeral robes by a pair of nervous attendants. They were standing in his father's small library courtyard: three halls forming three sides of a square, and the southern side enclosed by a high wall.

The courtyard was lined with bricks, and a few flowerbeds were heavy with plants that gave off a rich, sweet scent. Set into the walls were glass lanterns, shaped like fans or peaches or ornamental vases. They were all unlit, dark, extinguished.

Sir Te brought his attention back to his father's body. The funeral clothes were neatly pressed and folded, and one by one they were lifted and used to dress the corpse in the hat and shoes of a First Degree Duke of the Imperial Family of the Manchu Qing Dynasty.

He tutted and stood up, shooed the attendants to the side. "Respect!" he said. "This is the son of the Emperor himself."

He fretted over the set of his father's arms. It took a long time before he was satisfied. The two attendants didn't dare step forward until he gave them his express permission.

"Yes, put him in. But be careful, please!"

Duke Te was laid reverentially into the inner coffin, which had been packed with straw and herbs that would prevent decay.

"Would you like to have him remain in state?" the undertaker, a plump and gentle man, asked, bowing a little at the waist.

Sir Te, the eldest son, shook his head. He did not like to see his father dead. It reminded him of all the responsibilities that now lay on his shoulders. His father had tried to inculcate him into the world of wushu warriors, but Sir Te's attention had always wandered. He was more a man of books and learning than of action. Action panicked him. But his father had made him swear to keep his work alive. The safety of the Empire depends on it, he had said with his dying breath. Swear to me, and Sir Te had sworn.

"Sir!" the man said. "Would you like him to remain in state?"

Sir Te came back with a start. "No. Once the prayers have been said, please shut the lid," he replied, and the chief undertaker came forward and bowed.

"As you wish," he said, and hastily motioned to his assistants. "I find that it is better not to watch the nailing of the coffin."

"I understand," Sir Te said, "but this is my father and I want to see that all is done according to ritual."

The undertaker bowed again. "As you wish," he repeated.

剑

Shulien woke and found herself lying alone in the road. The net had been pulled off her. It was almost dark. The forest was quiet. Around her was a scene of devastation: dead men, some with black arrows sticking up from their bodies. Mule Wang lay at her feet. His throat had been cut. Only the pony was left, standing patiently, still strapped to the ruins of the two-wheeled cart. It snorted as she sat up.

Shulien pushed herself up. Her head was still sore. She felt a little sick. She soothed the pony. "Only you left. What happened?"

The horse snorted again, as if in answer.

The smell of blood had unsettled it. Shulien looked around; the ground had been tramped up. She leaned down. It was hard to see in the gloom but it was clear that a different horse had come. It was shod in the Mongolian style; a larger hoof, a heavier horse, judging by the depth of the print.

She could see how each man had died. Two lay with arrows in their backs. They had fallen forward onto their faces. The blood had pooled around them. The next had been the one who had smiled at her as the net fell. A great sword-slash across his chest had killed him. Two others had been trampled by horses, the last's head had been broken.

Their leader looked like a real warrior. His head was shaved and his weapon was a halberd with a serrated edge. She bent down, turned the body over. She did not know the face. He bore no sign, except for a red dragon tattoo on his body. Three arrows jutted out from his chest. She checked his pouch. There was a string of cash, but nothing else. No signs. Nothing that would identify him.

A quick and efficient killer, Shulien thought. But why had he left, and how had she escaped his cares?

Her head was sore and it was too much for her to take in. She cut the pony free, mounted up, heeled it forward.

She rode through the night, and at dawn was there for the opening of the city gates.

She approached Duke Te's doorway, strips of red paper with bold black characters, left over from New Year and starting to fade, two white lanterns on wooden stands marking the household out as one in the clutches of grief. She had not been back here since Mubai's death. She had said her farewells to the duke and turned away from the world of suffering. But the world had a way of pulling its hermit back from the wilds. And here she was again. She took a deep breath.

One gate was still shut, the other was propped open. In the street, on a stool, sat the gatekeeper, dressed in a long blue gown of office. He leaped up to take the reins of the pony. "Mistress!" he said, recognizing her despite the years between them.

"Gateman Shu," she said. He had a short forked beard, and gray above his ears, but she knew him well.

"I am glad to see you here," he said.

He hurried inside to summon the steward. Shulien followed him, stepping over the threshold.

剑

The Taoist priest came in and sang and danced. A Buddhist priest came in and droned on through the sutras. At the very end a Manchu shaman came in, with a knucklebone rattle, bizarre animal mask, and a black whip of horsehair. His chanting woke Sir Te from a dream where his father had been complaining. "You did not bury me with the proper rites," he said, and Sir Te had been mortified and fallen to his knees.

"Sir Te," one of the serving girls said. She was a pleasant little thing her father had adopted from a starving family. He had promised her a life and a job, and when she was old enough he had promised to find her a good husband as well: a hard-working man with a trade who did not whore or gamble. Sir Te beckoned her in. She was not tall, but slender and willow-waisted, and she seemed to sway toward him with all the languid grace of a candle flame, gently aroused by the draft of a half-closed door.

Her name was . . . he couldn't remember.

"There is a lady," the girl said. She had a pleasant voice. If he closed his eyes he could imagine her plucking a lyre, singing gently to him as she undressed. "At the gates. She has come to pay her respects to your father. Her name is Yu Shulien."

"She has come at last!" Sir Te said. "Make sure her old chambers are aired. Tell the kitchens to prepare some dishes. I shall come at once."

The girl pursed her lips and nodded, then turned and hurried out.

剑

Facing the doorway was the glossy-colored brick spirit screen. It blocked off all sight of the inner courtyard, and stood at the east end of the southern wall. To have the gates of the courtyards lining up with the front gate would have been bad *feng shui*, ghosts could have blown right through to the inner quarters.

Shulien passed around the screen into the wide entrance court, where Duke Te had entertained callers. She had many memories of this place, filled with voices and tables and laughter, but this morning, despite the pots of chrysanthemums, it had an empty and bleak feel.

A gray-haired serving girl, in blue cotton jacket and trousers, bowed quickly. "Mistress Yu," she said. "Sir Te is deeply honored to have you here to—"

"Where is he?" Shulien said.

The servant bowed. "He is busy," she said. "He thought you might want to wash before you saw him."

"No," Shulien said. "I should see him now."

"I will make sure your mount is stabled." The old lady nodded to the squint-eyed lad who smiled broadly, then bowed to Shulien. "This way, ma'am."

Shulien followed the maid through the first courtyard, past potted oleanders and pomegranates that lined the path, and gave a little shade, and then through a moon door in the west wall into the library courtyard, where Duke Te had entertained Shulien and Mubai in better days.

She remembered the glass lanterns Duke Te had lit around the courtyard, but it was not appropriate now, so what greeted her was not light and color, but the stark white of mourning. White cloth hung from the doorway, it was slung from the eaves of the gray tile roof, and filled the windows like blank eyes.

Sir Te was a poor copy of his father. He was tall and thin and affected a deliberately round-shouldered stoop, like a scholar. He fretted with his robe, and wrung his hands around and around, which gave him a nervous and prissy appearance. Obsessed, Shulien thought, with all the little details.

Sir Te returned her bow with as much gravity as he could manage. "Welcome, Master Yu Shulien! We have many mourners staying with us, but you are most welcome. I have had your old quarters swept and cleaned and the beds made with fresh sheets. You should go there and wash. Didn't my girl tell you? Oh dear. It is very hard. I have to do everything. I shall have to talk to her. I will have her beaten. I will do it myself."

"She told me," Shulien said. "But I insisted on seeing you."

Sir Te's eyes opened wide. "Oh. Really? Why? Is something wrong?"

"I think so," Shulien said, but he did not pause to let her speak.

"Oh dear. Let me sit down. Was the journey long?"

"No longer than before," Shulien said.

Sir Te stood back up again. Then he sat down, and stood up. Shulien waited patiently. At last the man spoke. "I had hoped you would come. My mother was sure you would."

"So were others," Shulien said. "I was waylaid, in Southbirch Forest."

He put his hand over his mouth. "Waylaid? Surely not!"

"Assassins," Shulien said.

He hurried to shut the door. "Assassins?" he hissed. "And you have led them here?"

"They are all dead. They killed my driver. They would have killed me."

"Thank heavens!" Sir Te drew in a quick breath. He sat down again. There was a long pause. "You as well!"

"What do you mean?"

Sir Te licked his lips. "You will not tell anyone?"

Shulien shook her head.

"Well. Since my father has passed away the martial world is uneasy. Gold Phoenix was waylaid in Wuhan City and killed. In Guangzhou, Mantis Li was found in a brothel, strangled with a silk rope. You know my father worked hard to keep the best warriors in his employ. A dozen of them have been killed since he died."

"The Iron Way is hard," Shulien said.

Sir Te hurried to the door and peered outside before shutting the door and bolting it. "It is not the Iron Way," Sir Te said. "It is organized. There is an enemy out there, a rogue house of warriors. One by one they are killing us all."

Shulien looked away.

Sir Te bowed. "I need your help. I do not know where else to turn. I think they are seeking something . . ."

Shulien saw the look in his eye and understood. "I should have come earlier," she said. "Is *it* still here?"

Sir Te nodded. "Would you like to see?"

"Later," Shulien said. "First things first. I must pay my respects. Where is he?"

Sir Te nodded. "This way."

He led Shulien through a small, intimate little courtyard, which had held Duke Te's study, and into the second courtyard, where family members were entertained.

"My father was moved here this morning," he said.

Shulien nodded and walked slowly, wading through memories that leaped out at her, held onto her, tried to drag her down. She had been here with Mubai, just before he had been killed. She had wished many times that she had been taken first. He could have found a girl somewhere: pretty, gentle, caring. It was not her fate to be happy in love.

She had sat with him as the poison slowly killed him. They had meditated together. Rationed out each slow breath, drawn out the time left for him. It had taken too long for the antidote to arrive, but it had been long enough for him to tell her that his ghost would remain with her. She had held him at the end. Given him her own breath, lip to lip, and her breath had kept him alive for a few moments longer.

She often wondered if his ghost was around her. Perhaps it was his ghost that had saved her in the birch wood. He had told her that he would follow her.

It will not be long now, my dearest Mubai, she thought. Then our ghosts can be together.

The eaves and doorways of the main hall of Duke Te's Palace had been hung with lengths of white cloth. Knotted white flowers hung down the side of each doorway and the faces of the family gods had been covered with red cloths. Scrolls of calligraphy memorialized the duke. Through the gateway a line of mourners was gathering.

Sir Te greeted them politely and led Shulien to the front doorway. Inside, the air was blue with incense and the flames from paper money, ingots and Duke Te's favorite food. In the middle of the room the coffin stood on high trestles. The red lacquer was carved with symbols of luck and longevity: double happiness, long swirling dragons and clouds and pearls.

Sir Te's brothers and sons and their wives sat along the side of the room, dressed in white with simple white caps. As Shulien stepped over the threshold an attendant, a middle-aged woman with a soft and concerned face, took a long white cloth and tied it around her waist.

Shulien felt all the eyes in the room on her.

That is her, they were thinking. That is Shulien the Warrior!

Shulien made her way around the rituals of mourning. As she reached the spirit tablet she was given three sticks of incense. The tablet was a piece of cedar wood, carved with two dragons at the top.

Spirit tablet of the illustrious lord Duke Te, who received the title of Grand Master for Governance from the Qing court. Respectfully set up by his pious son, Sir Te Songqing.

She lit the incense sticks from the smoky red candle and set them in the ash of those which had gone before. She knelt and bowed three times.

Shulien still had that sense that she was being watched. She turned and took the room in, half hoping to see Mubai's ghost standing at the back with his large sad eyes smiling at her. There were many looking at her, but it was a young noblewoman who caught her attention. Pretty, young, upright.

The girl looked quickly away.

"Who is that?" Shulien asked.

Sir Te wasn't sure.

"That one," Shulien said. The one with the white skin and black hair and proud bearing. Even though she was dressed in the same mourning white, to Shulien the girl stood out among the other noblewomen like a wolf amongst hounds.

Sir Te screwed up his nose. "She is the daughter of . . . someone. Why, do you know her?"

"No," Shulien said. *But I know her kind.* She leaned in close and spoke discreetly. "*It* is well guarded?"

"Oh yes!" he said.

Shulien did not like this sense of being watched.

"Maybe tonight you could take me to see."

"I shall," Sir Te said.

剑

Shulien had cleaned and washed, and was dressed in a simple green gown, the hem embroidered with swirling clouds. Curfew sounded from the drum tower, the boom rolling out over the Forbidden City to Duke Te's palace. The stooping sun filled the air with a gleaming golden light and birds were returning to their roosts as Sir Te took her through courtyard after courtyard, through the ornamental garden with its endless brick path, right to the private rear of the palace. They passed along a covered walkway, with beams painted in bold colors with scenes of scholars by thatched huts, lily pools and cloud-wreathed peaks. It led to a maze garden, with a low hedge winding around with the brick pathway. The next chamber was being used as a storeroom for winter furniture and braziers, and then they stopped before a blank red wall. Sir Te paused. He looked around, then quickly felt the wall, and pressed the third brick from the top. It slid back, and there was a soft *click!* and then the wall swung back like a door.

Sir Te stepped through quickly, and with a brief look behind them, he gently closed the door.

They were standing in a tunnel with an arched roof. The only light came from the paper lantern Sir Te held. "This way," he said. "It is not far."

The corridor was twenty feet long. It was level and dry, a heavy round moon door blocking the other end.

Sir Te took out a silver key, slid it into the lock, and it opened with a soft chime as the springs came free. He pushed the door open to a small, doorless courtyard, a dust floor and a single plum tree standing before a small locked pavilion with lattice windows. Sir Te stopped before it and fumbled with the keys. "I did not know about this place until just before my father died. He came here alone." He took the heavy brass lock in one hand and turned the key with a sharp click. The two halves of the lock sprang apart, and he unslotted the bolt and drew it back, pushing the doors open.

The air was dry and clean and dusty. It had an unlived feel to it. He lit the lanterns and they cast a dull red light around the room.

Shulien saw a small chamber, hung with ancient scrolls of landscapes of the finest calligraphy; cups of the finest Burmese jade; white porcelain vases and plates painted with blue willows and women and gardens for wise men; ancient statues of wrestlers, their bellies bound with thick sashes, their arms curled around their sides; there were silver cups, Tibetan *tankas* of silk and gold; brass lions from the Palace of Eternal Spring in the southern jungles of Yunnan; and a statue of the dying Buddha carved from black marble, that had been sent from some ancient king of Siam.

Shulien walked to a pair of scrolls that lay unrolled on a table.

"*The wise man teaches by action, not words,*" one scroll said.

"*Deviate an inch, lose a thousand miles,*" said the other.

She turned to follow Sir Te. He stood next to a high shrine table in front of a small jade statue of the Warrior God, Guanyu, standing on a high altar. On the table was a long ornate box. Sir Te undid the clasps and gently opened the lid.

There was the Green Destiny: a long straight sword, forged a thousand years before, eight steel rods folded nine hundred times by a master smith, the likes of whom no longer existed in the world. The sword that had once hung at Guanyu's waist. It was like touching myth. The blade was unblemished, unchipped, undented, a greenish tinge to the steel. It was light, a uniform width, three fingers wide from end to end, the edge as sharp as a razor despite the years. In the blade clouds swirled in intricate patterns of light and dark. Shulien got caught for a moment in their interweaving. She and Mubai had spent many evenings staring at those patterns, as if there were a meaning there.

She touched the golden hilt. She stroked the ironwood handle, stroked the finely plaited yak-hair grip. She shivered suddenly. Mubai had carried this sword for many years. After his death she had brought it here, but now the sight of it uncovered long-buried memories. She had thought her grief had hardened and grown thick, like an old scar, and was surprised how easily she could be cut again. When she spoke her voice was a whisper. "This sword has brought me so much sadness but still I cannot help but gape. Such beauty, such power. What warrior is worthy of wielding this blade?" Her voice trailed off.

She could feel Sir Te's nervousness and paid him no heed. Mubai had given the sword to the duke for safekeeping. If anyone could claim ownership of Green Destiny it was her, as Mubai's closest living friend, not Sir Te.

She sighed.

It was not right to blame others. Duke Te had hidden this sword for so many years, had kept it both safe and secret. Sir Te was clearly inadequate to the task of holding and guarding such a treasure, but when the strong are missing, the weak and inadequate and unlearned man must step forward.

Sir Te was only trying to do what was best.

She sighed again. More sadly this time. "This is where your father came to think?" Shulien said.

Sir Te nodded. "Only he came here, and only he was allowed to eat the fruit of this tree."

Shulien took in a deep breath.

"And this is where he kept Green Destiny?"

"Yes," Sir Te said. "But he would not let it go. It was too dangerous, he said."

"He never used it?"

Sir Te shook his head. "No. It must always be hidden, my father told me. He made me swear before he died that I would tell no one. History is the best hiding place. Forgetfulness. Dust. Lost to memory."

Shulien nodded, but she was not so sure. Memories lived long, she thought. Sometimes longer than the people themselves.

"Thank you," she said. "I am glad to see it once more. It reminds me of happier times."

Sir Te shut the lid and rebolted the door, and as the moon rose through the falling curled branches of the plum tree, he shut the gate behind them, and Shulien let out a long sigh.

This place was too full of ghosts, she thought.

"I am tired," she said. "I think I will sleep now."

11

There was a hush in the central hall of the second courtyard. It was time for the coffin to be nailed shut. Duke Te's four sons stood in a line, their silver ritual hammers raised to be purified. Each looked awkward and stiff and incompetent.

Wei-fang had joined the hired mourners. The place was deserted of warriors. He suppressed a smile. He felt cocky. If this was what the House of Te had fallen to, then, he thought, this should be easy. He had known from personal experience that the maids knew far more about what was happening in a household than the owners or the guards. He had paid one of the serving girls a bit of attention, and a combination of soft words and a winning smile and she had been very forthcoming about where Duke Te kept his most treasured possessions.

"Not in his study," she had said, shaking her head. "No. He keeps them in the northern courtyard. Past the storerooms. No one's allowed there, except the master of the house."

A little investigation and Wei-fang now knew which courtyard to try; he was almost giddy with expectation. He bowed his head as the funeral master aligned the lid of the coffin properly and then the silver nails, each stamped with the character for luck, were held in place. Sir Te fumbled with the first one. He muttered something and the funeral master's smile set a little too hard.

Such fumbles were inauspicious, Wei-fang thought. A father like Duke Te deserved better sons. For a moment he thought of his own father and mother, and the fiancée he had escaped from. He put such thoughts away and made his excuses to the other professional mourners, rolled up his personal scroll of funeral calligraphy and slipped outside into the front yard. The sun was setting. It was time to start.

Serving men and women were rolling round tabletops into the yard to be set up for the mourners. The Te clan was rich and wide and powerful, and there were many who claimed a connection.

One table was set without any seats. That was to feed the spirit of the dead and all the ancestors and wandering ghosts. A red lacquer tray held watermelon seeds, sugared plums, coconut and melon in separate compartments. Similar trays were being carried around by the blue-dressed household servants.

Wei-fang took a green sugared plum as the maid brushed past him. She smiled shyly at him and he gave her a quick smile back, and lost himself in the bustle of mourners and servants. It was easy to go unnoticed. He slipped behind a pillar into a side courtyard and pulled off his gown of funeral white.

Underneath he wore a black suit. He rolled his white gown up and stuffed it into a large blue and white ceramic flowerpot.

In the Palace of Duke Te everyone was making their way, like roosting birds, to the front courtyard to feast. The rear courtyards were deserted, except for a few nightwatchmen hanging lit lanterns between the buildings.

Wei-fang swung himself up to the roof.

The sky was darkening; the first stars were beginning to burn in the sky above his head. He paused for a moment to savor the view from the heart of the capital, just next to the Forbidden City.

Over him the great gates of the city reared up. Qianmen, Tiananmen, and the acres of *hutongs*: little alley-blocks of houses and halls and plum trees and families sitting down to their evening meals. To the east, between him and the rising moon, were the walls and halls of the Forbidden City, ranked one behind the other. Wei-fang felt he could almost see over them to the palace gardens, the scent of jasmine blossoms, pretty girls, the finest wine that only the Emperor himself could drink. And there was Coal Hill, where the last Ming Emperor had hanged himself for shame rather than suffer the indignity of conquest.

He froze as a young couple passed beneath, late for the feast. The man was a little unsteady with wine and he fell against the girl a couple of times, and she staggered as she took his drunken weight, and kept him moving forward.

Alone on the roof Wei-fang watched them pass.

He heard the laughter of the drinkers, the joy of friends drinking and eating together, and he felt an ache. Hades Dai banned wine within his camp, and many times Wei-fang had paused by an inn, or a sing-song establishment, and something deep and primeval had yearned to go in and drink. To drink the wine, to laugh and sing, and look into the almond eyes of some young and clever beauty. But beauties were only for Hades Dai.

He breathed deeply. Hades Dai's rule was wrong. It was unfair, but Wei-fang had sworn an oath. This was his first great adventure, and he would not fail, himself as much as the rest of them. If he did then what had been the point of leaving his mother behind? He would not fail.

He could not fail.

To walk the way he was going would not have taken more than ten minutes. But going along the roofs took Wei-fang more than an hour. He moved so gently the tiles did not even tilt under his weight. There was one place no one was allowed to visit. One corner of the great palace where no doors led to. That surely must be where the sword was hidden.

A moth landed on his cheek, fluttering its furred wings as it waited for the moon, and a bat plucked it from him as if he were a tree or a wall or statue. Other bats flittered oblivious around him.

The gibbous moon was a hand's breadth above the topmost tower of Coal Hill by the time he reached the hidden courtyard. There was the plum tree, there the locked moon door, and as he slipped along the wall, there was the empty courtyard and the Hall of Antiques.

Wei-fang felt giddy for a moment. He crept forward. He had learned much from Iron Crow. Discipline was chief among them. He swatted his worries aside and crept forward with the same discipline that had brought him here to the brink of success. A few minutes later his shadow stopped on top of the Hall of Antiques. He carefully lifted the clay tiles free. One, two, seven were enough for him to slip through the gap. He peered down. The rafters had been papered over. He lowered himself very gently, took a knife from the sheath that was strapped to his calf, and broke the surface of the paper, cutting a hole along the rafter's edge where the paper was taut and would cut the easiest.

He folded the square of paper back. A few rat droppings fell into the room below. He watched them skitter down. They were as loud as drumbeats in his mind. He cursed. Iron Crow would have looked sadly at him, and said nothing. Sometimes silence was worse than words.

Wei-fang breathed long and deep and slow. The rat droppings landed. They bounced. They scattered. They lay still. Wei-fang's blood pounded for a moment. But the room was still. No alarm was raised. Nothing happened.

There, on the altar table, was a long case. Wei-fang made sure there was no one around, and slipped down through the hole, landing on all fours, like a cat.

His palms were sweaty as he undid the clasp that held the case shut.

The silver clasp was warm to the touch. It flicked up, and he caught it in one finger and laid it silently open.

A little moonlight fell down through the hole he had made and lit the sword in its case. Wei-fang's mouth was dry. He swallowed anyway, and slipped off a black cotton glove. His ungloved hand reached out to touch it. His fingers closed on the grip, and he felt a thrill of power go through him, and his mind whispered to him: *Why give it to Hades Dai? You are the one who stole it. It is yours!*

Joy filled him—warm as a cup of wine—as he lifted the sword clear. It was light and balanced. He held it up to the moonlight, and it shone. As he moved the blade it gleamed cold and strange and green.

Wei-fang almost laughed.

"Don't," a voice hissed in his ear.

Wei-fang flipped back. He landed on both feet, hand still holding the sword. But however fast he was his opponent was faster. He flipped again, caught a roof beam with one hand, and swung himself across the room.

He was free, he thought, but as he landed he saw the shadow waiting: a small, lithe shape, blacker than the shadows.

A hand caught his wrist. He twisted it, kicked the owner and heard a gasp.

An unmistakably feminine gasp.

"A girl?" he hissed and the answer was a short hard kick to his gut.

For a moment his enemy crossed through the beam of moon-light and he had a brief glimpse of a masked face: smooth white skin, large black eyes, and long lashes. It was the painting of a beauty, he thought, not a mortal foe. And that was his second mistake.

"How did you get here?"

"I followed you," the girl said, and he had to knock away her fists.

They stood toe to toe, thrusting, kicking, parrying. It was bewildering and exciting. "Who are you?" he started to say, but did not get the first words out before another kick that almost crushed his manhood. He slapped the third kick away, but she had him by the hand and for a moment panic bubbled up through him as he remembered the night he had left home and the matchmaker had mocked him.

The girl drove at him with a frenzy of furious kicks and punches. He punched and parried until his forearm was sore. He would not let go of the sword, but having it in his hand was slow-ing him down. He cursed as he knocked a punch from his face, a kick to his ribs, one-handedly batting away another flurry of attacks. Remain calm, Iron Crow had taught him, but it was hard.

"Stop!" he hissed again, twisted and squirming from her blows. He was being driven back, step by step. Another low kick forced him back one more step and he knocked a rosewood table with a tall green vase on top. The vase wobbled. Both the fight-ers stopped.

"Wait," he said.

For once she listened. Her masked face nodded and without taking his eyes off her face he reached out and steadied the vase.

"Will you stop now?" he hissed.

"Give me the sword," she said.

There was something about the way she spoke that left him

tempted, but he shook his head. "If I could I would," he said, "but I can't."

"Can't, or won't?"

He frowned for a moment. "Both," he said, and ducked the first two kicks.

He saw an opening, but he hesitated. There had to be a better way out of this.

"Don't make me angry," he said, but she came at him in a flurry of fists and elbows and he let out an exasperated sigh and went onto the attack. She twisted away from his punch and kneed him in the ribs. He grunted as she kneed him again. The third time he felt as though his ribs were cracking and he desperately flung her back with a trick Iron Crow had shown him. She grunted in surprise and pain, and almost let go of his wrist, but not quite.

"You fight well," she said, already twisted as he aimed a stabbing punch at the inside of her arm.

"I'll teach you some time."

She laughed at him.

"No man ever taught me anything!"

"No?"

She roundhouse kicked and he ducked just in time. As he did so he caught a tall black lacquer stand. He saw the sudden alarm in her eyes, and turned to see the vase on top topple past the point of balance.

Wei-fang's fingers caught the bottom of the vase and he had a brief glimpse of it in the moonlight: a fat-bottomed pot, in dark blue and white, with a triumphant blue dragon coiling around the bottom. He felt the rough unglazed rim, the potter's marks stamped into the bottom, and he thought for a moment that he had enough of a grip to hold it up, before it slipped from his frail grasp.

It seemed to fall slowly before him. The other fighter swung her legs around in a two-legged kick, and he cursed her before he realized she was trying to put her legs between the vase and the floor. It was a wonderfully graceful move. The silk of her trousers was tight as she pirouetted around, but too late. There was a loud crash.

Pieces of five-hundred-year-old blue and white porcelain lay around them.

Both of them sprang to their feet.

"Why did you do that?" the girl hissed.

"I didn't do it," he said. She still had him by the wrist. He pulled his arm one more time.

"The guards will come," she said. All he saw were her large almond eyes and the frown in her smooth white forehead. The sound of shouting drifted through the compound.

"They'll find us," he said. He saw a moment's indecision in her eyes and twisted his wrist down and around. Free at last and with no more need for silence he leaped through the lattice window and jumped for the wall, caught the lip of the eaves and swung himself up.

"No, you don't!"

His opponent sprang after him and caught his feet.

"They're coming!" he hissed at her as he tried to kick her free.

"They're here!" she said as the guards banged on the wooden gate, and then the doors burst open and ten men tumbled in together.

Wei-fang gave his opponent an "I told you so" look. She tore the cloth from her face. He almost let go of the beam. She was beautiful. Not just beautiful, he thought, but *beautiful*. At that moment she opened her mouth.

"Thief!" she shouted. "Help!"

He kicked free. Wei-fang was almost regretful as he leaped ten feet from the ground. It was a great skill that Iron Crow had taught him, and he felt a strange sadness leaving his opponent behind. But he had the sword, and he would take it to his master.

12

Shulien heard the shouting, and within a moment she was up on the roof of her compound. She saw a shape using the Light Body Skill to jump effortlessly from roof to roof, gaining rapidly on the dark figure that was hurrying away from her. The thief leaped twenty feet at each bound, laughing down at the palace guards who watched impotently from below.

He was fast, but Shulien was faster.

She threw herself forward, as an arrow is shot from a bow, slammed into his side and, concentration broken, he tumbled down, a thud of air driven from his lungs as he landed.

"Who are you?" Shulien asked. He swatted at her, and she knocked him back down. "How old are you?" The thief said nothing. "Look at me."

He would not.

"Who sent you?"

"No one sent me," he said at last.

Shulien paused. There was much about him that seemed familiar. "You remind me of a warrior I once knew . . ." she said, almost to herself.

There was no time to ponder, for at that moment the chief of Sir Te's guards pushed forward. He was the eldest of three brothers whose name was Horse. They were known simply as Old

Horse, Horse Two and Horse Three. Old Horse was fat as a steamed bun, the other two were skinny and lean as noodles. Horse Two and Three caught the thief by the shoulder and dragged him down to the courtyard.

Old Horse bent down and grabbed his hair. "This was one of the undertaker's men. He was the one tying sashes around everyone's waists! What are you? What is this thief's garb you have on? Send him to the rear courtyard and bring out the big bamboo. We'll beat the truth out of him. I'll break every bone in his body, I shall!"

Shulien paused for a moment. Thieves wanted quick profit. There were many treasures here that would turn more easily into cash than this sword. She was about to speak when Old Horse knelt to bind Wei-fang's arms.

"Look!" he said. He exposed the thief's arm and held it up to the lantern light. A tattoo snaked about the thief's arm. The mark of the Red Dragon. Shulien's eyes opened. It was the same tattoo as the men who had attacked her in the forest.

"What does this tattoo mean, thief?"

The thief looked up. "Nothing."

"He is lying," Old Horse said. "This is the mark of the West Lotus Temple."

"Who is the master there now? Hades Dai?" Shulien saw the fear in his eyes, and she knew she had guessed right. "He will not be happy when he knows you have failed him. I would not want to be you. Hades Dai delights in cruelty. He needs little excuse to turn to evil."

Shulien squatted down. She stared at the young man as if looking for answers in the depths of his eyes. "He sent you, didn't he?"

"No," the thief said, but there was no conviction in his words.

"Hades Dai wants to rule the martial way. That is why he wants the Green Destiny?"

"I cannot tell you!"

"Cannot or will not?"

Wei-fang sighed. These questions made his head hurt.

"Tell me."

"Why?"

"Because it will be better for you," Shulien said. "I know something of the West Lotus warriors. Only I can protect you from Hades Dai." She paused for a moment.

"Let me take him to the magistrate's *yamen*," Old Horse said.

Shulien shook her head. "No. Send him to the east wing. Do it now. Chain him up, but do not beat him. Understand?"

Old Horse started to argue but Shulien was firm. All knew that she had the favor of the late duke and his son. Her word was as good as theirs. She did not need to bluster or shout. Silence was her strength. "Your late master, Duke Te, trusted me. If you do not trust me, then trust in his judgment."

Old Horse paused, looking for an argument, but not finding one that seemed likely to work, he nodded. "Yes, mistress."

剑

As the thief was led away Shulien walked over to the young woman who had disturbed the thief. She was young and pretty, with large dark eyes. The same girl she had noticed the day before at the funeral. The one who stood out from the rest of the pretty noble ladies. "Who are you?" she said. "What are you doing here?"

"I heard a disturbance," the girl said. "I came here and saw him escaping with that sword."

Shulien gave her an odd look. "It was lucky you were here," she said.

"Luck comes to us all at strange times."

"Indeed. But warriors do not trust to luck. It is too unreliable. Tell me who you are."

The young girl bowed. "I am just a humble servant of the house."

"I did not know Duke Te kept such fearsome warriors in his household."

Snow Vase bowed. She had come here to find Shulien, and now they were standing face to face. She was tempted to spill all her history, but then remembered what her mother had told her of Jade Fox and Jiaolong's role in the death of Mubai, and she held off from telling the truth. "I am not of this household. I am just a poor relative. A member of the Te clan. My name is Snow Vase." She inclined her head in a respectful manner. "I am at your service." The girl had picked Green Destiny up from the floor. She passed it, two-handed, to Shulien.

Shulien looked at the sword for a moment. The sword, she thought. *The* sword. Always bringing discontent into the world. "The guards have gone. You can speak truthfully to me. Lies make a poor start to a friendship."

At the word "friendship," the girl's eyes seemed to open wide for a moment.

"There is a saying, beware crouching tigers," Shulien said.

"I know. Under the calm water's surface a dragon might hide."

Shulien was calm. "You are not really of the House of Te, are you?"

The girl shook her head. There were tears in her eyes. She looked down and blinked them away. She did not look much older than the boy. It seemed a strange chance that two young warriors should both be involved in the destiny of the sword.

"Who are you?"

She looked up and the tears had gone. "I am a young warrior. I came here to find you," the girl said. "I am one like you, who takes the Iron Way."

"Then why come in disguise—like a thief?"

The girl looked up with her large black eyes. She was painfully earnest. No—innocent, Shulien thought, and she felt herself warming to this girl.

"I came to find you," the girl said again.

Shulien laughed. "Am I so hard to find?"

"Yes," the girl said earnestly. "I came here because I knew when Duke Te died you would come here to help bury him, if you still lived. There is no greater warrior alive than Yu Shulien. Please teach me. I want to learn the fighting techniques of Li Mubai. I will be your student."

Shulien was almost repelled hearing the name of Li Mubai from another woman's lips. She put her hand to her chest and shook her head. For a moment she was lost for words.

It took a long time for her to answer.

"No," she said at last.

"Please let me serve you."

Shulien backed into the wall. The girl knelt before her. She was young and earnest and Shulien hated that she could not fulfill this girl's wish. She shook her head and looked for the right words. "No," she said. "I cannot. I do not need servant or student. All I want is to return to the mountains to end my days in solitude. I have made vows I cannot break."

"Please," the girl said. The word hung in the air.

Shulien paused for a moment and looked at the girl, and was reminded of herself when she had begged her mother and father not to bind her feet, but let her learn wushu. The memory came back with all the intensity of youth. She thought of all the sadness the Iron Way had brought. Not for the first time part of her wished that her parents had bound her feet and married her off. A simple life might have made her happier.

"You do not want to follow the Iron Way," she said. "It does not make a girl happy."

"I do not want to be happy. I want to be a warrior! If it was not for me, the Green Destiny would have been stolen. Please!"

Shulien drew in a deep breath and turned and walked away.

The girl's eyes filled with tears. She wiped them away. She would not cry. She would become Shulien's student, and she would learn.

"My name is Snow Vase!" she shouted after the retreating figure, but Shulien disappeared from sight.

Snow Vase pushed herself to her feet. She let out a sigh. It had all been going so well, she thought, and looked up to the moon. Disappointment came in many guises.

13

Sir Te did not know whether to sit down or stand up, so Shulien put her arm in his and led him to his father's study and shut the doors behind them. The room was full of the traditional items that decorated a scholar's quarters: a carved bamboo brush holder, jostling with different sized brushes; the dragon stone slab, where ink was ground; the glossy stick of ink; a bronze peach, which Shulien knew Duke Te had used to hold the water with which he ground his ink stick.

Sir Te seemed a little overwhelmed.

"Let us drink some tea," she said. She had dressed in a loose gown of cream silk, buttoned at the side, and folded the loose sleeves back over her forearms as she spoke.

Sir Te looked somber next to her in a gown of colored wool. Shulien noticed that his hands were still trembling. He nodded. "Yes, tea," he said, and hung the lantern over the tea-drinking table: a wild hunk of trunk and root, cleaned and polished to a deep gold.

"Of all nights!" Sir Te said as he dusted at his seat. At last he sat down, stooping over his little round belly. "You think they might wait until my father was buried. My poor mother, she is as nervous as a mouse. She cannot sleep. I sent her opium. A little smoke will help her rest. I might take a little opium myself. I have never taken opium before. My father did not approve."

He let out a sigh and looked around the room. He seemed to forget Shulien was there for a moment, then forced a smile. "I dropped my hammer," he said.

Shulien's face was sympathetic. "It is not easy to bury a parent."

Sir Te nodded. The word "bury" seemed to go through him like a sword. He took a deep breath. "Tea," he said. "Let me get a pot."

Duke Te had been quite a connoisseur of tea and tea-drinking implements. He had silver tea caddies, porcelain cups, cups of swirling gray Dali marble, and even a Mongolian skull bowl, rimmed with silver.

"Which one would you like?" He stood by the rows of miniature teapots. Some were black, some pale gray, most were a deep terracotta red. Some were molded into the shapes of bamboo, one a dragon, and others inscribed with lines of ancient poetry.

"Your father and I always used that one," Shulien said.

She pointed and Sir Te followed her gaze. "Ah yes. This was my father's favorite."

The pot was small and made of the finest red clay. He cupped it in his hand for a moment, and held it out toward Shulien.

"I could never tell why my father liked this one," he said. "Look. See how the handle thickens toward the top. How fat the body and how small the lid! And this little fat spout! Reminds me of Yang Guifei. I always thought this the ugliest little thing. Perhaps that is part of its charm. I don't know. I could never see the appeal."

He put the teapot down on the table.

She looked at the wooden chests that were piled high against the far wall.

"What are those?"

"What? Ah, those. They are my father's scrolls. Pictures, calligraphy. We hang them at New Year. I'm sorry. I'm all a-jitter." Shulien looked at him. He caught her gaze for a moment and saw almost disappointment in her eyes. "You know I am not my father. I have not chosen the same path as he. I was not made for the martial life. I have quieter pleasures . . ." He sighed. "The sword. What can I say? I do not want this thing here, if this is what will happen. You saw the tattoo?"

Shulien nodded.

"So what my guards tell me is correct."

Shulien nodded again. Sir Te shuddered. "Hades Dai. Why, even the name makes me shiver, and I have heard only whispers. I did not know he was still alive."

There was quiet as the black cast iron kettle began to rumble to a boil. Before it did he took it aside and carefully washed the cups and teapot both inside and out. He did not touch the cups or implements with his hands but used a pair of cedar-wood tweezers.

Before him on the table he had a folded red towel, which he used to dry the bottoms of each cup and the pot. The sight of tea seemed to cheer him up a little.

"What would you like? I have oolong or *pu'er* tea. I had some *maojian* as well, but it is a little late in the year now. It has lost its freshness . . ."

He seemed consumed by the variety of teas he had to offer.

She put out a hand. "Your father always made jasmine with this pot," she said. "And jasmine is good for the soul. It has a cleansing and fresh quality, I find. And it will not keep us up too long."

"Jasmine," Sir Te said, and fretted back and forth as he opened caddies and found the wrong tea, or found last year's jasmine. He sniffed it. "Jasmine Pearl Balls," he said. "It is not as fresh as it ought to be. I know I had some white jasmine somewhere, but I think the steward steals it. I have caught him twice before drinking my father's oldest *pu'er*. What to do?"

"Make tea," Shulien said.

"Ah yes. Tea."

He refilled the kettle and set it to boil again. "This is from the spring at the back . . ." He stopped. "Oh, you must know this already. I'm sorry. I'm tired. The last thing I need is thieves breaking into the house. What am I to do with this thing? Why did Mubai bring it here?"

Shulien swallowed. "He did not," she said. "I did."

Sir Te's mouth fell open. "Sorry," he said.

She put up a hand. "I am sorry," she said. "I should have destroyed it. It has brought me more sadness than I can tell. Jade Fox killed Mubai for that sword. And now Hades Dai is seeking it. I should have destroyed it, but it seemed so beautiful. What can I say? Mubai and I both loved to see such beauty, such craftsmanship. It was like a child to us. We took it out and marveled at it. How little we knew. It was no child. We had no children. We never were anything but friends." She looked up and smiled as he put three scoops of jasmine pearls into the pot, filled it to the brim, and then poured the infusion away.

Shulien loved the smell of jasmine. The first brew washed the leaves and released the aroma. The second was the finest to drink.

She tapped the table with one finger to thank him as he filled her cup, took it in two hands and smelled it.

"A cup of wine takes your cares away," she said. "Tea is like wine, I have found. Jasmine is the queen of all teas."

They sipped the cups and then he refilled them. In this manner they drank three or four cups of tea.

"Will he escape?" Sir Te said.

"The thief? From that cage? I do not think so."

"My father used to keep his dogs there. It is a sad thing to see thieves locked up. What are we come to, I wonder? My guards tell me that he has threatened them. Is he mad?"

Shulien sipped the tea and set her cup down. "No, he is not mad. He comes from Hades Dai, that is certain. But he is only young. He is little more than a boy. Not all he said made sense to me. But one thing is clear. Hades Dai will soon learn that his thief has failed in his task, and he will either send more and better warriors, or he will come himself. That is what I fear." She idled her cup. "If he comes . . ."

"Hades Dai will eat your livers!" the thief had said to her. "You only have until the waning of the moon!" Shulien did not want to alarm her host. "How many men have you here?" she said. She tried to sound nonchalant.

"Just those you have seen."

"Where are the others?"

"My father used to command a hundred martial warriors. I have only half that number now, and all but ten are gone. When I heard of all the men who had been killed across the kingdom I thought I should reinforce them. I sent them out into the world. They are all on the Iron Way to subdue the bandits and terror-mongers." He sighed. "I fear also that my father was too successful. He maintained peace for too long. Our blades have gathered dust. We took too much to wine and poetry and the gentle arts, and now we have need of skill and speed and violence."

"What about this girl, this Snow . . . what is her name again?"

"Snow Vase."

"Yes. She can fight, it seems."

Shulien nodded. "Yes," she said. "I will keep her close. I want to keep my eyes on her. But still. We will need more." Sir Te refilled the pot once more. The brew was still green but it had lost its fragrance now.

He pursed his lips and waited.

"I suppose we could summon swordsmen. There might be wandering men who would come and help if the son of Duke Te asked them."

Shulien set her cup down. She forced a smile. It seemed a desperate move. "Why not?" she said.

She watched as he paced back and forth, rubbing his hands together, as if washing them. He stopped and put a hand to his head. He seemed heartened. "I will send notices out tomorrow."

剑

Sir Te seemed glad to leave the sword with Shulien.

"Will you be all right?" he asked as she walked him to the doorway of the courtyard.

She nodded.

"Oh good," he said. "If there is any problem . . . I suppose you will be fine. Yes?"

"I think so," she said.

That night Shulien sat alone. The sword lay on the table before her: unsheathed. It glowed in the light of the candle. She traced the cloud patterns in the steel until she lost herself. She had thought never to see this sword again, had hoped not to see it. But now she was here, alone with it and the candle, which was slowly burning itself out, and she found the presence of the sword almost comforting. She shut her eyes and she could feel it, and if she tried just a little she felt she could feel Mubai's ghost as well.

He was standing just behind her, in the long scholar's robe he liked to wear. It showed his accomplishment in fighting that he could best others without breaking a sweat, often with one hand behind his back. She remembered watching him fight with Green Destiny once, and he did not bother to unsheathe it.

"I feared for you," she had said to him and he'd stopped and looked at her in a puzzled, almost pained way.

"Why?" he had said.

"I thought they might best you."

He'd cleaned the sheath and cupped the sword in the crook of his elbow and walked toward her.

"Of course not," he had said. "It is not my destiny to die at the hands of men like those."

He had been so confident, so full of life and quiet power and energy that she had believed him. Believed him even when he had gone out to fight with Jade Fox. But it was the poison that had bested him, not her fighting skill, and that day they had both learned the hard way that there are some foes more powerful and deadly than even the greatest warrior.

"Hades Dai is seeking it." She almost surprised herself to hear her own voice speaking aloud. She kept her eyes shut, and imagined him walking to stand before the table, arms behind his back, half turned toward her, half turned away: one half lit by the candle flame, like the moon.

He cannot have it, Mubai's ghost said simply.

There was a long silence. Shulien breathed slow and deeply. She waited for the ghost to speak again.

You must stop him, his voice in her head said. *Just as I stopped Jade Fox.*

She opened her eyes suddenly, as if she might catch his ghost before it fled.

But the room was empty, except for the sword and the candle, which had started to drip. She was tired. She knew many warriors who could out-fight Hades Dai, but all of them were dead.

Now she did not know any warrior living who could beat him.

Not even herself. Once, maybe, she thought. But not now.

You must stop him, the words echoed in her head.

"I will stop him," she said, more confidently than she felt.

14

Next morning the broad streets of the poor southern quarters of Beijing were bustling with the early trade. All along Pig Market Street and Grain Market Street peasants squatted behind their spread of herbs and vegetables, arranged on scraps of sackcloth or wicker mats. Gangs of camel drivers just returning from the long and dusty Russian tea routes, their faces dark with sun and wind and sand, paused in the shade of Lama Temple. They traded banter with those who were getting ready to set out, brought tidings of favored watering holes, dangerous stretches, the movement of hostile tribes and bandits.

There were old mothers with baskets buying green clumps of coriander, lotus root, and small pieces of pork from the fat meat seller who waved the flies away. Traders, scholars, civil servants, poets, all mixed in busy crowds, and standing a little way apart was a man dressed in simple black clothes, stained with dust.

His hair was unbound and fell around his face in a wild mane. His chin low, he looked around him with eyes that were hard and small and threatening. Men kept away from him if they knew their business, and everyone knew their business that morning.

The warrior pushed himself off from the wall and strode slowly and purposefully across the street to where a crowd had gathered to read a poster that had been nailed to a gibbet post in the shade of a black-tiled old temple, grass growing from the eaves, the Ming Dynasty brickwork still straight and even.

Mule drivers and rickshaw men moved around him. The crowd parted like a knife through soft fruit as he stopped before the poster, and the people looked at him, not the poster. There was a weight to his steps that was at odds with his lean appearance, and when he set his feet shoulder width apart, it was like a tree being planted into the yellow earth.

The man was tall, with a hard face, deeply lined by weather and the years. There was a bitter air about him as he ignored the thronging people and stared at the poster so hard it was as if he were looking through it to a meaning beyond. His eyes followed the black characters descending from left to right. *Men of the Iron Way wanted at the House of Te*, the poster read.

The people were trying to work out what it meant. The stranger let out a snort of derision, reached up and tore the poster down, crudely folding it into four and shoving it inside his jacket. He turned and looked at the crowd around him and they averted their eyes and hurried on their way.

剑

A day's ride from the capital was a gateway where two tall cedar trees grew, their long-hanging needle fingers combing a low hiss from the breeze. The path ran through the arch the trees made, and inside was a wide courtyard, and a sprawling teahouse, named the Chan Li Inn.

It was a place shunned by peace-loving men and women. It attracted all the wrong sorts: sing-song girls, crazed herbalists, and wushu warriors who came here to exchange news, or to find a master, or pupils willing to study and learn. There were sleeping

147

halls to east and west, and across the north of the courtyard was the inn itself: a broad building with a tiled roof and a faded Imperial flag fluttering on top.

The second floor was full of private rooms where the sing-song girls entertained their guests. The bottom floor was a wide room, ringed with wooden cubicles, while the center of the space was devoted to round tables and pots of tea and rice wine. The inn was busy these days: abuzz with the news of Duke Te's death and the killings that had happened.

In the middle of the room sat Black Tiger.

He and his men had arrived the night before, the sing-song girls had been singing all night, and now he was on his third pot of wine and was shouting and bullying, throwing his prodigious weight around the place.

The rest of the inn was giving him a wide berth as Black Tiger clapped his hands and called for more meat.

"Beef!" he shouted, and pounded his fat fist on the table until the innkeeper brought a plate of cold roast beef slices, piled with coriander leaves and sprinkled with red chili flakes and drizzled with sesame oil.

Black Tiger glowered down. "There's too much coriander," he shouted, "and too little chili!" He picked a slice of beef, dabbed off the coriander, chewed slowly. "Too much five spice!" he shouted. "Too little salt!"

The innkeeper's daughter came out a few minutes later. She carried a plate of cucumber fried with egg. She slammed it down on the table. "Too much egg," she said. "Too little cucumber."

Black Tiger's eyes narrowed. Ever since he had tried to kiss her she had been like this. His scowl deepened and darkened, like the sky when a storm is brewing.

"More wine," he said at last.

She took the empty pot and sashayed off. She was a lovely

little thing, he thought. Plump, hard-working, feisty. Just the kind of woman his mother had warned him against.

"The best stuff," he shouted. "And ten catties of dumplings."

"Beef or mutton?"

"Mixed," he said. "With cabbage."

剑

Black Tiger chomped through the plates of dumplings as he heard the clatter of a horse approaching. The clip-clop grew steadily louder, right up to the door, the shadow of the horse darkening the entrance.

The stranger dropped lightly to the ground. His hair was unbound, his chin was low, and he strode silently into the room with all the menace of a mountain tiger. He reached inside his jacket and took out a rough scroll of paper, unfolded it, and used his knife to pin it to the beam above the bar.

Men of the Iron Way wanted at the House of Te, it said.

Some men watched the stranger, others watched Black Tiger.

Black Tiger scowled. He didn't like to be disturbed when he was eating. He didn't like to be disturbed, he didn't like strange horsemen, and he didn't like them putting posters up on the Chan Li Inn wall. He shoved in one more dumpling and pushed the table back as he rose. "Who are you?" he shouted.

The man ignored him.

"I said, who are you?" Black Tiger growled. His voice was so deep and resonant it made the teacups tremble on the tables.

The stranger continued to ignore him and turned to face the room. "The House of Te is fearful. They have called for warriors to come and help them."

The stranger had a quiet voice but it carried across the silence, and the whole room stopped and looked up.

"Help them against what?" Black Tiger demanded.

The stranger looked at him for a moment, and then turned to face the rest of the room. "They want warriors, not eaters."

There were a few chuckles from the far reaches of the room. Black Tiger's round face darkened. He strode into the middle of the room, right before the stranger. "You want warriors. I am Black Tiger. I lead thirty warriors. I will come and help this Te man for twenty ounces of silver each man." He belched a mix of garlic and mutton.

The warrior looked at him. "How much in total?"

Black Tiger tried to work it out, but he was better with his club than he were with numbers. "Seven hundred ounces," he said, as if he were bargaining in the market.

"Does that include your food?"

The laughter was louder this time.

Black Tiger pushed up his sleeves and showed fat forearms bound with vambraces of black leather, studded with brass. He drew himself up, and took up a fighting stance.

The stranger did not respond. He looked at the fat warrior posturing before him. "There was a time when warriors used to fight for honor," he said. "Not silver."

"Was," Black Tiger said, and belched again. He thrust out his belly. "Not now."

"That is sad."

Black Tiger forced a laugh. "Go home and cry then."

"What is your name?"

"I am Black Tiger!"

"I have heard of you. Men spoke more highly of you once. I had not known you had sunk so low."

"You have insulted me twice," Black Tiger said. "Which is twice too many."

He put out a hand. One of his men passed him his club. It

was a thick piece of polished wood with a large brass cannonball lashed onto the end.

"Speak your name, stranger!" he boomed. "Before I send you to meet your ancestors!"

The whole inn was filled with the rattle of teacups and plates as men scraped back their chairs and created a wide space in the middle of the room. The stranger seemed unmoved. He wore high Mongolian boots, a dusty black leather jacket and a belt of woven thongs. "My name is Silent Wolf," he said.

Black Tiger snorted and stood up. He was dressed in a long gown of black silk, frayed and weathered around the hem. "Impossible. He is dead."

The stranger did not move.

Black Tiger stomped forward. "Who are you to take his name? We shall soon see if you are real or a pale imitation."

"I am no forgery," Silent Wolf said. He spoke quietly, but his voice was full of menace.

Five of Black Tiger's men stepped up about their leader. "Show him the road," Black Tiger told them.

As they reached for their weapons, Silent Wolf was a sudden blur. With his sword still scabbarded he struck each man only a single blow, but each blow perfectly precise, striking vital pressure points that left them writhing on the floor.

"I thought you were showing me the road," he said. "It seems I showed your men the floor."

Black Tiger's eyes narrowed. He clicked his fingers and the other twenty-five of his warriors stepped forward.

"Let us see how one does against twenty-six of us," he said, and rolled his shoulders to warm them up.

"Not against one," a voice called out. "Twenty-six against two."

One of the men in the inn stepped forward and bowed. He was a tall skinny man with gray at his temples, and a slight, almost elfish look to him. His belt was hung with throwing knives and spiked stars. "I am Flying Blade of Shandong. I will serve with you."

Black Tiger's face grew even darker. "Twenty-six against two it is," he growled.

"Not two, three!" another voice called out.

A short gruff man came forward, put his fist to his palm in a martial salute. The sound of flesh meeting flesh was like two hammers banging together. "Thunder Fist Chan! Famed in Zhejiang! I will fight with you."

"Five!" called out a third voice.

A slender, cold-eyed woman stood as well. Her stool fell over as she rose. She kicked it away with one foot. She had an embroidered cloak over her shoulders, which hung heavy around her.

"I am Silver Dart Shi!" she said. "And this is Iron Turtle!"

Iron Turtle was a short fat man with a giant turtle shell shield on his back. He saluted, pulled the shield from his back, and pulled the sword from inside the shield.

Silent Wolf bowed at his new companions. "Thank you, friends, though please do not stand with me for fear of my safety. It shall not take me long to deal with these village brawlers . . ." Silent Wolf turned to Black Tiger and the bristling crowd of his men. "Are you sure you still want to fight?"

Black Tiger growled at him. "You mock me, little one!"

Silent Wolf smiled: a thin, unfriendly smile. "Shall we?"

Black Tiger roared as he came forward, his gown fanned out like a cloak, and the civilians fled screaming as the fight began.

15

Through the Chan Li Inn a whirlwind flew, scattering chairs, tables and thrown warriors. The center of that storm was Silent Wolf: a blur of movement, lightning strikes and the low grunts of impact. Black Tiger's warriors dived into the storm and flew back out again, like sparks from a spinning whetstone. Silent Wolf knocked them back with split kicks, jumping kicks, front and back, and double kicks. And throughout this he did not draw his sword. He did not like to draw a blade unless it was necessary. Blood was messy, a real warrior did not need to kill, for the true warrior the body was steel.

Silent Wolf's face was set, his pursed lips slightly open as he sucked each breath in and punched it out again with explosive force.

He did not fight alone. Ten of Black Tiger's men howled with pain as Silver Dart, her teeth in a tight clamped grimace, swung her spike-sewn cape and a hailstorm of missiles flew out. Iron stars swirled from Flying Blade's fingers, almost hitting Silent Wolf.

Iron Turtle grunted as he tried to keep up, pulling a heavy saber from the scabbard on his back and driving away with great whooshing swipes a few of Black Tiger's men who had got around Silent Wolf's back.

"Ya!" Iron Turtle shouted again, and Silent Wolf ducked.

"Careful!" he warned, in a low voice.

"I was going for the man on your back!" Iron Turtle said.

"I had him covered."

剑

It took only moments before Silent Wolf double kicked the last two fighters, who came at him from both sides at once. Iron Turtle laughed. The inn was carpeted with the groaning and wounded warriors who had followed Black Tiger.

"So much for your thirty swords!" Iron Turtle said. "How much silver did you want? Looks like they all need to go back to school."

"Who should listen to one fat man hiding behind his friends?" Black Tiger shouted.

"Who are you calling fat, baldy?"

Black Tiger growled and Iron Turtle strode forward to fight, but Silent Wolf held him back.

"He is mine," he said simply.

剑

Watching Black Tiger charge was like watching a standing water buffalo. He lumbered slowly forward at first, trampling his men as they lay wounded, crushing bones underfoot. He gathered speed with each step, roared once more as he swung up his mighty club.

Silent Wolf's face was set hard as granite as he crouched. He did not move until the club had started its descent, then he let out a short shout, his upthrust open hand meeting the cannon-ball club. His hand trembled as he pushed from his left heel right through his body. Black Tiger snarled and grunted as he tried to force it down. The roof timbers shook with their exertions. There was a loud crack as the shaft of the club splintered. Black Tiger was thrown back. Silent Wolf tried to follow, but the floor timbers beneath his feet had cracked, and they broke as he pushed off them.

Black Tiger saw his chance and with a shout he leaped forward and reached for Silent Wolf's throat, but Silent Wolf was no longer there.

Black Tiger's hands clawed as he changed his attack and raked at Silent Wolf's face; the other warrior parried each blow, twisted away as Black Tiger tried to drag him into a deadly embrace. It seemed to Iron Turtle that Silent Wolf flapped the blows aside with almost contemptuous ease. He stood open-mouthed, twisting and shadow-boxing as if he were the one landing the blows.

"I will help you!" Iron Turtle shouted and ran forward.

At that moment Silent Wolf stepped lightly to the side to avoid a bone-crunching heel-kick and knocked Black Tiger from his feet. The huge warrior crashed down among the bodies of his own men. Silent Wolf scowled at him, and the big warrior's courage left him. He scrambled up through the debris of his lunch and half crawled, half ran to the door, his men limping and groaning as they followed him out.

Silent Wolf stood in fighting pose, black leather jacket stretched tight across his back, until Black Tiger and his men had funneled through the door. Then he stood smartly and saluted the other warriors.

Iron Turtle clapped. "I have never seen better fighting!" he said.

Silent Wolf said nothing.

Thunder Fist nodded. Silver Dart's cheeks were flushed. "How come I have not heard of you?" she said.

Silent Wolf laughed briefly. "I've been dead for years," he said.

The five warriors drew around the poster that Silent Wolf had pinned to the wall.

Men of the Iron Way wanted at the House of Te.

Flying Blade winked. "Well, if you are looking for warriors, stranger, then it seems your call has been answered."

Silent Wolf looked at him. "So it seems."

"Well! Warriors! Look no further!" Iron Turtle said as he stomped forward. "I will join you, great warrior. What is the cause?"

Silent Wolf looked around. He spoke quietly, so that only his companions could hear. "It is of utmost importance. Do you know Duke Te?"

"Of course we do," said Flying Blade. "But the duke is dead."

"Indeed. Which is why their need is so great."

Iron Turtle snorted. "Who would dare attack the House of Te?"

There was laughter from Flying Blade and Silver Dart. Who indeed!

"Hades Dai," Silent Wolf said. "And the Temple of the West Lotus."

Silence. Silent Wolf saw a number of his new friends exchange glances.

"Hades Dai," Thunder Fist said, speaking slowly. "I will not fight him!"

"Hades Dai!" Iron Turtle said.

"Are you afraid?" Silver Dart said.

"No!" Iron Turtle stamped his foot. "But we do not want to pick a fight with Hades Dai, or the West Lotus warriors."

"No, who would?" Silent Wolf said. "But Hades Dai has picked the fight. And we must help the duke's family."

He looked at each one, and he could see fear in all their faces. Even Iron Turtle looked away and would not catch his eye.

Silent Wolf pulled the poster from the wall and started toward the door.

"Stop!"

Silent Wolf turned. It was Silver Dart who spoke. "My father was killed by Hades Dai. I will fight with you."

"Well, if she fights with you, I shall fight. I will not stand any man saying Iron Turtle hides inside his shell!"

"Well, if my fat friend will fight, how can I not? That just leaves you, Thunder Fist."

Thunder Fist's face had turned red. He scowled and looked away.

"Do not judge me," he said.

"I do not judge," Silent Wolf said softly. *There were many friends I looked for, who have disappeared. Black Mountain Bear. Gold Phoenix. Mantis Li. They are all dead. This cannot be chance.* "I offer you nothing but danger," he said aloud.

Thunder Fist took in a deep breath. "I remember Duke Te. He helped my master when I was young. But Hades Dai . . . He is evil. I faced him once, and was lucky to escape with my life. He is dark and terrible! Do not fight him."

"He must be terrible to scare a big man stiff with fear!" Iron Turtle said.

Silent Wolf stepped forward and put his hand to the big man's arm. "Hades Dai is a terrible opponent."

Silver Dart watched Silent Wolf closely. "You speak as if you know him," she said.

"I do," Silent Wolf said. "I know him very well. He was the man who killed me."

Thunder Fist put out a hand. "If you are dead, you should be cold, but you feel warm."

Silent Wolf smiled. "Death is not so final."

They looked at him, not sure of the joke. "How many men do you have with you?" Thunder Fist said.

"I had five two minutes ago."

"I said I did not want to fight Hades Dai," Thunder Fist said. "I said I would stand by you, Silent Wolf. I will do so."

One by one they nodded.

Iron Turtle picked a pot of wine from the floor. "Remember Guanyu, in the time of the Three Kingdoms? He and his brothers swore an oath together to fight one and all. Let us drink three cups too, and seal our pledge to fight this Hades Dai."

Silver Dart sniffed the contents. "Open Your Mouth and Smile wine," she said, and dropped it onto the floor, where the pot smashed. "That was what Black Tiger was drinking ... I don't think we want to drink that."

"Here!" Flying Blade said, picking another discarded pot from the floor. "Fenjiu wine."

The others all stepped closer to sniff the top of the pot.

Iron Turtle found five wine cups and set them on the table, where they were filled.

He handed each warrior a cup, and they stood in a circle and solemnly drank three cups, one after the other.

At the end Iron Turtle wiped his mouth with the back of his hand. "I hope Duke Te's sons keep a good table! All this fighting is hungry work."

剑

Wei-fang had not eaten for two days and the cage was so small that he could neither sit up nor stretch his legs. It was almost as if it had been designed as an instrument of torture. He peered out between the bars. The cage was in the stable yard. Beyond his sight he could hear the horses snorting as their hay was wheeled in.

"Food!" he shouted.

There was silence for a long moment. He shouted again.

A door banged open and Horse Three stomped forward into his field of view.

He bent down, hands on his knees, and scowled. "Shut up, dog!" he said.

Wei-fang bit back his retort. Fury led to weakness, Iron Crow had told him. The true warrior stays calm. He does not let anger lead him around by the nose.

"I said 'food,'" he said.

Horse Three stood up and shouted out to his brothers. "The dog is barking again!" Wei-fang crawled to the side of the cage and he could just see two other guards playing chess on a cloth board. Old Horse was winning and Horse Two had a despairing air about him. "Food!" Wei-fang shouted, but neither of them looked up from their game.

Wei-fang sat back.

He had been unable to sleep all night as he plotted the possible futures ahead of him. They all looked bleak. Beaten to death with a small bamboo; beaten to death with a large bamboo; death by a thousand cuts. He had seen it once, a man lashed to a post and pieces of flesh cut from him and tossed into a wicker bucket. It was not pleasant. The kind executioner would slip with the knife and stop a man's heart when the chest was cut away. The rest was all butchery. It had the same effect on the crowd. Perhaps, he thought, he would be chopped at the waist.

"The vital organs are all in the chest," he remembered his tutor explaining. "When a man is cut in half at the waist, then he lives long enough to feel agony and shock. And he will go to his ancestors in two halves, and have to explain to them how he ended his life so badly."

Wei-fang's mind went on like this for a long time. If Hades Dai came he would punish Wei-fang for failing him. If Hades Dai failed then Wei-fang would be turned over to the magistrate. His mind had time to ramble through the various punishments. The anxiety was as interminable as his hunger. He found himself less worried about what the magistrate would do to him; it was what Hades Dai would do that unsettled him.

"Food!" he shouted.

The Horse Brothers were on to a new game of chess and this time Old Horse was beating Horse Three. "Down, dog!" Horse Two shouted. This time he brought his pole arm: a long bamboo with a sharp metal spike. He thrust it through the bars at Wei-fang's face. Wei-fang caught it. They tugged back and forth for a moment, and then Wei-fang exerted all his power and threw the man across the yard and his two brothers fell over laughing.

"I'll teach you!" Horse Two said. His face was a snarl as he ran forward. Again, Wei-fang caught the pole and used his power to throw the guard back. The third time his brothers came with him, and the three of them brought their bamboo poles and beat him.

Wei-fang could not fight them all. Not like this, penned in a cage. He gave up and protected his head with his arms. The beating felt good; it was a break, at least. At the end Wei-fang's lip was bleeding. "Will you feed me now?" he said.

"No!"

"Even a dog gets a bone," he said.

Old Horse bent down and pulled an ugly face. "Shut up, West Lotus dog! We don't feed rabid beasts here! We beat them to death before they bite anyone. Just you shut up or we might forget what our master told us about keeping you safe. Understand?"

"Leave us," a voice said, and Wei-fang looked up to see Shulien, dressed in a simple pale gown, and a beautiful girl in a pale blue jacket and trousers, walking into the stable yard. The Horse Brothers bowed, and left them alone together.

Wei-fang straightened his clothes, ran a hand through his fine black hair. It was already getting matted. They would not even give him a comb. "It might be a weapon," Old Horse had said.

The two women stood over him. Shulien squatted down. "Did you sleep well?" She spoke so quietly, but with such authority. Wei-fang had not known anything like it before. He felt he trusted her. She had a way of speaking that made him want to tell her everything.

"Yes," he said, but he could not stop irritation from discoloring his voice.

She gave him a look, as if to say, really?

"You cannot keep me here. Not if Hades Dai comes."

"Then tell us his plans."

"I do not know them. I was barely even one of his men. Only long enough to get the tattoo. My master was one of his disciples."

"Why would he entrust a mission this important to a passing warrior? You expect us to believe that?"

Wei-fang nodded, though he didn't really. "It's true," he said feebly.

"Really?"

Wei-fang let out a long sigh. He looked away. There was no point to this. The women walked away and Wei-fang's stomach rumbled noisily as the beauty followed Shulien out of the yard, as light and graceful as a scarf of silk.

If anyone was the real threat here, he thought, it was Shulien's young student. Not him!

The student turned and caught his eye, almost as if she had read his mind.

She was small and young and very beautiful. Almost painfully so.

He thought of his mother, and how she would be crying, and then the girl turned away and they shut the gate behind them, and left him to his hunger.

16

"I always do this to calm myself," Sir Te said, as he dabbed the excess ink from his brush and then wrote the single character ke—刻—onto the page.

"*Ke?*" Shulien asked, a little confused. It meant "quarter."

"I like this character," he said. "It calms me. The brush strokes have a beauty to them, quite apart from the meaning. These strokes curve sideways, and these are straight. It is a pretty combination, I think. Like sweet and sour, spicy and sweet, crisp and soft."

She nodded, but seemed a little unsure.

"You would prefer something more literary. I will give you something more literary."

He pulled a fresh sheet of paper, dabbed ink onto his brush, and then smoothed away the excess.

He breathed for a moment, calmed himself, and then wrote in neat descending columns of perfect characters. When he was done he blew on the ink, then held it up.

Shulien recognized it right away. Mubai had liked to quote it to her. It was a poem by a Song Dynasty hermit.

> You ask me the way to Cold Mountain
> To Cold Mountain, no road goes . . .

"Beautiful," she said. "Very soothing. Now—any word from your spies?"

He put his brush down, careful that the end hung over his ink stone. "None." There was a pause. "Will he really come, do you think?"

"I do," she said.

"But we have so few men."

"That is why he is coming."

"You think I was mistaken to send my best men out? I did not know what else to do, there were killings across the kingdom."

"The rice is now cooked," she said. "But let us not lose hope. Much may yet happen."

剣

Shulien left him to his calligraphy and walked back to her yard. The palace seemed quiet. For someone whose only friend had been solitude, she found the stillness a little unnerving.

Snow Vase was in her rooms when she got back.

"What are you doing here?" Shulien said.

Snow Vase blushed. "Nothing."

She looked as guilty as a naughty dog.

Shulien strode into her room. Almost immediately she saw that things had been moved and put back almost in the same place. She turned on Snow Vase—her look said it all.

"I'm sorry," Snow Vase said. "I just wanted to see it again."

"It is better that it remains hidden."

"I understand," Snow Vase said. "I can hardly believe that this is the sword that Guanyu used. My mother used to tell me such tales when I was young, and the ones of the Three Kingdoms were my favorite. Even more than the Monkey King. Is it wrong to believe too much in stories?"

"No. I don't think so. I remember the Three Kingdoms, and how much I learned from Guanyu and Cao Cao."

"I heard tales of you, and Mubai, and the Green Destiny."

"Really? I don't know why. Don't put too much faith in *those* tales."

"Did Guanyu really wear the Green Destiny?"

"So the tales tell."

"Then how did he lose?"

"Fate," Shulien said. "Luck. It always runs out."

"Is the sword as great as men say?"

"It is finely crafted. Exquisite, in fact. There is no sword like it: light and lean and beautiful. A sage once said that only the man who could hold the Green Destiny could be the ruler of the martial world. So many have tried and died to claim it. That is why it is being sought now. By those who wish to command others, dominate, control. I have no interest in these. The sword has no power over me. I have never seen it display magical powers. I do not see the title it bestows upon the wielder, or the power, or the prestige; I see the pain it has brought. The constant squabbling among mighty men that brings them all down low."

"Why keep it then? Why only hide it when you could destroy it?"

"I tried to. But the blade is too hard for me. I could neither bend it nor break it. So I gave it to the finest swordsmith in the capital and told him to melt it down and craft a vase from it, or something that could cause no harm to the world. A week later, I thought the deed was done, but he came back to me, and I saw that the sword was unblemished and my heart was heavy. I took it back into my care because it was not fair to burden another with this thing. I sat in despair and then meditation, and occasionally in my despair I offered up incense to the Heavens, and looked for a sign or a message in the clouds or the flight of the wild geese in the blue winter skies. But there was none. No answer from without, only within. I saw that this was a test I must take, and pass or fail, but take nonetheless. 'There is nothing I can do,' I thought. 'This sword has defeated me.'" Shulien looked up. "So I think it is not our fate to see the sword destroyed. It is our fate to carry it through life, and by bearing it the best we can we show our true natures."

"And be the master of the martial world, as the sage has prophesied?"

"For me those words do not go with the sword. They are other men's words, and hold no power over us today. But enough of this. I was suspicious of you at first, but I see there is honesty within you. And goodness. Would you like to help me here, in this trial, and to be my student?"

Snow Vase's eyes widened. "Yes, mistress, yes!"

"Don't call me mistress."

"Master?"

Shulien frowned. "Nor Master."

"But—"

"No buts." Shulien turned away again. Snow Vase was not sure what to do. After a long pause Shulien said, "I have spent too long alone. The gentle arts of conversation rubbed away after a while. But some things remain. Titles have little meaning to me. If you must call me anything, then call me 'teacher.' For that is all I am. I do not seek to master anyone or anything."

Snow Vase nodded. Shulien turned quickly. "Good! So. Show me what you know."

Snow Vase opened her hands. "I am best with a sword or bow . . ."

"But you have neither . . ."

"No," Snow Vase said.

"So?"

Snow Vase held her hands open . . .

Shulien walked outside to the tree in the corner of the yard. "What tree is this?" she said.

Snow Vase shook her head.

"This tree," Shulien said, "is a magnolia, planted by the Buddhist monk Dashan, who lived in the Dajue Temple. He planted a sister tree there. The one in the temple has white flowers, but look, this one bears flowers that are both white and purple. Every March, for ten days only, this tree flowers, and it does so whether anyone is here to notice or not."

Snow Vase nodded as if this were a lesson, though she did not understand what exactly was being taught. Shulien reached up to stroke the tree, and as she did so she snapped off two branches, each one ending in a flower.

She smelled one as she walked across the yard and handed one branch to Snow Vase.

Snow Vase blushed. She was not really one for flowers or perfume. She was a warrior's daughter, a horsewoman, a fighter.

"Look at it," Shulien said.

Snow Vase looked. Each petal was deep pink at the base, fading to white at the tip. She wasn't sure what to do with it.

"What does it smell like?"

"Lemon."

"Look at it."

Snow Vase looked.

"What do you see?"

"A flower. Petals. They are deep pink at the base, white at the top."

Shulien said nothing and Snow Vase felt she had to keep on talking. "There are two layers of petals."

"The outer petals protect the inner ones," Shulien said. She had stepped very close. "From the frost and the snow."

Snow Vase looked back at the flower.

"Are you ready?" Shulien said.

Snow Vase looked up. "This is my sword?"

Shulien nodded.

Snow Vase took a quick breath before taking up a fighting stance, and using the stick as a sword, swished it through the air in the Wu Tang style. Petals flew off as she fought. At the end she held her stance, the half-stripped flower bobbing at the end of the branch.

Shulien nodded. "Your form is good," she said. "Your posture correct. It is a start."

Snow Vase held her posture for one more moment, before standing to listen. "Thank you, teacher," she said.

Shulien stepped forward. "But it is one thing to perform the movements, another to apply them to real fighting."

Snow Vase nodded. "I know," she said.

"Do not answer back," Shulien told her. "Students should listen, not talk, otherwise they learn little."

Snow Vase's cheeks colored, and she nodded and bowed her head and swallowed back her irritation. Acting like a demure noblewoman, dressing in constricting silks, being a student again. None of this was easy.

"Strike me," Shulien said.

Snow Vase shrugged. She was starting to feel irritated. "Do you want to see the crane style, or the mantis?"

"The only arrow that counts is the one that strikes the foe."

"So . . . Which form should I use?"

"The best one."

If this had been her mother, Snow Vase would have rolled her eyes, but she bit her lip and nodded curtly.

The spirit of the crane entered Snow Vase. She was long-legged, long-necked, her blade a beak to strike the snake. A slender girl, hair plaited to the sides of her head, in black trousers and top, suddenly assuming the stance of a striking crane. She was grace and elegance and then she struck and she was speed and power and penetration, then soft and flowing and graceful again, as the dancing bird.

Shulien was neither crane nor mantis, tiger, leopard, snake or dragon. She was all and none; she was hard and yet soft; yielding and firm. She batted Snow Vase's attacks away effortlessly, one hand behind her back, barely moving her feet. Snow Vase pursed her lips, and came faster and fiercer, trying move after move and improving. Shulien irritated her at first. Snow Vase worked harder and faster, her feet moving as fast as a fist-fighter. But however hard she tried, however fast she fought, she could not land a blow.

One by one the remaining petals were torn from her flower. Shulien's flower had not lost a single petal. Her teacher was not even breathing hard, while Snow Vase's forehead was damp with sweat.

Snow Vase abruptly stopped, and let her arms hang without form. She was furious.

"What does this prove?" she said.

"That anger is like wine, it harms your health." Shulien held the flower up almost delicately. "That fixed form cannot beat a fluid defense."

Snow Vase scowled. Shulien took up a casual pose. She did not move her feet before landing the first blow.

"One," Shulien said.

Snow Vase bit back her anger. She told herself to move faster this time but the older woman walked almost casually, flicking the stick against her arm and skirts. "Two. Three. Four," Shulien said, the last one a gentle touch on Snow Vase's left cheek.

No one had ever struck her face. Snow Vase's nostrils flared as she attempted to defend herself, but the number of strikes kept increasing. Eight. Nine. Ten.

Snow Vase stepped back and forth, desperately parrying, and failing. She tried to attack with a quick thrust to Shulien's face, but the older woman knocked it to the side and slapped her left cheek again.

Snow Vase tried to parry with her arm, but the strikes began to come thick and fast, so fast that all Snow Vase could smell was lemon, all she could feel was the soft kiss of petals on her cheek. Eighteen. Nineteen. Twenty.

Shulien stopped suddenly. Snow Vase paused, wary, but it seemed the lesson was over. Snow Vase looked at her own stick, and it was bare of buds and flower. All that remained were a few stamens. "Your flower has not lost a petal, but mine is bare," she said.

"Not true," Shulien said, and held up her stick. Snow Vase watched as a white petal broke off. Shulien caught the petal in her open palm, and she looked at it sadly, before turning to her student. She almost smiled, a brief and passing expression. "You have some skill," she said.

"Thank you."

"But think. You are faster and stronger than I. And yet I beat you."

"How is that?"

"The true sword requires more than speed," Shulien said. "More than power." She did not take up a fighting stance, but deftly landed a light blow with the flower to punctuate each sentence. The third time Snow Vase tried to parry, but the flower kissed her cheek regardless.

Her face grew dark with sudden frustration and anger. Shulien landed another blow on the tip of her nose.

"The master knows when to strike," Shulien said, stepping back and lowering her stick. She walked to the gateway. "Practice what I have taught you," she said, and then walked away.

Snow Vase called out, "Teacher. What have you taught me?"

"What have you learned?"

"That I am too slow, too tense, that I have much to learn. I am angry at myself for being beaten so easily."

Shulien nodded. "Never be angry. Be glad you came to someone who can teach you."

"I am, teacher."

"First lesson, then, is to control your anger, your energy, your *qi*."

"What is *qi*, exactly?"

"It is all around us. It is the air we breathe, the will that lifts us from the ground when we are tired, the thing that sparks our life within our mother's womb, the thing that we give up when our days are done. It is fierce, it is powerful, you must learn to summon it in and control it. Anger is wasted *qi*. Channel your anger. Make it soft . . ."

Shulien smiled gently, then bowed and left. Snow Vase was alone. She stood and stared at the magnolia tree as if it might tell her. The tree stood silent and uncaring, dropping petals. She sat down and threw the stick across the yard. She shook her head, let out a sigh. She had thought she was good, and Shulien had just shown her how little she knew.

She thought on her teacher's words. Channel, soft, anger, *qi*.

Snow Vase was determined to match Shulien. She pushed herself up, rolled her shoulders, and tried to loosen the muscles in her neck. She reached up and kneaded her right shoulder. She breathed deeply to slow her heart down, then picked up the stick and closed her eyes. She remembered the day her mother had first taught her, breathed in the *qi*, and felt it swirl within her.

"Stand with your feet together," her mother had said. Snow Vase had done so. "Shut your eyes." Snow Vase had. "Now, imagine the tip of your left little finger has become heavy with all the *qi* rushing there."

The five-year-old Snow Vase had frowned as she thought. She imagined the tip of her left little finger becoming heavy, so heavy that her body began to lean, and as it did so her mother's voice came close by her cheek.

"Let your stance open."

The tip of the little finger pulled Snow Vase down to the left, and as it did so her right leg came off the ground.

"Balance yourself," her mother said.

The weight slipped from her finger, and she opened her eyes and found that she was standing with her feet shoulder-width apart.

Her mother was seldom talkative, or even concerned with her daughter, but this time she seemed to speak from personal experience.

"Men will think that you are weak because you are a girl," she said. "That is their first mistake. The mind is stronger than the body. Remember that."

There were many tricks her mother showed Snow Vase to reinforce this point. She taught her the one-inch punch, which came from the heel, and which could throw a man across a yard. She showed her how a tense arm held out straight was bent easily by twisting the wrist inwards, while holding an arm out straight and relaxed, but imagining that a steel bar ran through it, made that arm stronger than iron itself, as long as she held onto that mental image.

But her mother never told her what to think of a teacher who would not even tell her what the lesson was.

Snow Vase lifted the stick as a sword, and imagined hitting

Shulien full in the face with each blow. Fifty, she thought, a hundred!

剑

Snow Vase meditated before she slept. Each morning she meditated before the sun was up. Then, dressed in a simple cotton shift, she trained harder and faster than she had ever trained before. She brought images to mind that would bring anger. Anger, she learned, was like a tiger, wild and clawed and unstoppable and deadly; she began to learn how to master it, subdue it, tame it, make friends with it, like a household cat, sit it purring on her knee, until the moment she needed its speed and focus.

As she trained, Shulien would come and watch her. They would spar, and Shulien would try to enflame her anger, and Snow Vase met her teacher's taunts and probes with gentleness, softness, and turned them all aside, as the oilskin sheds rain.

"Good," Shulien said one day, quite out of the blue. "Tomorrow take a wooden sword and train at the butts."

Snow Vase bowed deeply. She was so calm that it took a long time to realize that the feeling inside her was deep, bubbling joy.

She smiled only faintly. "Thank you, teacher," she said.

17

Wei-fang shook himself awake. He could hear the scrunch of grit, the slap of an open palm on a knee or a high-kicking foot. He pushed himself forward to the front of the cage.

It was the young girl. Shulien's pupil. The ice queen.

He hunched forward against the bars and watched her, skin pale as a ghost, her hair loosely tied up at the back of her head, effortlessly moving through the Hundred and Eight Routines. She was as slender and graceful as a willow wand, as cold as winter. It thrilled him just to look at her. She finished with a sudden shout as she kicked high then landed low to the ground, like a cat. She rose slowly, caught his eye, and looked away, picked up her towel from the floor, wiped her brow, and threw it over her shoulder as she walked from the yard.

The second morning she ran through the same routines, and did not look his way. As she left he called out to her but she ignored him. She ignored him on the third and fourth mornings, and on the fifth he lay back, closed his eyes and chanted lines of Lu Bai's poetry to himself, an old favorite about sitting with friends, drinking together by the gentle light of the full moon.

"Hush," a voice said. It was the girl.

He opened one eye, then the other, kept humming the lines.

"I'm trying to concentrate."

He stopped and sat up and smiled. "When will she let you train with a real sword?"

"Cocky, huh?"

He shrugged.

"How's your new home?"

"A little smelly. The previous owner apparently had fleas." He looked at a point just before him and clapped suddenly. He opened his hands and shook his head. "Missed it."

She was unamused. "What is your name?" he said.

"Why should I tell you?"

"Because it's your fault I'm here," he said, and he thought he saw the hint of a smile. "Next time I won't hold my blows."

"You didn't hold your blows."

"I didn't draw the sword."

"You couldn't," she said. "I had hold of your hand."

"So you won't tell me?"

"No," she said.

At that moment the door of the courtyard opened and a servant came in dressed in the blue livery of the Te household. She was short and plump and smiled as she came forward. She bent down and passed a bowl of cooked white rice through the bars. "There you go, my little duckling," she said, clucking like an old hen.

Wei-fang smiled. "You are too kind," he said. "May the Buddha bless you. Oh my! So much rice. And warm too, thank you!"

The kitchen maid half hid her smile as she made her way back out again. Wei-fang took the chopsticks and started to shovel in the rice, smelling the meat before he uncovered it, hidden under the rice: slices of fatty pork fried with garlic stalks. His grin was sudden and spontaneous. In his joy he held it up to the girl to show her.

"Look!" he said. "See, I am not all bad."

"Tell Hades Dai that."

剑

Snow Vase walked to her compound and used a damp cloth to wash away the sweat from the back of her neck. She dressed in a simple gown and went to the kitchens.

"Has Mistress Yu eaten lunch yet?" she said.

The cook was a gentle man also named Te, who spoke through an iron pipe, the end stuck with a wad of rolled tobacco. The pipe had gone out, but he did not remove it.

"No," he said. "Not yet."

He pointed to a round tray on the chopping table, where domed wicker screens covered four plates. "Mistress Yu Shulien likes simple dishes. No garlic. Nothing too strong. I used to make them myself, but she likes my son's cooking better now. His taste buds are still good. Me?" He put a thumb to his nose. "I smoke too much."

He waved his hand and kept chatting as Snow Vase picked the tray up and nodded as she hurried out with it.

Duke Te had liked to eat his lunch early, and even though he was gone, the routines he had set carried on beyond him. A few servants were returning with empty trays, but otherwise the lanes and courtyards were quiet, except for a yard where the grandsons of Duke Te were being schooled, and they were chanting together Hanyu's "Memorial Discussing the Buddha's Bone."

Snow Vase's mother had been classically educated, and she had tried a few times to teach her daughter, but Snow Vase had never had a head for dry treatises.

"The Buddha was a tribesman from distant lands," they chanted. "His tongue was incompressible, his clothes were for-

176

eign, he did not know the histories of our earl kings nor dress like our old masters."

Snow Vase rolled her eyes. She passed another courtyard where some other children were playing. Their laughter was sudden and delightful as sunlight through colored glass, but then she turned right and at the end of a long silent walkway was Shulien's yard.

Snow Vase paused, balanced the tray on one knee and knocked.

There was no answer. She knocked again, listened, heard nothing, and pushed it open with her foot.

She peered through and saw an empty courtyard, and felt a shiver of premonition.

"Teacher?" she called out and walked toward Shulien's chambers. There were three broad steps up. The door to Shulien's chambers were open. Snow Vase put the tray down and crept into the room. She jumped when she saw Shulien, sitting on her bed, eyes open, watching her.

"You frightened me," Snow Vase said, then saw that Shulien was not looking at her, she was looking through her. Snow Vase turned and saw a teapot on a tall vase stand. It was an ugly little thing: fat-bodied and short-spouted like an ugly woman with large flapping feet.

"Teacher?" Snow Vase said. "Are you well?"

Shulien smiled. "Look at it," she said.

Snow Vase did. "It's ugly," she said, then paused. "Is this a lesson?"

Shulien unfolded her legs and pushed herself off the bed in one movement. She came forward. "This teapot sat in the middle of us, Duke Te, Mubai and myself, many times. It is small and silent. We barely noticed it. But now, of the four of us, there are only two left, this pot and myself, and I wonder which of us will outlast the other. I think perhaps it will be the pot."

Snow Vase looked at the pot. It would be easy to pick it up and shatter it on the floor. She was tempted. It was a truly ugly pot. So ugly it drew attention to itself.

"Books have been written about Duke Te and Mubai. Men tell tales in the inns and way-houses. No one talks of the pot. It is silent, and it inspires silence."

Shulien smiled. It was a rare moment, like the flowering of a magnolia tree. "You should not listen to stories in inns," she said.

"What else can one do in them?"

"You have been to many?"

Snow Vase nodded. "Yes."

"Inns are not places for young ladies."

"I had to cross the kingdom to reach you," she said. "I came from Dunhuang."

Shulien stopped, and seemed to see the girl for the first time. "Dunhuang?" she said. "That is many weeks' travel."

"It took me six." Snow Vase's voice was cocky as she spoke, and she added quickly, "I ride fast."

"So you do."

Snow Vase nodded. "I brought you your lunch," she said, and went out and brought the tray in and set it down on the bed, then took the dishes off one by one, careful not to spill the sauces.

There was cucumber, lotus root, a plate of fried egg and tomato, and another of fried peanuts with salt. Snow Vase poured a little soya bean milk for her teacher, and then bowed and made her exit.

"Have you eaten?" Shulien said.

Snow Vase paused at the doorway. "No," she said. "But . . ."

"Come!" Shulien said. "Eat!"

"I could not."

"Look, there is enough for two."

As Snow Vase sat to eat there was a sudden shout. Shulien's gate banged open. In a moment her master was out of her seat and at the door. How does she do that? Snow Vase thought, and hurried to stand next to her.

Horse Three ran across the yard. "There are riders at the stable gate!" he panted. "My brothers are trying to keep them out."

Shulien turned to Snow Vase. "Bring your sword!"

剑

The two women ran through the palace. The sound of shouting came from the stable yard. He has come for Wei-fang first, Snow Vase thought. The rest of the compound stood in eerie silence. They ran through a screaming band of women, and at the next intersection they saw Sir Te. "I brought all I could," he said.

Shulien drew her sword and led them toward the stable gates.

"I am sorry!" Old Horse sobbed. "They broke the door down. I could not stop them."

"Mubai!" Shulien's war cry rang out as she ran into the stable yard. Her sword flashed in the spring sunlight as she took up a fighting stance. But then a tremor went through her, and she let out a strangled gasp, and took a step backward.

It was not Hades Dai, but five dirty warriors. The foremost of them was a grizzled, lean-faced man, with narrow eyes and a jacket of black leather, belted at the waist.

Snow Vase looked at her master. "Are these the best of the West Lotus men?" she said.

"No," the grizzled leader said. He looked sadly at Shulien, and then bowed and saluted Sir Te.

"Sir Te, I am Silent Wolf," he said. His voice was low and rough, like sackcloth. "I saw the summons you put out. I have gathered these warriors. We all pledge our service to you."

Snow Vase turned as Shulien stared at him. Her face went from disbelief to shock, then a flashing look of anger.

"You!" she said, and seemed lost for words. "How dare you come here?"

She did not wait for an answer, but turned and walked from the yard.

Snow Vase looked around her in astonishment. Sir Te looked back and forth, confused and nervous. "Well," he started. "Welcome! You must have traveled far, from the—er—smell of you all. Well! I'm a little startled, that is all. You must not take offense. I am deeply gratified for your service, and ... do you know Yu Shulien?"

The lead warrior did not smile. His eyes were looking at the moon door where Shulien had gone, as if he expected or hoped that she would return. "Do I?" he said. "No. But I did once. Long ago." He spat on the floor. "You might say I knew her ..."

He paused for a long time.

"In another life."

18

Next morning Snow Vase's horse snorted as she entered, lifted his long face, and nuzzled her. She held the horse close. He was the only friend she had left, she thought. The only family.

She held his head up, and the horse snuffled at her. "So much has happened," she said. "I cannot even begin to tell you. I am learning. So much!" The horse snorted again as if in answer. "Yes. We will ride again soon," she said. "I promise!"

As she came out, Snow Vase saw Silent Wolf training in the yard.

She turned her face so that she would not accidentally catch Wei-fang's eye, but try as she might she could not stop herself from watching Silent Wolf.

The grizzled warrior was stripped to the waist, a broad black leather belt around him. He was a true master. He moved as smoothly and effortlessly as a flag that is carried through the air, but when he connected with an object there was a loud *crack!*

Such power, she thought. Such control!

She took a step closer, and waited.

At last Silent Wolf stopped, and she tilted her chin and started to speak, but he looked at her, said nothing and turned away.

"Snow Vase!" a voice called at the end.

She shook herself and turned, and saw Wei-fang.

"He is good, huh?"

"Yes," she said.

"He's teaching me," Wei-fang said.

"Teaching you? What—how to fetch a stick?"

Wei-fang smiled. "I close my eyes and imagine . . ."

"I bet you do."

This morning the kitchen maid had brought him two bowls of rice, each one stuffed with chili pork tendons, boiled to tenderness. He bent over them and picked his way through, savoring each morsel. "No. Just watching him I am learning. I may be imprisoned here, but my mind is free to wander where it will. I think when Hades Dai comes I will need to fight him, so I am watching this master, and going through the moves in my mind."

"You would fight your master?"

"He's not my master," Wei-fang said.

"No?"

"Not anymore."

She gave him a look.

Wei-fang sighed deeper this time. "If it wasn't for the threat of my master, I might enjoy this sojourn," he said. "I am like the mountain hermits. The wind is my fellow, the rain is my shower, and as I sleep the stars watch over me."

Snow Vase looked at Silent Wolf. "Does *he* ever speak to you?"

"Yes," Wei-fang said.

"What does he say?"

"He thinks I am innocent."

"He is a fool."

"Maybe. He is in love," Wei-fang said.

Snow Vase's pulse quickened. "Is he?"

"Yes," Wei-fang said. "You mean you don't know?"

"No," Snow Vase said. "How would I know?"

"Didn't you see how Shulien looked at him?"

"Yes," Snow Vase said. "You mean—he and Shulien?"

Wei-fang winked.

"What do you know?"

"Ah!" Wei-fang said. "That is private."

"Idiot!" she said, and slammed the gate behind her.

剑

For the rest of the day, whenever Snow Vase was passing the dog cage she made studious efforts to ignore him, but she was almost disappointed when he shouted out to her no more. Two days after that she stopped and said, "How do you know my name?"

Wei-fang looked up in surprise.

"I asked," he said.

"Who?"

"Ah!" he said, and grinned.

She shook her head with irritation and carried on with the sack of millet grain.

剑

That night Shulien and Snow Vase sat together in her yard to eat.

"The new warrior," she said. "He said he knew you."

Shulien turned sharply. The two women had started training in Shulien's own courtyard, and she had become strangely sharp. "Who?"

"Silent Wolf," Snow Vase said.

"You have been talking to them?"

"No, teacher," Snow Vase said. "You told me not to talk to them, and I am your student. But . . ."

"But what?"

Snow Vase's cheeks colored. "Wei-fang asked me about it. He mocked me because I did not know."

"What business is it of his?"

"It is not."

There was a long pause. "Leave me," Shulien said.

Snow Vase saw from her teacher's face how she had transgressed, and nodded. Silently cursing Wei-fang, she hurried from the courtyard.

"Stop!" Shulien called out. She stood up and walked toward Snow Vase. "I am sorry," she said and took a deep breath. "All this is hard for me. I came here, out of my solitude, to grieve quietly for my old friend. And instead all I have been beset with is troubles. I remember something Mubai once said to me. It is the things one does not want to happen that teach us the most. I am sorry, I have been hard on you. Unnecessarily, perhaps. You are young and talented and you are a good student. I wish I could be a better teacher for you."

Snow Vase saw the look on Shulien's face and she nodded.

"Yes," she said. She smiled. "I will go and practice!"

"Good," Shulien said, and smiled back. She was so pretty when she smiled, Snow Vase thought. "You should smile more often," she said, before she had thought whether this was a good thing to say.

Shulien smiled again. "You are not the first to tell me that," she replied.

"Silent Wolf?" Snow Vase said.

"Go and practice," Shulien told her.

"Yes, teacher."

Shulien watched Snow Vase walk from her yard.

Silent Wolf, she thought. That was the biggest surprise of all. Mubai had always said that if you were afraid of something you must confront it, lest it control your life thereafter.

This was the last thing she wanted to do. She took in a deep breath and threw a simple black cloak around her shoulders. Silent Wolf and his men were staying in the courtyard next to the stables.

19

By the time he had paced the entire perimeter of Duke Te's palace, Thunder Fist's face was gloomier than a chained hound. "How can we protect this place?" he said. "This is a hopeless task. It is like asking a man to stop the ocean with his hands."

"The man without hope has lost before the first blow is struck," Silent Wolf said.

Thunder Fist glowered at him. He waved an arm at the size of the place. "I am brave but I am not a fool. It took me two hours to circle this palace. If Hades Dai comes with all his men, then we cannot hope to patrol the walls."

"We do not need to," Silent Wolf said.

"What do you mean?" Thunder Fist said.

Silent Wolf pulled a stool over and sat down on it. "I will explain," he said.

The others looked up. Even Iron Turtle thrust his chopsticks into his rice and set the bowl down. "We do not need to protect the palace. All we need to do is protect the sword. Hades Dai is only interested in that.

"Hades Dai is a cobra. He is a man of great strength and power, who puts more faith in craft and cunning and guile. He will not come at the head of his warriors, but he will try subterfuge and lies. Such are the things he delights in. It is what has made him evil, and made his evil grow deeper and blacker. He seasons his food with cunning, drinks it down like Iron Turtle drinks wine.

"No, when he comes it will be in secret, at night. Otherwise he will rouse the whole city against him, and the soldiers … Well, they may be weak but they are plentiful. And I doubt even Hades Dai will escape once the Imperial Cavalry are set on his heels. There are only so many arrows one man can dodge."

Silver Dart laughed. She had seen men dance. "I have never known a man who could dodge all my shots," she said.

Silent Wolf nodded. "I believe it, Silver Dart Shi. I would not like to be put to the test."

Thunder Fist was unmoved. "Then what are we to do?"

Silent Wolf stood up. There was a long pause. "Our weakest points are not the gates or the walls. Thunder Fist is right. We cannot hope to guard the walls of the palace. And the place is already full of mourners. As far as we know, Hades Dai's men could already be within the walls. No. The only place we need to guard is this courtyard." He swung himself up and strode to the roof-ridge of the hay store. "If you see the palace from here, the roofs are a walkway. These will be Hades Dai's roads."

"So what do we do?" Iron Turtle called up. "I am not one for running over tiles all night. I will break them, for one."

"We can lay traps," said Flying Blade. "Tripwires, bells."

"What happens if Iron Turtle is sleeping off a pot of ale? You think a bell will wake him?"

"Who said you were allowed to sleep?" Silent Wolf said.

There was a long pause.

Iron Turtle looked at Silent Wolf. "You're joking, yes?"

Silent Wolf almost smiled, but the look quickly faded. "No," he said with a sigh. "I am not joking. Hades Dai will come, that is the one thing of which we can be sure. We will stay here. We will keep watch. Not a single person shall enter this courtyard without my permission."

"The sword is here?" Iron Turtle said.

"Yes," Silent Wolf said.

Iron Turtle looked around him. All he saw were the three single-story buildings that formed the north, west and eastern sides of the courtyard, their gray brick façades and papered windows staring blankly back. Across the southern side of the courtyard was a wall of the same gray brick, as high as the buildings, through which the gateway ran. To the left of the courtyard, in the crook of the west wing, was an old plum tree, wizened and bent with a few scraggly branches, their last pink blossoms still clinging on.

"It's not in my room, and it's not in Silver Dart's room."

"How do you know?" Thunder Fist said. "Been spying on her?"

Iron Turtle's cheeks colored red. "No," he said. He glowered at the bigger man.

"It is hidden," Silent Wolf said. "And it is better that way. All you need to know is that it is here, and that no one comes into this courtyard without my say-so."

They nodded their agreement. "Beware spies," Silent Wolf said. "Hades Dai will have many plans. It is the fool who relies on one arrow when he has a full quiver."

剑

That night Shulien stood in Sir Te's study, the Green Destiny on the desk before her. She moved the candle closer. The sword seemed to glimmer with an inner light, as if it were made of glass, or jade.

She knew she was being watched. Knew an intruder was there. Only one, and he was very good. He thought she could not tell he was there. He was patient, she gave him that. Patient and almost silent. One of the best. But it was the little things that gave him away. The cricket that suddenly stopped. The way the bats veered above the intruder's head.

Shulien did not know if she was trained to this, or whether her knowing it was natural. But she knew he was armed, male and deadly. But she remained calm. She had Green Destiny. And there was almost no one in the world who could outclass her in sword-play.

"I know you are there. Why not step out of the shadows?" she called out.

The figure stepped forward through the shade of the doorway. An armed warrior, his sword sheathed across his back: Silent Wolf.

Shulien turned to face him. "I thought it was you," she said.

"How did you know?"

"Because you were so good," she said. Her voice remained calm, but it took on a hard edge as she looked at him. "You were dead," she said. "Why did you come back?"

He stopped and swallowed and did not seem to know what to say. She saw him struggling for words, and an odd mix of relief, justification, satisfaction and despair came over her—and she could not hold on to one long enough to give her a sense of exactly how she felt. "What is the point of appearing now, after all these years?"

"I swore an oath," he said.

"Is that an answer?"

"It is my answer."

Damn him, she thought, he is as infuriating as I remember.

"An oath. What for? Me, or the sword?"

"I swore an oath to protect both. I have come to fulfill that oath."

"I do not need protection."

"You did in the birch forest, when Hades Dai's men waylaid your wagon. I remember them catching a choice fish in their net. And yet it was they who lay dead at the end of the fishing trip, not the fish."

"That was you?"

Silent Wolf nodded.

She moved so there was a wide stretch between them. "How long have you been following me around?" she said.

"Years."

"And you never came to speak to me?"

"I was tempted."

"Tempted?"

He nodded. She shook her head at him. "What does years mean? How many? Where? How have I not seen you?"

Silent Wolf had an odd light in his eye. She backed away from him. "Does it matter?" he said.

"Yes," she told him. "It matters."

The two stared at each other across another man's study, across the years, across all that might have been. Her anger was like a tumbling stream that pooled for a moment. She shook her head. His eyes seemed hard. Glossy as a black pebble in the hand. But there was no sign of madness about him. He was calm. Measured, much as she remembered him, except the lines of age around his lean cheeks and eyes.

"I do not like this," she said.

He sat down again. "I understand. I . . ." He paused. "I may not have handled this well."

"No you have not. Explain how you survived on Vulture Peak."

Silent Wolf nodded. "When I fell from Vulture Peak I landed on a wide, rough ledge. My body was broken in many places.

I was like a wild beast that crawls into a corner to die. But somehow I survived. Life kept burning within me. The flame would not go out. I healed slowly. I licked rainwater and dew from the rocks. Chewed moss. Ate whatever grubs and beetles I could find.

"I do not know how long I remained on that high rock. My bones healed. My body grew thin, but I was not weak. In that time I brought my *qi* to a new point of excellence. I refused to die. I thought of you and Mubai. I thought of my former life, and that hope kept life burning within me. But when at last I found a way down from the crag where I had sheltered, and made my way back to civilization, I heard that you and Mubai had gone off together, and I was glad for you both." He paused. "Though it hurt me too. For I knew that I had lost the two people most dear to me.

"I thought you would marry. I imagined your children. Sons like him. Daughters as beautiful as you. And that brought me happiness. I was never one for weddings or wives. My father knew that. I traveled south. Far, far south to where the coconut trees grow along the broad sands. I lived in Hainan, and even made my way to Yunnan. I lived for a long time like a hermit. My home was Tiger Leaping Gorge. A river cuts a path through a mountain. The cliffs are beyond counting, and so close that a tiger could leap across. It was far, remote, magnificent. And then one day when I came to the town of Lijiang I heard a tale about a woman named Jade Fox, who had poisoned the great Li Mubai, and I dropped my chopsticks and called the speaker over to me. 'Mubai is dead?' I said. 'How can that be?' I was told the tale and set off at once, even though I did not believe it. I crossed the entire kingdom: by sled, by boat, and on foot. I crossed every river, every mountain range, and came at last to Beijing, where I heard the tale in full. That was nine years since. I knew it was true then. In my heart. And I wept. I wept for my best of friends. I wept for you. And I wept for me, for I learned also that Mubai had been unmarried when he died, and that the great Yu Shulien had gone back to her father's house and was no longer seen."

Her anger cooled. She stepped closer to him, sat down opposite and looked at those hard black eyes as if they could tell her more. "But why did you disappear in the first place? We both missed you so much. Mubai never forgave himself."

"I died for you," he said. "And Mubai."

"How?"

"I saw how he looked at you. And I knew his feelings, and why he hid them. Our parents had arranged our marriage. You were my betrothed. He would not marry you while I was alive."

"So you pretended to be dead."

He nodded.

"We never married," she said. "Mubai and I."

"I know."

The sigh seemed to take the last of her anger away. She shook her head and buried her face in her hands. When at last she looked up, there were no tears, only a deep sadness and weariness. "I see you tried to do good. But you were mistaken. You should never have done what you did. Mubai felt he had let you down. He had his honor. Of course he would not marry me. He could not."

Silent Wolf sighed and shook his head. "If Mubai had a fault, it was that he loved his honor a little too dearly."

Shulien slammed her open palm onto Sir Te's black lacquered desk. The brushes rattled in their ceramic pot. Her anger came back stronger than before. "How dare you! We mourned you," she said. Part of her was outside herself, watching her lose her temper, lose her control, lose her discipline. She almost enjoyed the feeling of anger, the freedom of the outburst. She hit the table again. "We lived in mourning. We never loved. Never loved each other properly because of that. We kept to more than just our vows. We kept ourselves honest to *your* memory. And you were on some great adventure!"

"It was not like that—" Silent Wolf tried to say, but she shouted over him and he stopped.

It took a few long moments before she could calm herself down enough to speak. "You should not have just appeared like this. You have done wrong. You have done me wrong, and Mubai wrong, and I do not think I can forgive you."

"I do not want forgiveness," he said. "But I also owe a debt. That is really why I am here. To fulfill my debts to Mubai."

She turned her back on him. "I am sick of honor and duty," she said. "When this is over you shall leave. When this is over I shall tell myself that you are dead. I do not want to see you again. Understand?"

Silent Wolf nodded. "I understand."

She stared at him across the room, her wide eyes as wild and fierce as a stormy sky.

"I have told my men the sword is hidden in my courtyard."

"Why?"

"In case any of them are untrue."

Shulien turned to shut the case on the Green Destiny. How she hated this sword. It was for this that Mubai had died. And here it was, still tormenting her. She looked at him. "Two West Lotus warriors were caught entering the capital yesterday. They are drawing close. It will not be long."

"How many days until the full moon?"

"Four."

She paused. She wanted to be clear. "All that was between us died on Vulture Peak. Really died. Gone, and cannot come back."

"I understand," he said again.

He followed her gaze to the sword. "I will keep it here," she said. "No one will know except you and I."

He nodded and bowed, and disappeared as silently as he had arrived.

Shulien sat down abruptly. She felt weary with all the emotion inside her.

Mubai, she thought. You would never believe this . . .

She imagined him standing and laughing at the absurdity of it all. She put her hands to her face and took in a deep breath. She started to rock back and forth, and as she did so an odd sound came from her: half crying, half laughter.

20

The moon was rising, and through the gloom Iron Turtle saw a palace servant approaching. The closer he came the slower he went. He paused and looked back, as if losing his courage, and at that point Thunder Fist stood up. "Who goes there?" he shouted.

The man jumped. He was a young lad, maybe twenty years old, with a patchy beard beginning to grow on his chin. He held his hands together, and moved forward sideways, like a crab. He stuttered for a moment, then called out. "Sir Te sent me," he said. "Please do not shoot. Sir Te has said that there are messengers from the palace, and he wanted to talk to you."

Silent Wolf's face appeared. "The palace?"

The man nodded. He didn't know who to address, Thunder Fist or Silent Wolf. "Shulien has asked for you."

"I will come. Iron Turtle!" he called. Thunder Fist opened the gate, and the two warriors walked out. "Lock the gate behind us," Silent Wolf said. "And remember, no one goes in or out without me there."

Sir Te had his hands together, as if he were in prayer, when Silent Wolf appeared.

"Shulien." He nodded toward her.

Shulien's face betrayed no emotion. "There is a summons from the palace," she said.

On the black lacquer desk a scroll lay before her. He bent down to read the characters. Sir Te's eyes looked from one warrior to the other. "Has the Emperor heard what is happening?" he asked.

Silent Wolf bent to read the summons. "No, I think not," he said at last.

"But if the palace demands this thing ... just imagine what will happen to it once the eunuchs get their hands on it," Sir Te said. The eunuchs were a plague on the palace. They knew more than the Emperor, they schemed and plotted with corrupt officials and stole and thought of nothing but their own comforts.

Silent Wolf seemed to shiver. "The palace eunuchs must not be allowed to seize it. Listen, Shulien. Will you go to my compound and ensure the sword is safe? I will go with Sir Te.

"Iron Turtle, you shall come with me."

剑

Noblemen were required to wear formal robes in the presence of the Emperor. As Sir Te dressed, his palanquin was brought out, dusted down, and the lanterns on the corners lit and hung. At last eight Te clan servants, two to each shaft, lifted it to their shoulders, and before them came four men carrying yellow lanterns on long bamboo poles, and a last man carrying Sir Te's banner.

They set the palanquin down for Sir Te to step in. He was tense. Summons at this time of night were never good. "Do you think the palace has heard? How can I explain it to the Emperor? I will deny everything!"

It was a short way to the gates. Silent Wolf and Iron Turtle paced far ahead of the palanquin to open them.

The gatekeeper was asleep in his shed. The door was open, but inside it was dark. "Gate Wang," Silent Wolf said. "Sir Te is leaving. Up you get. Open the gates!" He had to shout three times before there was any sign of movement inside the gatekeeper's hut.

Gate Wang came out, a thick padded coat thrown over his naked shoulders. He was a friendly man, but he did not like to be woken, and he yawned and squinted at them all. "You?" he said. "Open the gates?"

"Yes," Silent Wolf said. "The minister's guard are waiting outside for him."

Gate Wang squinted at the minister and bowed his head in a brief greeting. "Open the gates," he mumbled to himself and went back into his hut.

They could hear the voice of the gatekeeper's wife, and they could hear his answers.

"It's Sir Te," he said. "He's going to the palace. It's one of those warriors. I don't know . . . I just open the gate when they tell me."

Iron Turtle saw the palanquin approaching. He could still hear the man talking with his wife, and he let out a short sigh. "Come on!" he called. There was the jangle of keys. Gate Wang came out and walked to the gates. He fumbled for a moment in the dark, then the large brass lock clicked as it sprang open. The gatekeeper put both halves into his pocket, hauled one gate open, and then pushed the other.

As the gates opened the palace guard were revealed. There were ten men, all wearing the blue and yellow robes of the palace. "Is Sir Te here?" their leader asked.

Silent Wolf nodded. He stepped forward to shake the man's hand, when he saw that under his robes the man was carrying a bow and quiver. The palanquin started forward, and suddenly Silent Wolf drew his sword.

"Stop!" he shouted. "West Lotus!"

剑

He was too late. The palace guard threw off their yellow robes. Their faces were ugly and fierce, their arms each had the red curling dragon of the West Lotus warriors.

The air hummed with arrows. The men were here to attack and kill. Silent Wolf somersaulted forward, knocking the first man back, seizing his sword from his hand, and beheading the second man. "Defend Sir Te!" he shouted to Iron Turtle, and Iron Turtle, who had been running forward to help, now ran back as two of the West Lotus warriors scattered the men carrying the palanquin. There was a furious battle. Silent Wolf held the gateway alone, filling it with his sword strikes, as Iron Turtle killed the first man, and then the second, just as he pulled the curtains apart and Sir Te yelped with fear.

At that moment the leader of the warriors pulled a black-fletched arrow from the quiver on his back. His composite bow stretched its arms backward, like a confined prisoner, until the string was drawn back to the warrior's ear and the arrowhead met the bow. In his sights was not Silent Wolf or Iron Turtle, but Sir Te.

Silent Wolf saw the danger just as the arrow was released, but he was overstretched and off balance. He swung at it with his sword, but the arrow flew too fast. It flew so close to Gate Wang that he thought he had been hit and fell down in terror.

Sir Te turned at that moment and saw the archer, drew an invisible line between the archer and himself, saw the bow straighten, and understood that he was the target. He closed his eyes and awaited his doom. There was a thud and a low, pained grunt. Sir Te put his hand to his chest. He felt no pain. His heart was still beating. He opened his eyes and looked down. The arrow had not hit him. It had struck another. He turned and looked to see who had taken the shot that was meant for him.

剑

Silent Wolf killed the last attacker with a savage down-cut. There was a dull thud, and a spatter of blood as he looked for the bowman, but he saw the broad street was empty and dark, and the rest of the enemy had fled. "Shut the gates!" he roared, and he and Old Horse pushed them closed.

The women of the Te clan were shrieking and swearing as they huddled together for safety. Sir Te had his hand to his mouth. At his feet lay Iron Turtle.

A black-feathered arrow stuck out from his gut. Half the yard of shaft was hidden. Blood trickled from Iron Turtle's mouth. His eyes were desperately looking around, trying to find a familiar face.

Silent Wolf knelt by his side. Iron Turtle grabbed hold of his hand. He started to speak, but all that came out was a rush of blood. "Hush, my friend," Silent Wolf said. "Hush!" He saw that the arrow had gone right through Iron Turtle's shield.

The blood that stained his front was dark and arterial. It would not be long, he thought. Some wounds were fatal.

"You took the arrow," Silent Wolf said. "That was a brave deed!"

"I took it on my shield," Iron Turtle managed to say. Silent Wolf wiped the blood from his mouth. "I feel no pain. Is that a good sign?"

"Yes," Silent Wolf said gently, cradling Iron Turtle's head as he lay him back.

"I will live?"

"Yes," Silent Wolf said. "The names of brave men will always live on."

Iron Turtle smiled. "We drank the best wine here," he said. "Save my wine pot. Don't let Thunder Fist take it!"

"I shall not," Silent Wolf said. "No one will drink your wine."

Iron Turtle smiled. The life was gushing out of him, and his eyelids fluttered—like a spring butterfly that has just emerged into the sun—then he was gone.

剑

Snow Vase heard the sound of fighting drifting over the night air, pulled her sword from its peg and vaulted the wall in one great leap. The palace compound seemed to be in chaos, with torches hurrying back and forth and panicked shouting from north and south.

"Where is Sir Te?" Shulien was suddenly standing next to Snow Vase.

Snow Vase had ceased to be surprised at her teacher's skills. "I don't know," she said. "I heard screams and grabbed my sword. The Green Destiny . . ." she started.

"It is safe," Shulien said. In a moment she read the commotion. "There's an attack at the gate. It is Hades Dai's men. Follow me!"

Shulien ran up the wall and across the roof-ridge, leaping from one roof to the next. Snow Vase jumped after her but slipped as she landed, broke a tile with her knee and winded herself. Her knee hurt, and as she limped along the rooftop there was an unearthly scream. She froze and turned. Shulien was already far ahead, jumping the gaps between buildings with all the smooth grace of a deer that runs for joy across an open plain. She looked to the stables, and heard the horses snorting and neighing in fear, and her mind was set. The screams kept coming. There was horror and desperation in that voice. The pitch of the terror was rising. The voice was that of a man, and it came from the stable yard.

21

"Don't get used to that cage."

Wei-fang snapped awake. The dream clung to him, like spider webs. He waved his hands and heard a low chuckle.

"I am no dream." The voice was now behind him.

Wei-fang turned and saw a dark shape. It was like a fox spirit, dark, hunched, rattling with bones.

"You!" he hissed, and scrabbled back until he hit the bars and strained against them.

"Yes," the voice of the Blind Enchantress whispered in his ear, behind him again.

As he watched, the shape of the Blind Enchantress began to shift. It seemed not to be a human shape any more, but unfolded, like a giant cockroach that was curled up and slowly straightens out. He saw an open mouth, dripping fangs, and from the mouth came a stench of dry death, decay, the long-imprisoned air of the tomb.

"What do you want?" he said, but the creature laughed at him.

"You failed," the voice said.

"I tried," he said.

"Trying is not enough."

Wei-fang's hair began to rise as the thing moved with an inhuman gait.

"Where is the sword?"

"I will not tell you," he said.

"Will not?"

"No!" he said. "What are you?"

"Your nightmare." The answer seemed to come from all about him. Wei-fang moved to the center of the cage. He put his hands out. He felt safe within the cage. "And I will show you what failure means!"

The Blind Enchantress reached through the bars. The arm was long and skinny. The skin had a green tinge. He struck at it, thinking to bat it away, but it shrugged off the blow and stretched forward, impossibly, inhumanly long, the hand unfolding six fingers, each with a black claw.

He pressed himself so hard against the bars that he heard the bamboo start to creak and crack and still the arm reached for him. The thing laughed. It was not a woman's laugh. He kicked at it, but the hand was dry and papery, and hard as the dried carcasses of sheep or horses that men found long exposed to the steppes' wind and cold.

Wei-fang shouted as the six-clawed hand closed around his ankle and started to drag him. He kicked and fought and held onto the bars above his head, but he was inexorably drawn across the cage. Another hand reached through the bars. And another. And another. He gripped the bars and strained them to breaking point.

Then they snapped, and the cage was rent open, and that was when Wei-fang screamed.

剑

Shulien landed in the yard right next to Thunder Fist.

"What?" he shouted, and swung at her with his pole arm. She

parried that blow, and the next two, and it was then he understood who he was fighting. "You?" he said in surprise.

"Yes."

He frowned. "I'm sorry. I was told not to let anyone in."

"Well," she said. "I am here. Where is Silent Wolf?"

Silver Dart came toward them. She seemed to sway across the yard, hips first. "He is not back."

The sound of fighting grew louder. There was the sound of clashing steel and men's shouts. Shulien ran up the wall and saw black figures running along the rooftops. West Lotus warriors were coming from all directions, all of them heading for this yard. There had to be twenty or more.

Shulien's sword rang out. "They're coming!" she said.

剑

Sword before her, Snow Vase leaped past the bolting horses and straight toward the cage where Wei-fang was desperately battling. She shouted as she ran forward. The smell made her retch, but the thing retreated before the blur of her steel.

"Do not come between Hades Dai and his prey!" a voice said, and Snow Vase felt two hands behind her back, pinning her arms. She felt fetid breath on her neck. She threw the monster over her shoulder with a move her mother had taught her, and the thing laughed.

"You should not fight me," the thing hissed. "We are bound together. Master, student, daughter."

"You are no master of mine!" Snow Vase said defiantly.

The thing hissed and struck out again with a flurry of hands. Snow Vase did not step an inch backward but parried each one, and with her last strike she nicked a hand, and the blood that dripped out was red.

"I see you bleed just like any other man or woman, if human you be. Now get you gone. I am Snow Vase, foul six-armed beast. If you do not leave now then you shall be a six-armed creature no longer. I shall clip those claws!"

The thing swayed menacingly but it seemed almost pleased. "I see, you really are Jiaolong's daughter. But less her daughter than this is her son."

Snow Vase heard her mother's name and it gave her more courage and strength as she came forward now, sword a lightning blur. "Enough!" she shouted. Her first blow cut through one arm. The second lopped a stabbing claw from the limb. The third whooshed through air as Wei-fang fell heavily to the ground, and the thing was suddenly gone.

It had not fled or climbed onto a wall, it had simply, impossibly disappeared.

剑

Wei-fang looked at Snow Vase, and Snow Vase turned. The yard was empty, though the smell of the thing—if thing it was, not nightmare—lingered.

"What was that?" Wei-fang said.

Snow Vase shook her head. Her breath came in deep slow gasps. Her heart was pounding. "Whatever it was, it has gone."

She looked at her sword, and there was no stain upon it. She cleaned it regardless, and thrust it back into its sheath, pushed the hair from her face. She had never felt more alive and charged and in the present moment; not in the past or the future. She had never felt so connected to her sword. Never so powerful. So calm in the face of horror. "I beat it," she said to herself, almost in wonder.

She looked at the prisoner. The cage was a ruin. Snow Vase

didn't want to speak. She didn't want to break this moment. For a moment it seemed the world was them alone.

"That will not keep you prisoner any longer," she said. "You had best come out. But do not attempt anything."

Wei-fang's face was pale. His hands were bleeding. "I thought I was dead," he said.

"You were."

He asked again. "What was it?"

She shook her head. Even the limbs she had lopped off had disappeared. "I have never seen such a thing," she said. "Though I have heard of fox spirits, or ghosts that lie undead and crawl from the grave to take vengeance on the living. But it spoke to me . . . You did not hear it?"

Wei-fang shook his head and Snow Vase frowned. "You did not hear it speak to me?"

"No, I only heard you speak."

Snow Vase let out a long breath. As she turned she saw an odd look in his eyes. "You know what that thing was?" she said. She looked at him, and for a moment it seemed that there was only Wei-fang in the world, and his eyes.

He was about to answer, when a shout made them both turn. "Snow Vase!" It was Shulien. "Come away!"

Snow Vase bowed and stepped back.

Wei-fang stood calmly as Shulien strode toward them. Her nostrils were flared. There was blood on her sword. The pupils of her eyes were wide and black and fierce. Shulien turned from Wei-fang to her pupil. Her eyes were wide and furious. "Why did you not follow me?" she demanded.

"I did," Snow Vase said, feeling badly done by. "But I fell and you were too quick for me. I shouted, but you did not stop. That was when I heard the noise."

"What noise?"

"There was ..." She paused, and gave Wei-fang a look that seemed almost gentle. "I heard shouting. Wei-fang was trying to raise the alarm."

Wei-fang raised his eyebrow as she spoke. "He was shouting 'Attack! Intruders!' I came here in case the front gate was a diversion ..."

Shulien looked from one to another. They both met her gaze.

"I did warn you they would come before the moon was full," Wei-fang said.

"It seemed more like a threat at the time," Shulien said, stepping forward and inspecting the ruins of the cage. "Who did this?"

"Not who," Snow Vase said. "What."

"I know it," said Wei-fang. "It was sent by the witch Hades Dai keeps. Or it was the witch itself, in its true form. It was not human. It dragged me from the cage. It was trying to kill me. I have never seen such a thing. It had six arms. It smelled of death. It wanted me to lead it to the sword."

Snow Vase looked at his face.

"I refused," he said.

"Why?"

"Anyone who uses such beasts should not have the power of the sword."

Shulien said nothing as she assessed Wei-fang's words. There was a long pause. "That is late in occurring to you," she said.

Wei-fang looked at her.

"I would like to trust you," Shulien said, "but I would not entrust the sword to a man whose loyalties change with the wind."

"You can trust me," Wei-fang said. "I will leave this place and never come back."

"Hades Dai will find you. No, I think you should stay

here. Though it seems that the cage will no longer hold you. If you want to prove yourself, let us set you to guard the sword."

"Show me where it is and I will ensure no others touch it."

"Prove yourself first," Shulien said. "You have much to make up for."

Wei-fang seemed disappointed, but he nodded.

Snow Vase watched him and heard the words of the creature in her head as clearly as if it stood behind her and whispered them in her ear. *You should not fight me. We are bound together. Master, student, daughter . . .*

剑

Wei-fang had left the stable yard and the ruins of the cage behind, and now he was chained to the plum tree in the courtyard where Silent Wolf's men slept.

He looked up through the spring leaves, rattled the chain that Shulien fixed firmly to the tree. "So where is the sword?" he said.

"Hidden," Shulien replied.

At that moment Thunder Fist and Silent Wolf carried Iron Turtle's bier into the west hall. They set the body down onto the bed. Silver Dart Shi had a bundle of white cloth. "This was Duke Te's," she said simply, as she draped the cloth around the door where the body lay.

A maid brought a tray of food from the kitchens. There were a few simple dishes. All that could be rustled together at this hour: *dofu* skins with garlic, tomatoes with sugar, boiled peanuts, sweet pickles, and a plate of deep-fried eggs, and Silver Dart brought out the pot of wine that Iron Turtle had been keeping.

"His ghost will not begrudge us this," she said.

"Stop," Silent Wolf commanded. "I promised him we would

not drink his wine. Let us pour it for him, and leave it as an offering for his ghost." He poured three cups into Iron Turtle's cup and poured the libations onto the ground.

"Here," he said, finding another pot. "Let us drink to his memory."

They stood in a circle and raised three cups to Iron Turtle. The wine was fierce and sharp. Silent Wolf looked at Wei-fang. "Why is he here?"

"I brought him," Shulien said.

"Why?"

"He says he wants to fight for us."

"Does he need to be chained up?" Silent Wolf said.

Shulien looked at Wei-fang. "He is your guard dog. Look after him."

She turned and walked from the yard. Silent Wolf watched her go. When the door was shut and bolted behind her, Silent Wolf strode toward the prisoner. Wei-fang had kept his head down as they grieved for their fellow. He looked up as Silent Wolf approached. He wore his jacket over his shoulders, the arms hanging empty and loose.

"Hungry?" he said.

Wei-fang nodded. Silent Wolf looked to Flying Blade and Flying Blade filled a bowl with food. Silent Wolf took it over to him. Wei-fang gulped it down.

"What happened?"

Wei-fang shrugged. "I told Hades Dai's witch that I would not work for him to find the sword."

"Why?"

Wei-fang shrugged. "He is on the wrong side."

"That's a revelation that's been a long time coming."

"I spent my life dreaming of the martial way. When I found Hades Dai, I thought that he was the best that this world could offer. But I have seen a better vision. Finer fighters. More up-standing men."

Silent Wolf ignored the compliment, looked up at the moon to see the time. "You know, I fought Hades Dai once. On Vulture Peak. He bested me. Though, in truth, I was trying to die."

"You didn't manage it."

Silent Wolf laughed. "No. Though I came close." He opened up his shirt and across his chest was a puckered scar, white as a tooth, that went from one side of his chest, angling down to the bottom of his ribs on the other. "This was Hades Dai's broadsword," he said. "It took me six months to recover from the wound. Longer to regain my confidence. Many dark years divide me from that fight."

Wei-fang tried to imagine what it would be like to take that wound and live. He puffed out his cheeks. There was a long pause. "So you want revenge?"

Silent Wolf laughed. "Partly," he said.

"What else?"

Silent Wolf stood up. "Revenge is never a good reason to do anything. It is more about oaths I made, and the future. All that," he said. "Shulien must think there is hope for you."

"Really?"

"Yes." Silent Wolf winked. "You're the decoy."

剑

As Wei-fang and Silent Wolf sat in the library yard, Shulien sat alone in her room, brushing her hair before a silvered mirror. Snow Vase stepped through the door, dressed in a simple night-gown, her hair already unbound and combed. "So, Iron Turtle is dead," Snow Vase said. Her face was pale.

The comb paused. Shulien nodded, before pulling the knot through. "Such is the Iron Way. It takes us all in the end. There is no escape. Does it frighten you?"

Snow Vase stepped up behind her and nodded. "May I?" she said, and took the comb from Shulien's fingers. The knots had already been combed out, so it was more like stroking through Shulien's hair. It was calm and simple and soothing.

"Were you frightened?" Shulien asked.

"By the creature that came for Wei-fang?"

Shulien nodded.

"Yes," Snow Vase said, and frowned. "But not until afterwards. Until now. When I got undressed I could barely untie my clasps. Even now my fingers tremble. I have never seen such a thing."

Shulien held her gaze for a moment. "You did well," she said.

Neither of them spoke for a long while. They heard the drum tower strike the second watch. So much had happened since the sun had set it felt like a week had passed.

"Thank you, teacher," Snow Vase said.

The silence stretched out again. Snow Vase's voice was soft when she said, "I hope I grow as wise and graceful as you."

Shulien seemed surprised. "But you are young and beautiful. Why would you wish for what I have?"

"You have wisdom."

"I have age," Shulien said.

"I would trade beauty for skill and wisdom," she said. "Beauty is a gift, but it does not last. It is like relying on the block of ice. It will melt. Wisdom and skill and grace seem more valuable to me." She trailed off. A shadow passed over her face. "I fear that creature will return in my dreams. I am tired."

"Why don't you sleep here tonight?" Shulien said. "It might be safer that way."

"Thank you," Snow Vase said, and yawned. She lay down, and in a moment her breath had slowed, her eyelids flickered like butterflies, and she was lost in dreams. Shulien stood over her for a long while. Snow Vase seemed so young and frail and frightened. Shulien put a hand out, but did not touch her, just lifted the sheet so that it covered Snow Vase's body.

As she listened to the night noises, Shulien sat down again before the mirror. She looked at herself and saw all that age and the years had done to her. Only her eyes remained unchanged: dark brown, gleaming, hard. She looked sadly at herself, saw a gray hair and quickly isolated it with her fingers, then plucked it out.

She held it for a moment, smiled wryly, then let it drop to the floor. She blew out the evening candle, lay down on the bed, and tried to sleep.

22

Death was like a bad dream that did not go away when morning came. Wei-fang could see the moment each of the warriors woke, and then remembered Iron Turtle was no longer with them.

Thunder Fist stood and shook his head, then sat with his head in his hands before shaking himself and standing up. Flying Blade lay on his back for a long time, his eyes open, staring through the rafters. Silver Dart walked out into the yard with a weary determination. She paused before Iron Turtle's shield, which was propped up against the wall where his body lay. She picked up the empty wine pot and placed it next to the shield. It seemed a fitting memorial.

Silent Wolf was the only one who showed no visible reaction. He woke, he sat up, he swilled out his mouth with cold green tea, and then sat with his broadsword, cleaning it with a cloth. The broad blade gleamed with a cold blue light. Last night it had killed seven West Lotus warriors. It looked almost as if it were alive, waiting for the next battle.

Once they had eaten and stretched, the fighters began to spar.

Silent Wolf and Thunder Fist sparred with a grim seriousness. Silent Wolf won the first three bouts and Thunder Fist shouted at himself in anger. The death of Iron Turtle had cast a somber, serious air on the morning routines.

But as the fights went on it was as if the fighters were working out the sadness, as you worked out stiffness after a hard day's training. Their moods lightened, they began to smile and joke. Wei-fang watched eagerly. It was fabulous to see masters at work. In the third bout he saw Silent Wolf's move before Thunder Fist did, and clapped when the move came and Thunder Fist was thrown onto his back.

Thunder Fist grunted with anger as he pushed himself up. "What are you grinning at?" he said.

Wei-fang held out his hands. "I was just admiring the contest."

"Well shut up, you distracted me."

"I think Silent Wolf knocked you over," Wei-fang said.

"Who asked you, snotling?"

"No one," Wei-fang said.

Thunder Fist stomped toward him and Wei-fang jumped to his feet.

They butted, Thunder Fist's belly against Wei-fang's chest.

"Think you can do better?" Thunder Fist said, chin outthrust.

"Yes," Wei-fang said, and kicked the chain away from his feet.

"Prove it."

"Give me a weapon."

"Here," Silent Wolf said, and tossed a quarterstaff across the yard.

Wei-fang caught it one-handed. He balanced it in his fist. It was ash wood, strong and flexible, with a good weight to it. It was similar enough to the nunchaku for him to get the feel of the weapon. His muscles had become stiff in the cage. He stretched them, flexed his fingers, spun the staff around, flipped it into the air, and caught it with the hand behind his back, his other hand held out in warning.

Wei-fang sniffed cheerfully as he swung around to face Thunder Fist.

"Ready, boy?" Thunder Fist said.

"Ready," Wei-fang said.

Thunder Fist had a spear. His anger had cooled a little. He came forward with a few simple jabs that Wei-fang avoided easily. Thunder Fist saw the grin on his opponent's face and came at him more fiercely this time. Wei-fang batted the blows away. He was clearly enjoying himself. He had a smug grin on his face as he looked at his pole and twirled it around his head again.

Thunder Fist came at him a third time. His anger was up and he fought hard. Wei-fang moved smoothly and surely. There was a blur as the two fighters came together, batting and parrying. Once, twice, three times the two fighters clashed, halberd and quarterstaff ringing off one another, then the halberd was knocked out of Thunder Fist's hands.

The big man let out a cry of anger, which stopped short as Wei-fang's quarterstaff drove toward his face, stopping an inch from the end of his nose.

"You got lucky," Thunder Fist said and batted the pole away. He grunted as he turned his back.

剑

Shulien spent the morning perfecting Snow Vase's moves.

"Good," Shulien said at last.

"Good?" Snow Vase grinned. That word was like a blessing. Shulien didn't seem to understand. "Yes, fairly good."

The word "fairly" tarnished Snow Vase's smile.

"Well, 'fairly' good from Shulien is worth gold from another," Snow Vase told herself.

There was a knock at the door. Old Horse came in. He bowed

stiffly. "Madam," he said as he tiptoed into the yard. "Sir Te is ready to see you now."

Shulien sheathed her sword and nodded.

"Keep practicing," she said to Snow Vase. "Maybe you should go to the warriors' yard to work on that new move. See if Silent Wolf can spot it."

Shulien seemed strangely cheerful this morning. Snow Vase bowed. It seemed a great honor to say that she could now go and practice with another master. She tried to walk slowly as she paced across to the fighters' courtyard. When she got there the yard was empty, except for Thunder Fist and Wei-fang.

Thunder Fist looked quickly up. He was restrapping the grip of his halberd with a fresh leather thong. "My, my," he said. "Hello, pretty."

"I'm looking for Silent Wolf," she said.

"He's not here."

"Do you know where he's gone?"

"No," Thunder Fist said without looking up.

Snow Vase paused. She didn't like being ignored like this. "I'm not just a maid," she said. "I, too, am a warrior."

"Really?" Thunder Fist said, sniffing. "Go fight the dog then."

"What dog?"

Thunder Fist nodded across the yard to where Wei-fang sat in the shade. "There," he said.

Wei-fang was watching her. She thought of what the creature had said, and walked over to him. The chain rattled as Wei-fang stood up. He had been chained to the plum tree. He reached up and broke off a stick. He brandished it like a sword.

"Shall we?"

"No," she said.

"Stick against steel," he said.

Snow Vase looked at him. There was a hint of amusement in her eyes. She turned toward him. "I might hurt you."

"Ow," he said.

Snow Vase thought she would try the new moves she had learned that morning. Her sword flashed as she drew it. They saluted each other and then came together, stick and sword rubbing along each other, and having sampled each other's skills they came apart again.

"You're good," she said.

"You sound surprised."

"Beauty," he said, as they fought again, "skill. A heady combination."

She didn't like being patronized, and he had to shut up as she attacked again. The only sound was the scrape of wood on steel and the rattle of Wei-fang's chain.

He attacked around the plum tree, but the chain caught on the trunk and she jumped into the branches, landing behind him.

"Damn!" he said, as he dragged the chain free, then swung it at her and almost caught her foot.

Their fighting became wilder, more extravagant as they showed off their abilities. He ran lightly up the wall, she ran after him; he lunged, whirled, flipped over, and she was no longer there, but was on top of the wall, jumping to knock him down.

Wei-fang parried. Their blades came together again, but this time he stepped in close and pinned her up against the wall, in the shade of the plum tree.

"I think I have just won," he said. Dappled sunlight fell on her upturned face. Her lips parted as she breathed with the exertion.

"Oh dear!" she said, mimicking the voice of a helpless beauty. "What should I do?"

"Grant me a prize?" he said, and bent forward to kiss her.

She did not reciprocate. "Look down," she said.

He did and saw her sword between his legs.

"I think I won," she said.

He smiled. Their bodies were still pressed close. He could feel the softness of her breasts and thighs. He looked at her lips as they parted.

Snow Vase let him bend and kiss her, but as he smiled and closed his eyes, she was reminded strongly of her mother. The words of the nightmare monster came back to her. *Jiaolong's daughter. But less her daughter than this is her son.* She pulled away, bowed and turned, and hurried from the yard.

剑

That night Snow Vase could not sleep. She lay with her eyes closed and waited until Shulien's breathing had slowed and become regular.

"Teacher?" she whispered.

Shulien's breathing did not change. Snow Vase waited, slowly slid from the bed, careful not to disturb Shulien with an elbow or a knee, or a tilt in the mattress. She slipped on an embroidered silk shawl and went through the doorway.

The air outside was chill tonight. She shivered for a moment, put her head down and kept going. She did not take the gates and walkways but ran lightly up the wall and leaped from rooftop to rooftop, dropping down into the courtyard beside Wei-fang. He was asleep. As she landed, a hand caught her arm: high up, above the elbow.

"You should be careful," Silent Wolf said.

"Yes, master," she said.

Silent Wolf's eyes were dark. "What brings you here?"

"I wanted to talk to him," she said. Wei-fang remained asleep. The more she looked at him the more obvious the resemblance became. It was eerie, she thought.

"How is your teacher?" Silent Wolf said.

"She is well."

Silent Wolf nodded slowly. "Good," he said. "Serve her well."

She bowed. "I shall, master."

剑

Snow Vase couldn't help herself. She crossed the yard where Wei-fang was sitting with his back against the plum tree.

"Which is better," she said, "cage or chain?"

"Neither," he said.

She sat down next to him and looked at him. "I keep thinking of that fox spirit."

Wei-fang looked at her with a strange intensity. "Don't ask me about it."

"Why?"

"I feel it's going to find me. I can barely sleep for fear of its coming. What happens if I sleep? Or they sleep? Or if you are not there? If I had the sword at least I could fight it."

"Is that what you would do?"

"Yes," he said. "Do you know where it is?"

She shook her head and sat back on her heels. "I have an odd feeling about you."

"Love?"

"No."

"Ah."

She looked at him, and he wasn't sure what she was going to say. "I feel I know you."

"Really?"

She nodded. He frowned. "You know, when you look at me I feel the same way too," he said. "It's not a good feeling."

"Why?"

"You remind me of my mother. It's a long story."

"What day were you born?" she said.

"Why? You have a matchmaker who wants to find me a bride?"

Snow Vase gave him a look. "Well," he said slowly. "My mother was always a little odd about the date of my birth."

Snow Vase looked at him. "Really?"

"Yes," he said. "That's how my mother speaks. *'Really?'*"

"I'm flattered."

He smiled. "Did I tell you why I left home?"

"No."

"My mother was trying to get me married. She had a matchmaker come and take my horoscopes. She became odd when the matchmaker asked the date of my birth."

Snow Vase nodded slowly. "So when were you born?"

He sat up. "On the twenty-eighth day of the twelfth month in the tenth year of the Guangxu Emperor."

"The Year of the Snake?" she said.

He nodded, and looked up from the pebbles, and saw Snow Vase was biting her lip, her eyebrows coming together in a frown.

"What is it?"

"What was your mother's name?"

"Yu," he said, and drew the character in his hand. It was the same character for "fish."

"Was she a wife?" Snow Vase asked.

"No," Wei-fang said. "Why?"

Snow Vase took in a deep breath and puffed out her cheeks. "Where are your family from?"

"Luoyang," he said, and Snow Vase felt the tightness wash away from her.

"Oh, that's good," she said. "I had a horrible feeling about you."

Wei-fang looked at her. "Horrible?"

"Well. You remind me of my mother. And that nightmare thing said some things about us. About my mother. I feel it knew about me. Private matters." She laughed and sighed and felt the tension falling from her. "I was adopted, you see." Suddenly there were tears in her eyes. She did not know where they had come from, or why they had welled up at a time like this.

Wei-fang looked sympathetically at her. "There is no shame in that," he said softly.

She nodded, blinking the tears away. "I know. But there is more. I think my mother loved me. She was never unkind, but she was hard sometimes. Too hard. She was a wushu warrior. Well, I say I was adopted. But really—" She stopped. "The problem was that she had a child at the same time. A boy. And that boy was taken by the concubine of a local magistrate. Her name was Fang. Though I do not know the character. He was born the same day as you. I saw you and thought, perhaps you might be him.

"I *feared* it," she said, and took a deep breath. "But you can't be. She was in Gansu when her child was stolen. So I think it cannot be you."

Snow Vase smiled. Wei-fang paused. He looked down at the stones in his palm. He let them drop, then picked them up again. He took in all that she had told him. "Gansu?" he said. His voice croaked as he spoke. He coughed and forced a smile. "My father was a magistrate in Gansu," he said. "His name was Han. We moved to Luoyang when I was two years old."

"Where was he a magistrate?" Snow Vase said.

They were both speaking in whispers.

"Liangzhou."

Snow Vase reached out and took his hands in hers. "Fate has brought us together," she said. "I wonder why?"

Wei-fang looked at her and thought she was very beautiful. "I wonder," he replied.

23

Sir Te's voice was rising rapidly in volume as he paced back and forth. "I have just buried my father," he said. "I have buried my father and the night of his funeral feast my halls are attacked. A man is killed at my gateway. I thought I was dead. I was almost dead. Is this what my family needs? No. This is all a disaster. I cannot imagine anything worse. The magistrates have all been here asking questions. The palace will hear soon. Next time it will be no ruse. And then, what will I say? How can I explain myself? I did not do any of this. My mother has taken to her opium. She hasn't eaten for two days now. The Te clan elders have asked for a conference. And my wife. Oh! My wife. She refuses to sleep with me unless I get rid of 'that damned sword.'"

"You told your wife?" Shulien said.

Sir Te stopped. "Yes," he said. "Of course. How could I not? A man cannot keep secrets from his wife. You know that."

Shulien and Snow Vase exchanged looks. "I don't, actually," Shulien said.

Sir Te sat down and stood up again. He was too caught up with his own problems. "It cannot stay here," he said.

"You are right," Shulien said.

Sir Te seemed not to know what to say.

"You agree?"

Shulien nodded. "It cannot stay here, but it cannot be taken away safely."

"I don't understand," Sir Te said.

"I will think," Shulien said.

Sir Te sat down again. It was an abrupt movement that seemed more like his legs had collapsed under him, or like a puppet when the puppet master drops the strings. He looked from one woman to the other and wiped the sweat from his face. "Oh, that is good news. Yes, Shulien. I am sorry. I have spoken hastily. It has all been too much. But your words hearten me. Please do think," he said. "My wife cannot sleep with that sword here. I am sure there is a solution."

"Do not worry, Sir Te," Shulien said. "We will find one."

剑

Snow Vase walked slowly behind Shulien. Shulien was thinking hard.

"Teacher, do you have a plan?" Snow Vase said.

Shulien shook her head. "No, not yet. Well, I have an idea. I must go and speak to Silent Wolf." They paused at the courtyard where Silent Wolf and his fighters were housed.

Shulien went into the courtyard, and Snow Vase followed her through the gateway, then stopped. As she did so Wei-fang looked up. Their eyes met. His face was grim. She saw the anger in his eyes, and he turned away.

I knew she was not my mother, his glare said. I got a damned concubine, and you got my *real* mother!

"How are you?" Snow Vase said as she stood over him.

"Fine," he said.

She squatted down and reached out to him. They were

connected through Jiaolong. She felt it. It was a new and strange feeling. She spoke gently. "Do not be angry at me," she said.

He looked at her. He was angry at his mother. His adopted mother: the child thief. More angry than he had been before.

"I'm not."

He said nothing more.

"It's not my fault," she said.

He nodded. "I know. I'm sorry. I am not angry at you. I am angry at my mother for never telling me the truth."

"How could she?"

"She could have tried. She wanted to control everything. She *knew*. She knew my mother was a wushu warrior. She banned me from practicing. If it hadn't been for her I would be a great warrior now."

Snow Vase didn't know what to say. Truth hurt at first, before its edges were blunted. Since she had learned of her adoption she had imagined her mother many times—the opposite of Jiaolong, soft, caring, gentle, loving.

She felt sorry for this woman she did not know but who had borne her in her womb.

She sighed. "She wanted a son," she said simply.

"She stole me," Wei-fang said. "It was better for her. But you had my childhood! You had a wushu warrior as a mother. I had a stupid concubine! Do you know how I yearned for a master? My mother banned me from even reading stories about fighters. Now I know why!"

Snow Vase let him talk. He was angry and jealous. She had known his mother, while he had not.

Finally Wei-fang stopped and looked up. "I am sorry," he said. "I did not think." He paused.

They could hear Shulien and Silent Wolf's voices from inside.

"Do you know who my father is?" Wei-fang said.

Snow Vase nodded. "I know a little," she said.

"Tell me."

Snow Vase paused. She didn't want to say anything that might upset him more, but the truth was good sometimes, even when it hurt.

"Mother only talked about him a couple of times," she said. She watched his reaction carefully. "He was a great warrior. He was an outlaw. His name was Dark Cloud."

"Dark Cloud?" Wei-fang said.

She nodded.

"Never heard of him." Wei-fang puffed out his cheeks. "Why didn't they stay together?"

"Mother was not an easy woman. I do not think she could have stayed with one man. I don't think she liked the feeling of being tamed. She was an angry woman. There were times I didn't like her much."

"What was her name?"

"Whose?"

"My mother's."

Snow Vase shook her head and laughed. "Her name was Jiaolong."

Wei-fang looked away. "I met her," he said.

"Impossible."

"No. I met her. She came to West Lotus. She was sick. Hades Dai demanded she fight him. I had been there only a month or two when she was brought in. She had blood on her lip. She knew who he was. She spat at him when he touched her. 'Jiaolong,' he said. 'I knew your teacher, Jade Fox. Think you can fight better than her?'"

Snow Vase bit her lip. She shook her head. She didn't want to hear the rest, but Wei-fang kept telling her, detail by detail.

"She fought well. But she was weak. She was surrounded, and she had already fought the West Lotus warriors."

"She was sick," Snow Vase said. "But she was determined to find you."

Wei-fang shook his head. "She did," he said. "Although she did not know it. And I saw her die. I was there when she was killed." Snow Vase shut her eyes. "It was Hades Dai," Wei-fang said. "He cut her down. I cheered him on. We all cheered."

Snow Vase opened her eyes. Wei-fang was looking at her as if he were cursed.

"You know," he said, "I wonder if she did know. Just as she died I heard her voice in my head, 'Do not fear. Take your destiny.'" He stopped, and remembered what she had said at the end, "Take the Green Destiny!" But he did not repeat that.

"We have to take revenge," Snow Vase said, but she jumped back as Shulien paced toward her.

"What are you doing?"

"I . . ." Snow Vase said. "I . . . I . . ."

"Come with me," Shulien said.

Snow Vase gave Wei-fang a look, but he would not catch her eye, and that hurt more than Shulien's fury. Finally he looked up from his thoughts and their eyes met.

We will take revenge, her look said, and he saw and understood, and nodded.

剑

That evening the wind was northerly. The trees in the bamboo garden rattled with the cold. A brazier had been carried into Shulien's room, but it had been brought inside too soon, and the room had the acrid smell of charcoal. It failed to warm the uncertain air of waiting, and the hurt to Snow Vase's pride. She had not left home to be mothered, she told herself. She did not like to be reprimanded like a child. There was so much that Shulien thought she understood. If only Snow Vase could tell her half of what she now knew, but it would bring up the past, and Mubai, and his memory upset her teacher, so she decided against it.

Shulien liked to eat early and retire early. It was still light outside when the two women ate in silence. At the end Shulien picked out a dumpling and put it into Snow Vase's bowl. "You eat," she said.

Snow Vase refused the honor but Shulien insisted, and at last she gave in.

Snow Vase felt guilty then, for taking such offense. Your teacher honors you so, she told herself. Her mood improved and it was clear that Shulien's earlier silence had not been anger but distraction.

As the shadows deepened Snow Vase trimmed the wicks, lit the lanterns and hung them at each corner of her teacher's room. The darkness drew on. Soon the stars were out, and the moon was rising.

Shulien had not spoken. She paced back and forth, her footsteps softened by the red carpet.

"What are you thinking, teacher?" Snow Vase asked at last.

"Nothing," Shulien said.

There was a long pause. One of the candles burnt itself out. Snow Vase took the lantern down and relit it. "Perhaps we should ride out and meet Hades Dai," she said.

Shulien must have heard something in her voice, because she looked up and caught Snow Vase's eye. Snow Vase feared for a moment her teacher would see her thoughts. Her heart was pounding, her palms were sweaty. But Shulien's expression softened. "Silent Wolf thinks the same," she said.

"Maybe he is right," Snow Vase said. "It would stop Sir Te fretting."

Shulien walked to the door and leaned against the doorpost and looked out. Darkness had fallen. The air was chill, the sky clear, a few white stars glimmered in the west. The moon rose in the east. Each night it had changed—no longer a sickle, the circle was now nearly complete.

"Shall I get you a coat?" Snow Vase said.

Shulien shook her head and turned away from the open door again.

"When I was a girl I used to love Mid-Autumn Festival, when the moon was full and all the family gathered to eat." Shulien half smiled. "Whenever I see a full moon I think of those nights. My father was a warrior. He worked as a guard. He would escort merchants north and south. He was so good even the chief of the Shanxi bankers, an enormously fat gentleman named Goldtooth Wang, begged him to accompany him as he transported his silver." She paused. "But now they are all gone, and I am no longer a girl. I see the moon growing in size and I feel like a bow that is stretched tight, or the rope that lashes the boat to the shore and is almost at snapping point from the weight of the barge that tugs against it."

"Waiting is never easy," Snow Vase said.

Shulien nodded. "It's odd. When I think back I don't remember my father leaving, but I remember so many times waiting for him to come back."

Snow Vase felt a sudden sadness for her teacher. She looked old and weary and worn out. "It's here, isn't it?" Snow Vase said. "The sword, I mean."

Shulien looked sideways at her, but said nothing.

Snow Vase kept going. "Silent Wolf and the others. It's not with them. They're just decoys. They are there to die, when Hades Dai comes."

"Not decoys," Shulien said. "I would lament the loss of any of them. But you are right. The sword is not with Silent Wolf. It was his plan. It is not how I would fight this battle. But Silent Wolf likes secrecy." Shulien took in a deep breath. "If Mubai was here, we would fight Hades Dai differently. But he is gone, and so we must make do. Silent Wolf has many skills. I am alone. We must depend on him."

Snow Vase stood next to her teacher and watched as the moon cleared the rooftops of the east courtyard. It seemed to shrink a little as it rose into the air, to grow more distant, less yellow. "Two more nights," she said softly.

Shulien looked up and half smiled. "Yes, then it will all be over."

剑

Snow Vase went to bed early. She lay with her back turned to the room, eyes closed, breathing slow, but inside the stillness of her head her mind was like a caged monkey swinging from bar to bar, looping and jumping.

All she had to do was find the Green Destiny, then she and Wei-fang could end this. Tonight.

Shulien had not argued when she said that Green Destiny was in this room. But did that mean it was true, she thought, or just another decoy in the plot? She began to think of all the places Shulien might have hidden the sword. Under the bed? Too easy. In the rafters? Perhaps. In her chest? Too obvious? Under the floorboards? Not safe enough.

As she thought she listened to the sounds of her teacher as Shulien went through her evening rituals. She was methodical, always going through the same steps. Shulien always threw off her simple gown before brushing her hair by the mirror.

Snow Vase listened to the sound of the stool being drawn in under the dressing table, the almost imperceptible sound of a comb's bone teeth raking furrows through long black hair; the sound of a middle-aged woman looking at herself in the mirror, and wondering how she got here, like this.

"Snow Vase?" Shulien called out softly. "Are you awake?"

Snow Vase's eyes flicked open. She held herself rigid, and after a moment's thought "ummed" in a sleepy way.

There was a pause. Snow Vase turned. Shulien was standing over her. Her teacher's face was soft. "Can't sleep?"

Snow Vase shook her head, feigned a yawn, and then snuggled into her hard round pillow. "I keep thinking about fighting Hades Dai," she said.

"I hope it will not come to that. I do not think you could beat him."

Snow Vase bit back her retort. I *will* beat him, she thought. I will show you.

"I'm tired," Shulien said, and blew out the lanterns, and then crossed the room and lay down next to her, eyes open, staring at the ceiling.

There was something about Shulien that reminded her of her mother, Snow Vase thought. Both women seemed loners. It seemed a waste for any woman to cut herself off from friends, family, lovers. Snow Vase looked at Shulien and knew that she did not want to end up alone, hidden, waiting for the end with all the patience and calm of a Buddhist nun.

24

The night passed quietly, with no hint of the West Lotus warriors. But Sir Te could not sleep. He paced back and forth, and by the time morning came he had worked himself into a state of nervous exhaustion. As the moon set over the western halls of his courtyard, Sir Te summoned Old Horse, who came rubbing sleep from his eyes and failing to suppress a long slow yawn. "Any word?" Sir Te said. He saw the look on Old Horse's face.

"No," Old Horse said. "I was awake all night. I barely shut my eyes. But I can go and check, if you wish."

"Let us both go," Sir Te said, going quickly inside to fetch his coat.

His wife had still not unbolted her door. He listened to see if she was snoring, but there was no sound, so he found a fur-lined jacket and buttoned it up as he walked down his steps toward his gate.

Sir Te's yard lay next to the bamboo gardens. He decided to take this route to where Shulien was quartered. It would be faster, he thought.

Spring was a good time to walk through the garden. Wet plum blossoms lay splattered under the trees, buds bulged as the first leaves opened, and the bamboo shoots were a hand's breadth taller than they had been the day before. They were clean and pale green, highly polished as emerald porcelain.

When he was young Duke Te had taught him and his brother to carve their name in the smooth green skin of the young bamboo. "*Te*" he and his brother had written, and the scratches beaded with sap as the young bamboo bled. Now those stalks were grown tall, the scratches had healed, though the *Te* character was still a pale line on the bamboo segments. But they were like old friends and rattled gently as he passed through them, with Old Horse hurrying behind. For a moment Sir Te had been lost in memory, but then he remembered the Green Destiny again, and he wished he could put it out of his head for longer.

His father should have found a solution to the sword before he died, Sir Te thought. He should not have left this problem to his son.

On the way to Shulien's hall Sir Te rehearsed what he was going to say to her many times. He imagined her protests, he countered them, contradicted them, and eventually, when she refused politely to take that sword out of his palace, he drew on his rank and demanded she leave. All this meant that by the time he reached her yard he was in an unusually aggressive mood, such as he normally reserved only for his mother.

He paused at the gateway to Shulien's hall and waited for Old Horse.

"Shall I?" Old Horse said.

"Yes," Sir Te said.

Old Horse knocked smartly on the wooden gates. There was no answer. Old Horse knocked again, louder this time. He pulled a face. Maybe she is asleep ... maybe she is in trouble. Sir Te drew himself up. He motioned with his head. Old Horse put his shoulder to the door and gave it a shove. The door was unlocked, and Old Horse fell through the door, and a hand reached out to catch him.

"Good morning," Silent Wolf said.

剑

"Why is he here?" Sir Te whispered.

Shulien looked at him. Her face was drawn. It appeared that she had spent much of the night sleepless as well. "He is here to help us, remember," she said.

Sir Te nodded, but he took Shulien's elbow as if he meant to lead her away.

She stopped and looked down at his hand.

"I am sorry," he said, and let go. "But I cannot sleep. My mother has been taking opium for three days solid. She will die of hunger soon, and still the sword is here. What happens when the full moon passes? Can we really believe that Hades Dai will go home? And I don't feel comfortable with this man and his helpers. Look at him."

Shulien turned toward the nobleman. "Sir Te," she said, "you can trust Silent Wolf. I trust him as well as any man alive. He gave his life for me once. He has done much to help me and you and your father, and your whole house."

There were times when words unpacked thoughts that had not previously been spoken, and when Shulien heard herself say *I trust him as well as any man alive*, she understood something about herself that she had not known before.

Silent Wolf heard the words as well. He looked at Shulien but she would not return the look. She was at the gateway, he was standing in the doorway of the central house, the open yard between them, each wondering what the other was thinking.

Sir Te had been expecting this response and he switched into a more aggressive way of speaking. "I cannot allow this. This sword was brought here. Who knows what Hades Dai will sink to. You must take it away before my whole household is destroyed!"

Shulien looked at her student. "Snow Vase," Shulien said, and her voice sounded tense, even to herself, so she smiled to try to compensate, "can you wait outside? Please."

Snow Vase bowed and nodded.

The air was tense as she walked to the door and shut it behind her.

Then the raised voices began.

Snow Vase crossed to the far side of the yard. The night's chill had gone and this morning the weather was close, a hazy sun white behind the low flat clouds. It was just strong enough to cast a shadow, and her padded jacket felt a little too warm.

As she worked through her stretches she wiped the beads of sweat from her upper lip. The arguments continued, and at last the door opened and Sir Te marched out.

"Thank you," he said. "But I will walk myself to the doorway."

She bowed as he marched from the courtyard. He did not shut the gate behind himself.

Snow Vase pushed it shut. Silent Wolf and Shulien remained inside.

Their voices were hushed. Snow Vase took off her jacket and planted her feet just a little wider than shoulder width, in the horse stance. Her mother had always taught her that the true skill of a fighter came from their internal energy, their *qi*, and that it was a lifetime's work to achieve control over it. She closed her eyes, took in a deep breath and imagined the breath was her *qi*, moving through her mouth, down into her stomach, which swelled with power, then shrank as she breathed the energy out again.

In a wide, slow, circular motion, Snow Vase put her palms together and touched the tip of her tongue to the roof of her mouth, and as she breathed she moved the air, the *qi* around her body, down her legs, and through the bottom of her feet, the *qi* slipping into the ground like the roots of a tree and fixing her there, spreading out, until she was as much part of the earth as she was a human atop it. The feeling was so intense she found herself leaning forward, but she did not sway or fall, she was like an overhanging crag where the wizened tree grows.

Snow Vase drew the *qi* back from the ground. She drew it into her stomach, where it swirled and swelled, boiled within her like a lightning strike that she could hurl from a fist or foot, she brought it up to her head, straight out of the top of her skull, like a line on a puppet, and then plunged it back down through her feet again.

Her breathing slowed. The world's *qi* flowed in through her nose, down into her stomach, out through her barely parted lips. Everything in the world was circles. Life, death, rebirth; love, loss, longing; youth, power, old age. Everything had its proper place and time.

She had become more and more adept at controlling the *qi*, more skilled at drawing energy from the world around her. She could pull so much that it made her almost dizzy.

At last Snow Vase opened her eyes, let her tongue drop and rest behind her teeth, and let all the energy blow out from her puffed cheeks. She heard the door open as Silent Wolf stepped out. She shook the *qi*, like clinging webs, from her fingers. While she was breathing she had forgotten to listen.

Silent Wolf gave her a curt nod. "Good," he said, as he shut the gate behind himself.

Snow Vase walked back to Shulien's room.

"Just a moment," Shulien called out.

Snow Vase waited.

"Come in," Shulien said, and Snow Vase heard a tinny click as she stepped toward the door and paused, heard the chest being softly closed. She waited for a moment, then stepped inside and bowed. "Teacher, I have done my breathing exercises," she said. She noticed the carpet had been straightened out. There was a pause. Shulien looked up and frowned.

"You have done your breathing exercises. Right. I think it is time for practice with a sword."

Snow Vase bowed.

Shulien had given her two moves to practice, and after they had sparred for half an hour, Shulien sheathed her sword and said, "Good."

"Good?" Snow Vase said.

Shulien saw the look in her pupil's face. "Yes," she said. "You learn quickly. That was good. Well done." The servants had just brought their midday meal and set it on the table inside. "I'm hungry," Shulien said. "Shall we eat?"

Snow Vase gave a deep bow.

Two sets of chopsticks had been laid out, next to two dipping bowls. In the center of the table, on porcelain plates, was a selection of cold pickles, boiled peanuts, spicy pieces of chicken and two covered bowls of boiled mutton dumplings, the meat flecked with dark green chives.

Shulien liked hers dipped in vinegar. Snow Vase liked hers dipped in a bowl of minced garlic. What we eat reflects our nature, Snow Vase thought. She is sour and I am fiery.

Snow Vase made sure she put the best pieces of chicken into her teacher's bowl.

"No," Shulien said.

"Please," Snow Vase said. "You have taught me so much. I want to show my gratitude."

Shulien smiled, and ate quietly.

The silence had a different feel to the meal they had shared the night before. The distance between them was gone, and now there was a closeness in the silence, like an old village couple who do not need to speak anymore.

"Done?" Shulien said.

Snow Vase nodded and stood up. There were seven dumplings still uneaten.

"Have more," Shulien said.

Snow Vase shook her head. "I will take the others to Wei-fang," she said.

Shulien gave her a look that implied any man tattooed with the Red Dragon was not worth her time or effort, but she said nothing.

Snow Vase put a plate over the bowl, and tied a cloth around both. She pinned the cloth closed with a hairpin, turned right out of the courtyard, keeping to the narrow line of shade along the southern wall, and then turned left, along the side of the courtyard where Wei-fang waited. She could see the plum tree's tallest branches as she walked along the wall. She tried to go slowly, but she was so excited she forgot to stop.

"Who goes there?" a muffled voice shouted.

Snow Vase stopped twenty feet from the gateway. The peephole was dark as someone peered through. "Me," she said.

Light showed through the peephole; a frowning warrior let her in. He had a tired face. She smiled brightly. "Brought me some food?" the man asked.

"No," Snow Vase said. "I'm here to feed the dog."

"What with you and the kitchen maids, he's fed better than any of us," he said.

剑

Wei-fang was asleep. Snow Vase woke him with her foot. He squinted up at her and she squatted down next to him. "I brought you some dumplings. Mutton. I put garlic on them. I like garlic, so I thought you might too. You don't have to thank me."

He frowned, and thanked her nonetheless as he yawned and reached for the bowl. She was so eager she was almost giddy. "Are you getting plenty of rest?"

"Not much else to do," he said. He pushed himself up and ran his hands over his face.

She watched him eat. He began to feel unnerved by her attention. She was staring intently at him.

"What is it?" he said. "Did you make these?"

She shook her head. She looked briefly behind her and saw that the guards were not close. "I know where it is," she whispered.

Wei-fang put another dumpling in his mouth; he tried to speak but his mouth was full of food. He looked confused. She rolled her eyes. "I know where *it* is hidden."

"What?" he hissed back, even though he was not sure why they were hissing.

"The sword," she said, as if he were stupid. Wei-fang looked around, as if he thought it would be lying in the yard somewhere. "I know where it is," she repeated.

"And?"

"If you help me I can kill Hades Dai. Shulien says I am very good. I almost beat her this morning in our sparring. We take the sword. You lead me to Hades Dai. I will kill him."

Wei-fang put the bowl down. "No."

"What do you mean no?"

"I'll kill him," he said. "He would break you and your teacher."

"You have not seen me."

"I have seen him," he said. "He beat Jiaolong, remember."

"She was sick."

"I should have the sword."

"Why?"

Wei-fang sighed. "I have watched him. I know his weakness."

"What is it?"

"If you want me to take you to him, you have to agree that I fight him."

"No."

He smiled at her and Snow Vase shook her head, but he seemed so confident that at last she looked up and said, "Can you really beat him?"

Wei-fang rubbed his palms together. "This might sound crazy," he said, "but I have been thinking a lot about what

Jiaolong said to me. I have been reliving that moment again and again. Hades Dai was towering over her, and she had no fear. She looked and caught my eye. 'I am happy,' she said to me. 'Do not fear. Take your destiny. Take the Green Destiny!'"

"She said that?"

He nodded. "I think she foresaw this moment. She was touched with prophecy. Surely the gods could not want anyone to deal the death blow other than I."

Snow Vase had fought Wei-fang, and she had a lingering doubt. "I'm worried."

"'Do not fear. Take your destiny. Take the Green Destiny.' That is what she said."

"Are you sure you can beat him?"

"Yes," he said. "If you come with the sword, you will not be allowed within fifty feet. Not even Silent Wolf could break through the West Lotus warriors. If I take it, he will not be surprised. I am one of his men, remember. I will have surprise on my side. I can run him through before he realizes."

Snow Vase was slowly persuaded by his talk.

He smiled and belched as he finished the last dumpling.

"When will you take the sword?"

"Tonight."

"So we leave tonight."

"I do," she said. "If you think you can kill Hades Dai, first you must free yourself."

Wei-fang looked at the heavy brass lock, and held the chain in his hand in a gesture that spoke of resignation. "You're not going to help me?"

She shook her head and rose from a cross-legged position to standing in a swift movement.

"What? You're going to leave me?" he said.

She smiled at him and nodded. She had taken the bowl of dumplings but she had left the silver hairpin that had bound the cloth closed. He looked down and saw it lying in his lap, and he quickly hid it up his sleeve.

Right, he thought, and sat silently, waiting for sunset.

25

That night Shulien dreamt of a day when she had been young and begging her mother not to bind her feet. She had knelt before her. *I do not want to get married*, she had said to her mother. *I want to be a warrior.*

You will be alone, her mother warned her. *I will not*, she started but at that moment she woke suddenly. She was immediately alert. The door was ajar. Snow Vase was not in the room. The carpet had been thrown back. In a moment Shulien was standing at the door. She saw a flutter of black robes, a black-clad figure leaping from rooftop to rooftop, a sword in her hand. "Stop!" she shouted.

In a moment Shulien understood that she had been betrayed. Her anger was explosive. She leaped across the yard, took a short-cut across the bamboo garden, skimming from bamboo to bamboo as effortlessly as if she were using stepping stones to cross a stream. "Stop!" she shouted again, her anger growing.

Snow Vase leaped harder and faster. Shulien saw that she was going to reach the stables. She felt angry and desperate, "Stop!" she shouted and for a moment Snow Vase paused. "Stop!" she shouted once more.

Damn her, Shulien swore: Snow Vase was no longer her student, she was an enemy—a faithless, treacherous, lying thief.

剑

Shulien dropped lightly into the stable yard.

Snow Vase turned to face her teacher. Green Destiny was in her hand. A look of deep calm was on her face.

Shulien strode to her. "What are you doing with the sword?"

"Teacher," she said, "I need it."

The word "teacher" soothed Shulien's anger a little. "You cannot have it," she said.

"I will keep it safe," Snow Vase said.

"You cannot have it. Give it back to me."

"I cannot," Snow Vase said, and a fierce spark of possession flared in her eyes.

"What do you mean, you cannot?"

"I cannot," Snow Vase said simply.

"That is Mubai's sword."

"No. It was Guanyu's sword first. But he is dead."

"Mubai left me in charge of that sword."

"It was not his right to give this sword to anyone." Snow Vase spoke matter-of-factly, but Shulien was stung by the words and moved to attack.

Snow Vase drew the sword. It cast an eerie green light across her face. "Mubai is dead. I need the sword. I will look after it. I have been a good student to you. You should trust me."

The sword tip pressed against Shulien's throat. She moved half a step back. She had not seen Snow Vase as wild and furious before, and she believed her student would strike. "How can I trust you," she said, "when you have stolen the sword from me?"

Snow Vase's eyes were hard. "A student cannot be cheerful under the sky of her teacher's killer. A child cannot live under their parent's killer."

"What are you talking about?"

"Hades Dai. He owes me a blood debt."

"Hades Dai killed your father?"

"He killed my mother."

"Why would he kill your mother?"

"My mother was Jiaolong." Snow Vase wanted to tell her that her mother regretted the sorrow she had caused Shulien, but Jiaolong's name had a visible effect on her. Shulien shuddered. She drew her broadsword.

"*You* are Jiaolong's daughter!" Shulien spat the words out.

"Wait!" Snow Vase said, but Shulien attacked.

Sparks flew. Snow Vase parried once, twice, three times. She felt *qi* building within her. It directed her arms, gave them the strength and speed to hold Shulien's fury back.

"Good," Shulien said.

"Thank you."

There was no warmth in the words. Shulien wanted to take her alive. Good, she thought behind the cold smile, but not good enough!

Her teacher was a blur of steel. How she managed to balance the heavy broadsword with such effortless grace was amazing. Snow Vase took a step back. And another. Shulien slowly drove her back against the brick wall of the stables. Snow Vase was trapped and she knew it. It took all she had to catch Shulien's broadsword. Green Destiny held Shulien's sword stationary for a moment. The two women channeled their force through the swords. Snow Vase pushed with all her might, but Green Destiny was being held back, and it seemed that Shulien was barely using any of her strength.

Snow Vase struggled to stay on her feet. Shulien was pressing her student back and down. She was beaten. She was helpless. She had failed.

As Snow Vase fought, an image came to her mind of her mother: sick, old, desperate to find her son, being cut down by Hades Dai. Jiaolong. Her mother's name gave her a moment's strength. Anger flared within her and she held it back and focused on justice.

She breathed deep and she felt *qi* pressing in on her orifices like a flood of water. She feared it for a moment, and stopped her breath, but as her knee touched the ground she opened every gateway to the world.

Green Destiny called out to her to open herself up. Snow Vase gave in and *qi* poured through the crown of her skull, through the palms of her hands, through her mouth and nose. And as it swelled through her feet and through her groin she almost collapsed with the power within her. She tasted metallic blood in her mouth and knew that she was losing control. She felt she would explode with the power and let out an incoherent shout of rage, and drove at Shulien, and the world went dark for a moment.

剑

Snow Vase staggered as the world came back into focus.

Green Destiny was heavy in her hand. Blood streamed from her nose. She blinked and saw Shulien across the yard, a crumpled figure, and she felt a stab of fear and grief, until she saw her teacher stirring.

Shulien pushed herself up. She knew she had been beaten. Her eyes were wide with shock. She saw Snow Vase, who looked unsteady on her feet. She put her hand out to the wall.

She had never seen such power before. Not even Mubai could summon such power. She held out a hand in peace as she stepped toward Snow Vase. She felt fear. It was her student, but such power needed skill to use. More skill than Snow Vase had.

She spoke more gently now. "Snow Vase. Do not take the sword to Hades Dai. He is terrible."

Snow Vase drew herself up. She was wild and defiant. She wiped the blood from her upper lip, spat red saliva on the ground.

Shulien *feared* her student. It was a new feeling, and she swallowed back her panic. She could not let them take the sword to Hades Dai. Even with such power, she did not know if Snow Vase could beat Hades Dai.

She came forward slowly. "Snow Vase. There is a better way."

Snow Vase shook her head.

"I trusted you," Shulien said.

"And you can trust me," Snow Vase said. "Your foe is my foe."

"You are going to kill Hades Dai?"

Snow Vase nodded. "We are."

"We?"

"Wei-fang and I. Wei-fang will wield the sword."

Shulien shook her head. "Don't. Hades Dai has powers you cannot imagine."

"He is old," Snow Vase said. The sight of Shulien's crumpled body across the yard had filled her with confidence. She had such powers, no one could stand against her. She laughed at Hades Dai. "His time is done. In the morning we will bring the sword back. I swear this to you."

剑

Wei-fang appeared. Snow Vase waved him back. "You have the horses?"

He nodded.

247

"Are you all right?" he said.

"I am," she told him. Snow Vase kept her eyes on her teacher as she moved toward the horse.

"Do not do this," Shulien said as Snow Vase swung herself up. Her nose had stopped dripping, but she was still a little unsteady. Shulien's voice was no longer commanding, but imploring.

"I am sorry, teacher," she said as they heeled their horses toward the open gates.

In the corner of her eye she saw Shulien sprinting after them. She urged her horse forward, almost effortlessly propelled it with her *qi*, as the stride lengthened into a gallop.

For a moment she felt a hand clutching for her stirrup, but then it fell away, and the horses ate up the ground with powerful strides. She wiped her nose, sniffed the last of the blood away, and turned to Wei-fang and saw wonder and fear there. Her hand was shaking. Her whole body was shaking.

Wei-fang was staring at her. "What did you do to her?" he said.

Snow Vase shook herself. "I beat her," she said, and found that she was laughing. "I *beat* Shulien!"

26

The moon was setting behind the cedars on the hills above the valley. At the top of the Twelve-Sided Pagoda, Hades Dai waited as the Blind Enchantress bent over the fire that had been lit on its open roof. The band was wrapped tight around her head, but she stared into the flames as if she had sight. "The sword is coming," she said. "I said he would bring it. Look! The moon is not yet full. You doubted me."

"Yes," he said. "I doubted you."

She shuffled her feet in an odd dance, like an old lady going through the steps of a young girl. There was something macabre about the creature.

Hades Dai's eyes were wide with excitement.

He turned to his men who waited as far from the enchantress as they could manage.

"You!" he said.

Iron Crow stepped forward and bowed.

"You are his teacher?"

Iron Crow nodded sharply. "Yes, lord!"

"Go out and greet him, and bring him and the sword to me."

Iron Crow nodded and disappeared into the doorway of the stairs that led to the bottom of the pagoda.

Snow Vase and Wei-fang rode hard until their horses were steaming with sweat, then they slowed to a canter before pausing at the edge of a lake, letting them hang their heads and drink.

"Where is the sword?" he asked.

"Why?"

"I want to see it."

She pulled it out and showed it to him.

"Can I hold it?" he said.

"No," she said.

"Why? You can trust me."

She looked at him. She was being silly, she thought. "Here," she said. "Just feel it!"

He flicked it through the air; it was as light as a willow switch. "Beautiful!" he said.

She bit her lip as he held the sword. At last she couldn't wait any longer.

"Come," she said. "We should keep going."

"I'll carry the sword."

She didn't like the way he spoke. "No," she said. "I should carry it."

But he had not heard her. "What could a great warrior not do with this sword? How he would make a name for himself!"

"Wei-fang," she said. "Remember why we are here. What we are doing. We are going to kill Hades Dai." A dark light flared in his eyes; she put her hand out and he flinched, then shook himself, as if waking from a dream.

"Here," he said. "Take it."

Snow Vase took the sword and slung it on her back.

"We are together in this, remember."

He swallowed and nodded. She held out her hand and he clutched it.

"Together," he said.

剑

Snow Vase and Wei-fang rode hard through the night, heading north, until they could see the towers of the Great Wall that lined the mountain ridges ahead, black against the northern stars. They passed sleeping villages, heard dogs bark, a few men shouting a warning, and once they passed a roadside inn where a drunken man was singing a village song.

To either side the fields fell away, and when there was dusty grassland, Snow Vase and Wei-fang let their horses open up and gallop forward. She felt exhausted.

Wei-fang had been talking excitedly for more than an hour.

She was reluctant at first, but he had piled reason upon reason, and at last she had said, "You are sure that you can do it?"

"Yes," he said.

Snow Vase remembered the power that had flowed through her in the stable yard, and she did not trust herself. She did not want to draw on such power again tonight.

"Agreed then," she said. "You shall take the sword."

She presented the Green Destiny to him, two-handed.

He took it with both hands, and thrust it into his sash belt, then turned and heeled his horse forward.

"The Green Destiny!" he half laughed. "In my hands."

They slowed as they approached the mountains. Wei-fang had to look carefully to see the opening. It was marked by a white-painted *stupa,* where prayer flags fluttered stiffly against the wind.

"This way," he said.

Snow Vase nodded. She was alert and tense, like a drawn bow.

"This is it," Wei-fang said. "I am sure."

The valley was narrow and wooded. The long cedar needles combed a pleasant note from the wind. It was like ocean surf, a gentle white sound that filled the night.

As they came closer to the head of the valley they could see a dull red light.

"I shall go ahead," Wei-fang said.

They paused briefly. "Are you sure?" Snow Vase said.

Wei-fang nodded. "He owes me a blood debt," he said.

She let him go, and wished all the things she could not say.

Come back, she thought, as his horse dwindled into the night shadows.

剑

Wei-fang rode through the white walls of the temple and let his horse slow to a canter. Warriors slipped from the shadows but he ignored them, and turned only toward the leader—Iron Crow.

"You have the sword?" his old teacher said.

"I have."

"Give it to me."

"No," Wei-fang said. "The task is mine. I am the bearer of the sword. It is fitting that I should take it to Hades Dai."

Iron Crow took his student in for a moment. He had judged him wrongly. He nodded and stepped back, looking up to the top of the pagoda where a baleful red glow lit the night. "He is waiting for you."

Wei-fang looked up. Sparks swirled into the night air, hot and red against the blue-white cool of the stars, and silhouetted against them a huge black figure awaited. Hands on hips, Wei-fang shivered involuntarily as he saw his enemy. His horse paused. It seemed reluctant to move. Wei-fang had to kick it twice before it started forward again at a slow and deliberate pace.

剑

Shulien could not run anymore. She heaved in each breath and put a hand to the wall. She had been beaten and betrayed. She felt tears in her eyes, and swallowed them back in anger.

She dragged in each breath, and then started back toward the stables. She needed horses. She needed Silent Wolf.

As if he were summoned by her thought, Silent Wolf appeared, pulling on his black leather jacket and tying up the waist. "I heard fighting," he said.

"They've taken the sword," she called out.

"Where have they gone?"

"They are going to kill Hades Dai."

"He will kill them."

"I know that," she said.

"Why didn't you stop them?"

"I tried."

Silent Wolf's horse swished his tail as he pulled it from the stables.

Shulien rushed into the stable and looked along the line, scanning the horses for a good courser.

At the end she saw a dark head and recognized Duke Te's favorite mount: Dama, a strong black hunter. The horse had a melancholy look to it. Dama snorted as she came close and scratched the top of his head. "Will you carry me? I am going after the sword."

Dama snorted again, and stamped a forehoof.

"Come," she said. He came forward willingly and she leaped lightly into the saddle.

The night air echoed as Shulien and Silent Wolf set out into the night. Their horses pounded after the young warriors, the freshly turned sod showing where the other horses had passed.

Silent Wolf leaned low in his saddle to follow the tracks. They had gone through the night gate. The tracks were clear in the bright moonlight, heading north, toward the mountains.

When they were far from the gate, and the towers of Beijing were small behind them, the two paused to let their horses run on the soft green turf to the side of the road. When the tracks left the road, and turned toward a dark mountain valley, the two of them paused.

"Do you know this valley?"

Shulien shook her head.

"Let us go carefully then."

Silent Wolf slowed the horses to a walk; they were both lathered. He looked at Shulien and saw that her lips were pursed.

"Did she really beat you?" he said.

Shulien said nothing for a long time, but then she turned to him and nodded.

Their horses snorted the cool night air.

"It will happen to you someday," Shulien said as they entered the dark forest that filled the steep valley.

"What?"

"Being beaten."

27

The brick staircase was tight and close and dark as it spiraled around the inside of the pagoda's circumference. All Wei-fang could hear was his own breath, his own footsteps echoing back at him as he wound around and up, one hand running along the inside of the staircase. He reached the top and paused for a moment, then bent as he pushed through the cloth curtain, stepped out onto the top of the pagoda, felt the wind on his face, and the heat of the fire.

Hades Dai was a great shadow, his fists gripping the parapet as he stared down. Wei-fang had forgotten the size of him: he was massive, like a bear: huge, powerful, deadly.

Wei-fang felt his hand trembling. He drew in a deep breath and took a hesitant step forward. "Master," he called out. His voice faltered and was caught by the breeze. He coughed and called out again. "Master. I have the sword!"

Hades Dai turned. It was like seeing a stone statue turn. The flames shrank back before him, then leaped up as he stepped closer, the pagoda shuddering with each step. Flames underlit his face as he stared at Wei-fang, his eyes deep and demanding; red with reflected firelight. His fists opened and closed, large and fearsome. "Come, my child," he said, and beckoned with his hand.

Wei-fang stepped forward. A shape jumped out before Hades Dai. It was the Blind Enchantress. Wei-fang had not noticed her before. She stepped before the shadow and Hades Dai swatted her aside.

"Enough, hag!" he said as she landed with a thud against the wall. "See, the sword has been brought to me. Child!" he called out. "Come to me. Bring the Green Destiny here!"

Wei-fang stepped forward. A voice inside his head told him to give in, to hand the sword over and become the chosen one of Hades Dai.

For a moment he saw how it would turn out. He would place the Green Destiny into the hands of his master and his master would touch his head in blessing. "Well done, my child," he would intone, and Wei-fang would be glad.

But he hesitated. His feet would not move, even as Hades Dai beckoned to him again, and the air rumbled with his voice. "Come, my child. Come to me."

From below came the shouts and cheers of the West Lotus warriors. Their voices buoyed Wei-fang up, propelled him forward. His right leg began to shake. It wanted to bend, a voice in his head told him insistently: *Obey me.*

"Come, child," Hades Dai said. His voice was so deep it made the sword tremble in Wei-fang's hands as he proffered it. "Bring the sword to me, my son."

The Blind Enchantress moaned as she lay. Still Wei-fang hesitated. A shadow passed over Hades Dai's face. He stepped through the flames and they leaped up as he crossed them. Wei-fang felt the heat, like a furnace blast on his face, but Hades Dai seemed untouched as he passed through the fire.

From below the sound of cheering changed. There was the clash of steel on steel, the shouts of men dying.

There was a sudden war cry from below. "Jiaolong!"

Wei-fang had forgotten himself, forgotten where he was. His world was Hades Dai's face that looked down on him. But he knew that voice. It was Snow Vase. All of a sudden he remembered her, and remembered himself, the touch of Snow Vase's hand.

His courage rekindled. It burned fiercely, like embers that are bellowed back to life.

He shook himself. "I am not your child," he said. His voice sounded weak in his own ears, and Hades Dai looked down at him, almost with curiosity, as a bear would consider a dog. Wei-fang shouted, louder this time, and the sound of his own voice gave him courage.

"I am not your child," he repeated, "I am Jiaolong's son. I am Dark Cloud's child. Heroes of the Iron Way. It is in my mother's name that I bring this sword here to you!"

Hades Dai paused. He spoke slowly and carefully. There was command in his voice. "My child. Bring me the sword. Give it to me, my son!"

Wei-fang pulled the sheath free and flung it away. The sword flashed with an inner green light as he came forward with furious attacks and Hades Dai stumbled back, parrying the blows with his steel vambraces so fast that red sparks flew.

Three steps back, Hades Dai pulled his own broadsword free, the monstrous weapon of heavy steel that was the Hellfire Blade.

As he drew it the whole blade was wreathed in red fire. Hades Dai breathed on the flames, and the sword began to glow red. Red against green fought in a furious battle.

Wei-fang felt the heat of the metal as he ducked the first and second swipes. Hades Dai laughed. He handled his broadsword as if it were as light as a stick. This was good sport. Within moments all Wei-fang could do was defend himself. Hades Dai laughed louder. His eyes gleamed like red coals. "Come, my child!" he roared, and his filed teeth were needles of red flame in his mouth. "You want fame. I will give you fame. Jiaolong and her spawn. I shall fix your head to the spikes on the West Lotus temple, next to your mother's skull!"

Wei-fang ducked as the Hellfire Blade hit the parapet where he had just been standing. The brickwork exploded, shards raining down. He jumped again, and again the parapet exploded. Hades Dai was tireless. Blow after blow rained down, the blade glowing hotter with each swipe. Wei-fang jumped back again. He stumbled on the shattered brickwork and swung his arms around to try and balance himself.

A moment's opportunity was all that was needed.

Hades Dai laughed as he stepped casually forward, put his foot to Wei-fang's chest and shoved him out into the night.

剑

Snow Vase galloped out of the forest, composite bow drawn to her ear. "Jiaolong!" she shouted.

Her skill was immaculate, her timing was innate. At the moment the horse's four hooves were all off the ground she let the first arrow fly. It punched a West Lotus sentry back off his feet.

Snow Vase already had the next arrow slotted. A West Lotus warrior started to run at her. She opened her chest out, the arrow fletching brushed her cheek, the second arrow hit him in the throat and he fell with a strangled gasp. The third arrow was deflected by a leaping warrior, but the fourth came so fast after that it caught him full in the gut, and he pirouetted as he fell.

As the other West Lotus warriors ran at her, Snow Vase

swung her leg over the horse's head and landed on her feet. For a moment she saw Green Destiny flash at the top of the pagoda. Her next shot knocked over the lead warrior. Two more felled the next attackers, and then they were upon her, and Snow Vase let out an incoherent shout as she drew her sword.

剑

Wei-fang was falling. He tried to catch the parapet, but it was too late, the earth was rushing up to meet him. The pagoda narrowed as it went up, so as he spun he reached desperately out, felt the fingers of his left hand brush the lip of the sixth floor, then the fifth floor. On the fourth floor his fingers were cut as they caught the sharp brick edges, but on the third floor there was enough purchase. He reached for the ledge, cried out as his bleeding fingers caught and held and he swung hard, slammed face first against the brickwork, grunted with pain, almost let the Green Destiny slip from his fingers.

He felt his fingers slipping, kicked wildly, held himself for a moment, looked up, and saw Hades Dai grinning through a staircase window.

He was a floor above. "Oh good!" Hades Dai said. "Wait just there! I need your head intact."

剑

Hades Dai leaped down the stairs with terrifying speed, his howling eager as a wolf that scents its prey. Wei-fang looked desperately around. One hand on the sword, one hand clinging to the third level of the pagoda. The bricks formed a narrow ledge that ran around the pagoda. If he could just swing himself up . . . His foot slipped and failed to gain purchase. Hades Dai was coming.

Terror gave him strength. The third time his foot caught, and he pulled himself up, hauled himself up, shaking as he looked for a way of escape. He screamed as Hades Dai's fist punched through the bricks. And again. The broken wall swatted the sword from his hand.

It tumbled down, end over end and Wei-fang cursed out loud. The realizations beat down on him. He had failed. He had lost the sword. He was going to die.

Hades Dai's head appeared.

Wei-fang crawled desperately away and looked down. Snow Vase was holding the West Lotus warriors at bay. He crawled to the lip. It was better to jump, he thought, than to be torn apart.

Hades Dai's hands were gripping the sides of the hole and pulling the brickwork inwards, then his head thrust out.

"There you are!" he grinned.

剣

Wei-fang swayed as he stood on the edge of the pagoda. He was about to jump when he saw a green light from where the sword had fallen. The light grew brighter and closer. It was rising toward them. He saw a hand, then the hilt, then the face.

Hades Dai looked down and saw the face as well. It was Silent Wolf. His eyes opened in shock. "You," he roared, and tore a hole in the wall big enough to step through.

剣

The Hellfire Blade licked with flames as they circled the outside of the pagoda, Silent Wolf driving Hades Dai higher and higher.

The sparking swords lit up the night like fireworks as the Wudang masters gave a display of supreme martial skill. Block, slash, chop.

"I killed you once."

"I was never dead."

"You will be soon."

"Not as soon as you."

Hades Dai grinned. "I've missed you."

"I cannot say the same."

Hades Dai's sword flashed and whistled. Silent Wolf caught the Hellfire Blade with Green Destiny, and the two shuddered as they met. It was clear Green Destiny was winning the battle. Before the Hellfire Blade shattered, Hades Dai let his *qi* surge through him, and threw Silent Wolf back. As Hades Dai concentrated, he came at Silent Wolf faster and harder.

It was true, Hades Dai had missed fighting Silent Wolf. He had relived his fight on Vulture Peak so many times. He had never been so tested, so pressed, so unsure of victory. It was a feeling he had missed. Battle became less satisfying, less joyful, when victory was sure. He tasted blood in his mouth. This was mortality. This was life. He laughed wildly as the two swords met and clashed almost faster than he could follow. Every strike was wild and instinctive. It was glorious.

剑

Snow Vase was beautiful as she fought alone: dressed in white, her mouth grim, her face wild and furious.

"I am with you!" Wei-fang shouted as he dropped to the ground. She caught his eye for a moment and they shared a glance. At his feet was a West Lotus warrior with an arrow sticking out of his chest. In his hand was a nunchaku. Wei-fang pulled it out of the warrior's clasp and twirled it around his head. It was made of heart of ash—heavy, solid, reliable. Not flashy or historic. It was a weapon that reminded a man of his simple origins. It felt good in his hand.

He sighed. He had overreached himself with Green Destiny. Snow Vase should have wielded the weapon. He cursed his pride and twirled the nunchaku once more. *This* was his weapon, he told himself as he swung it to get the feel of it before stepping toward the fighting. He swallowed back the fear. The battle was far from done.

剑

Shulien hitched her horse's reins to the tree, then drew her swords and sprinted after Silent Wolf. He had disappeared into the shadows, but as she looked she saw Snow Vase trapped within a ring of fighters, shouting her defiance.

She paused for a moment. Silent Wolf could look after himself, she thought. Snow Vase was alone and surrounded. She needed her help. She was impressed with how Snow Vase kept the West Lotus warriors back. She was clinical, calm. She was controlling her anger.

"Back!" Shulien shouted as the West Lotus warriors fell back to let Iron Crow fight.

"No!" Snow Vase said. "I will take him."

It was at that moment that Wei-fang somersaulted into the combat. He landed at Snow Vase's side. Shulien turned away. Now he was there she had to help Silent Wolf. Shulien had a grim determination as she climbed the pagoda. She had lost one man in battle; she was not going to lose Silent Wolf this time.

She took the steps three at a time and almost fell into the chamber on the sixth floor.

"Yu Shulien," a voice said. A black crouched thing blocked the staircase. It was a woman, she thought, though a black cloth bound its eyes.

"Who are you?" Shulien said.

"I am the one who sees the future."

"Stand aside," Shulien said. "I have no cause to fight you."

"No?"

For a moment Shulien shook herself. For a moment she saw Jade Fox before her, pale and haunting and hungry as a ghost.

Then it was the blind hag again. "You see clearly," the hag said. "You see what binds us together with this sword."

"What are you?"

"I was born of her hatred. Even beyond the grave she has thirsted for your blood. She has been waiting all this time. Waiting for your death."

"Who?"

The voice of the hag changed, and this time it was unmistakably that of her old foe, Jade Fox, the woman who had killed Mubai. "Join me in the dark, Shulien. I've been waiting for you. Mubai is waiting. I have his soul . . ."

Shulien shook herself again as the hag came at her, spinning like a dervish, each hand holding a whip with links of razor-sharp steel. Each one was a whirl of death. Shulien knocked them back. One, two, three—the blades kept coming. Six razor blizzards that whipped at her. She held back for a moment. There was a thunderous crash from the top of the pagoda. Shulien's eyes looked up. The Blind Enchantress laughed. "I have seen it. Your man is not dead yet," she said, "but it will not be long."

Shulien leaped forward, her sword licking through the blizzard of blades. The Blind Enchantress yelped with pain. Her blood hissed as it fell. "Not fair," she said, and her hands moved in a wide circle. Drapes fell from the ceiling and covered the windows. The room was black.

Shulien did not have a moment to react. She heard the thing come at her and was blind to defend herself. She yelped as the blades began to bite and the thing began to laugh.

"Now we are equal," it said.

28

Silent Wolf fought harder and faster than he had ever fought before, his straight green blade battling against the enormous broadsword of Hades Dai. He was losing himself to fury, and he knew it. Twenty years he had relived his death. Twenty years he had waited for vengeance, and now as he fought, all the dammed-up grief and loss and waiting began to overspill. It would get him killed.

As if to reinforce the fact, there was a noise from within the pagoda. A woman's voice, shouting in pain. It sounded just as Shulien might if she were cut.

The sound distracted Silent Wolf and Hades Dai's broadsword slipped past his guard. He jerked back, bending almost double at the waist, but still the blade nicked his left cheek. The skin smarted, he felt warm blood on his neck. Hades Dai grinned.

"Next time, the whole head," he said.

Silent Wolf breathed in deep. He was listening for Shulien. She is in trouble. You are here and he is better than you remember. He will kill you. He will put your skull on his pile.

Silent Wolf tried to force his thoughts to silence. Be calm, he ordered himself, but he was fighting with his heart today as much as with his mind.

The Hellfire Blade got past his guard again; the flames roared as it crashed into the bricks where his head had been.

Silent Wolf needed time. He somersaulted down and landed where the heaps of West Lotus dead were beginning to pile up into mounds at Wei-fang's and Snow Vase's feet. Hades Dai came down like a gibbon from a tree, swinging his great mass on his long arms and landing with a thunderous thud on the ground. There was not a moment's pause. He bounded straight into the fight, Hellfire Blade leading.

Silent Wolf cursed as he fell back. He had hoped for a longer respite to calm himself. This is the fight of your life, he told himself again, and you are going to get yourself killed for your feelings! The absurdity of it seemed almost fitting. Silent Wolf, dour, taciturn, granite-cold, lost his last fight because he let his feelings get the better of him. His face was grim and set as he backed away. Hades Dai could tell his opponent was weakening. He stepped deftly for such a massive man. His footwork was impeccable, his speed terrifying, his skill deadly. Silent Wolf had to allow him that. And he had the reach, and the weight of the Hellfire Blade. Blocking it was beginning to take its toll on Silent Wolf's arm. He could feel the muscles in his shoulder beginning to burn. His forearm was stiffening. Silent Wolf had always thought the Green Destiny to be the finest blade ever forged, but if that was so, there was little between it and the Hellfire Blade. *All that is between them is the wielder,* the voice in his head whispered.

He gritted his teeth to shut it up. This is no time for doubt, he told himself, but words were one thing, reality another. He began to realize that not even he could best Hades Dai with the sword, and at that moment Hades Dai caught Green Destiny. It was a child's trick, a slow swipe, catching the hilt and twisting the grip from his hand. It was too simple, too easy. Silent

Wolf misread it and Green Destiny was ripped from his hand, flying across the clearing and embedding itself into a tree where it quivered, like a steel arrow.

Hades Dai shook his head and sighed theatrically. "Sometimes the straightest road is the best, the simplest tricks beat the best masters."

Silent Wolf did not step back this time. Hades Dai looked down on him, almost sadly. All life was theater, his expression seemed to say.

Tragedy, comedy, farce.

His muscles gleamed with sweat, but there was nothing weary about the way he took the Hellfire Blade hilt in both hands, and swung the blade up above his head for a mighty, killing blow.

Silent Wolf knew that this was it. There was no running now, no fighting. He opened his arms wide for the blow, closed his eyes, and at last he felt calm, like warm water, rise within him.

剑

Shulien was fighting blind—she had acute senses but they were not enough to ward off the Blind Enchantress. She parried one, two, three blows, and on the third a stray spark gave her enough light to see where her attacker was, on her left, and moving around to her side.

The spark lasted only a moment, before the darkness returned.

Shulien swiped at where she guessed her attacker was, but her swords caught nothing.

She tried again, and there was laughter this time.

Shulien swung both swords at the noise, but again caught nothing.

A third time she tried, and this time she gasped and dropped a sword.

She had been cut. She scrabbled in the dirt for the dropped sword, fearing a sudden blow, as blood dripped from her fingers.

There was the sound of ripping cloth, and moonlight suddenly spilt through one of the drapes on the walls. It was pale moonlight, not enough to be able to thread a needle, but it was enough for Shulien to see that her foe was nowhere to be seen. Which meant that . . .

Shulien leaped to the side and rolled, and heard the metallic clang of a blade striking the spot where she had just been. The Blind Enchantress was behind her, all six arms swinging as she clanged her way across the room.

Shulien was wounded and she only had one sword to hold the six blades off. They were a whirlwind of steel sweeping toward her.

剑

The light streamed in as the last of the drapes were torn down, and into the room jumped Snow Vase. Her sword stopped the killing blow an inch from Shulien's neck, turned it aside, then caught the next three blows and knocked them aside.

Shulien froze and Snow Vase spoke one word. "Teacher."

Her voice was low, breathless, almost imploring. It spoke to Shulien, begged her for help, begged her to be the master warrior she was, and it gave Shulien the confidence and determination to keep fighting.

The enchantress muttered in frustration, speaking to herself. "She has come! You did not see that. The young can be so hard to see. Their choices are hard to anticipate."

Together Shulien and Snow Vase, master and teacher, met the storm of steel, held it and then drove the thing back. It was a beautiful fight, almost a dance, between the inhuman insect-like enchantress and the two human shapes, twirling, spinning, pirouetting.

One mistake was all it took. One mistake was death, and it was the Blind Enchantress that faltered first.

Snow Vase's sword cut a hand from an arm, and it crumbled into dust as the sword fell to the floor. The thing still did not slow or show any signs of pain, though when Snow Vase sheared another arm just below the elbow it let out a gritted snarl of fury.

One by one they picked off the arms, like plucking legs from a daddy longlegs, until the thing was a squirming body with thrashing stumps of limbs.

Snow Vase looked down in horror, but she did not deliver the death blow.

She turned to Shulien and bowed. Judgment was for her teacher to deliver.

Shulien was wounded. Her left hand was thick with her own blood. "You have beaten it," she said. "You kill it."

Snow Vase paused.

"Quick!" Shulien said. "Before it rises!"

Snow Vase did not look away. She drove her sword through the thing, driving straight for where the heart should be.

It was a quick, clean blow. Merciful, in its way. The thing thrashed wildly for a moment, then a great shudder went through it as Snow Vase pulled her sword free, and it kicked a circle on the ground, like a headless chicken.

"It is gone," Shulien said as they watched it grow still. Its robes came free and beneath was not the body of a person. The skin was green, the back was hard and glossy, the underbelly was a brown-green color, like the belly of a cockroach.

"Heavens!" Snow Vase said. They stared at it in horror. Neither of them wanted to go closer.

剑

There was a furious battle as the remaining West Lotus warriors tried to reach Hades Dai. Before them Silent Wolf's men stood resolute. Silver Dart was cut down. Thunder Fist died with his foe dead in his hands.

Flying Blade lay wounded. "Water," he gasped.

"Here!" a voice said, and someone put a flask in his hand. He looked up. It was Wei-fang.

"They're coming again," Flying Blade said.

"I can see," Wei-fang said. He was bloodied and weary beyond belief, but he stood alone and held the enemy back.

There was a gasp, and the fighting lulled for a moment.

Wei-fang heard a ring of steel, a clean light sound like a small bell ringing.

He turned and saw the Green Destiny flying through the air. It struck a tree and quivered.

He turned open-mouthed and saw Silent Wolf standing with his arms wide open, welcoming the death blow.

"No!" he shouted. But as he began to shout the Hellfire Blade began its terrible downswing.

Wei-fang turned his back on the West Lotus warriors. He leaped forward, still screaming, as the Hellfire Blade kept swinging down. Wei-fang saw that he could not possibly hope to make it in time. He ran regardless, hurled his nunchaku, and the three links of wood twirled around and around, impossibly slowly as the world went quiet. It was one last, desperate, futile effort.

And now you have disarmed yourself, Wei-fang cursed as he saw that there was nothing he could do to help Silent Wolf.

"No!" he shouted again, or was it still the same shout, he could not be sure, but Silent Wolf did not react. He stood, bent a little backward, arms outstretched, eyes closed, breathing calmly through his nose as the Hellfire Blade whistled down in the breeze of its own passing.

剑

Wei-fang turned away. He could not bear to see this. Silent Wolf would be cut from shoulder to waist, his carcass cut into two pieces, like some common criminal. But, despite himself, he kept one eye half open.

As the Hellfire Blade descended, Silent Wolf brought his outstretched palms together and caught it within them.

It was a glorious effort, but there was nothing that could stop that blow from a man with such power as Hades Dai. But the Hellfire Blade slowed. Silent Wolf drew on all his *qi*. It was a rope holding his two palms together. The *qi* passed straight through the sword. It was stronger than muscle and bone, stronger than steel, stronger than silk.

His *qi* was a rod of pure power. His arms were a circle. Within them was trapped the Hellfire Blade, and even though Hades Dai grunted and strained there was nothing he could do to tug his blade free. He let go of the hilt and drove at Silent Wolf with bludgeoning fists.

Fist met palm, palm met kick, thrust became pull. The two warriors battled without weapons, closer and faster than before.

With size and strength and reach, this should have been Hades Dai's killing ground, but Silent Wolf, looking small and childlike, was holding his own. More than that, Wei-fang saw— he was matching each blow and thrusting them away.

Hades Dai's weight shifted to his back foot. Silent Wolf came forward, and Hades Dai took a first step back.

There was a brief moment's pause before Silent Wolf put both hands together and stamped as he pushed into Hades Dai's gut, shouting a blast of *qi*.

The giant flew back, as if he were no more than a rag doll. He rolled backward as he landed, and came back onto his feet. There was blood on his lip. He dabbed it with the back of his hand and smiled.

"I always dreamed of fighting you again," he said.

"Your dream will be over soon."

Hades Dai looked at him. "I see the power in you, my child. I gave you that. I am the spring from which you flow."

Silent Wolf laughed and Hades Dai's look darkened. "I killed you too quickly last time. I have enjoyed our fight. But now it is time for you to die again."

Silent Wolf saw his mistake too late. Hades Dai had rolled next to the tree where Green Destiny was impaled. He leaped as Hades Dai pulled the Green Destiny free, caught the giant's arm with both hands. He flung Hades Dai from him, and the two men rolled over and over, one, two, three times. And then they lay still. From the point of Green Destiny red blood gathered, and began to drip.

剑

"No," Hades Dai said, as he looked down. It was his own hand that held Green Destiny, but Silent Wolf had turned his wrist so that Hades Dai had rolled onto the blade and driven it deep through his guts. The bigger man was on top. He frowned as he shook his head. "That was a child's trick and it has done for me. But I have you." He reached down, both hands clamping around

Silent Wolf's neck. "We shall visit Hell together. Just one little tug, like a chicken . . ."

Wei-fang caught Hades Dai's hand and pulled with all his body. The bigger man groaned as he was slowly thwarted, and at last he was peeled off and Silent Wolf rolled away. His clothes were torn, there was a bite on his neck. The flesh was raw and bloody.

Hades Dai fell back, and the sword went deeper. At last he pushed himself up, and sat on his backside with a surprised look on his face.

"I killed you once," he said. "And now I think you have had your turn."

Silent Wolf staggered. He was bleeding from a dozen small cuts. He swayed, but managed to remain standing. His foe was beaten.

"We each won one battle," Hades Dai said. "Though I do not think there will be a third."

"The fighting is done," Silent Wolf said.

Hades Dai tried to stand but the pain was too much, and he gritted his teeth. His liver was bleeding. His guts were torn. He could feel the *qi* draining out of him. "I thought I would beat you. I beat you once," he said. He looked up. The anger, the fury had all gone. He looked almost sad as a cushion of blood spread around him.

"You fought well," Silent Wolf said. "Your name will live on when men speak of the Iron Way."

"The Iron Way," Hades Dai said. "I thought Green Destiny would give me great power, great fame. But look what it brought me." He looked down to where his lifeblood was draining away.

"You have won fame," Silent Wolf said.

Hades Dai laughed, but all that came up was blood, bubbling at his lower lip. Life was all a game, his eyes seemed to say.

剑

Silent Wolf stood over his enemy. Hades Dai frowned as his last lifeblood drained away, then he closed his eyes and Silent Wolf saluted as his enemy's ghost departed the world.

Silent Wolf looked up. Wei-fang was coming toward him. He had a cut on his arm. He stopped a spear's length from Hades Dai.

"Is he dead?" he said.

Silent Wolf nodded. "He is gone ahead, on the road we all must travel."

Wei-fang looked down. "When our time comes."

Silent Wolf smiled. "Yes. And we should enjoy ourselves until then."

Wei-fang saw a flash of silver as Iron Crow hurled a silver dart. He could not tell if he was the target or if the dart was meant for Silent Wolf, but he shouted a warning, shoved Silent Wolf aside, and leaped before the blade.

剑

Snow Vase saw the dart hit Wei-fang in the chest, and she shouted with fury.

She leaped from the window and landed before Iron Crow, sword flashing in attack. She drove him back with ferocious blows, caught him once, twice, three times, but he would not fall.

Snow Vase stopped only when a hand gripped her wrist. She yanked her hand away and saw Shulien's face. "He is dead," her teacher said.

Snow Vase looked imploringly at her teacher. Shulien nodded. "Look," she said, but she was not pointing toward Wei-fang, but to Iron Crow, who had fallen back against a tree. His eyes were open but his gaze was blank, and as they watched he slid slowly down.

Snow Vase turned. Wei-fang had fallen, and Silent Wolf was crouched over him. The wounded warrior did not move.

"No!" she said, and ran across to him.

Shulien was faster. The older woman bent down and turned Wei-fang over. She pulled the dart out, and a gush of blood came with it. The image of her mother's mouth stained with blood came back to Snow Vase, the sound of that cough. The red arterial blood. Snow Vase had a sudden fear and stepped back. Wei-fang's eyes fluttered as Shulien sat him up, and he coughed; there was red froth on his lips.

He's going to die, she thought, and cursed her luck, but she knelt down beside him.

"Her words were true," Wei-fang said. His lung was punctured. Blood was rattling in his throat. It was a ghastly sound.

Snow Vase held him. She didn't know what to say. Didn't know what or who he was talking about, just wanted to let him know that she was there for him. He looked at her and forced a smile. "She said he would get the Green Destiny by the end of the full moon. Silent Wolf gave it to him."

"We saw," Snow Vase said. "Hold your breath."

He shook his head feebly. "I'm sorry. I failed. I thought her words would come true. I believed in her. She was my mother."

Snow Vase shushed him as she frantically tried to stop the blood.

His movements became weaker. "My road has ended," he said. "It is the Iron Way. We all must travel it."

Snow Vase held him close. His blood was foaming on his lips and his breath rattled. His fingers clutched at her; blood freckled her cheek but she did not pull away.

Wei-fang's eyes were wandering but as the dawn began to brighten around them, they found Snow Vase and he forced a smile.

"I am glad that you are here," he said. "We were meant to meet, I think . . ." He coughed, and Snow Vase held him and her and Shulien's gazes met.

Shulien's eyes were wide with horror and grief and sadness. Snow Vase understood with cold clarity. This was how her teacher had held Mubai, as he breathed his last.

29

Sir Te placed his hands together as if in prayer, and touched his fingertips to his nose. He was pacing back and forth in the bamboo garden. His heart was racing, his palms were sweating, he was so nervous he felt exhausted. His breakfast tray of steamed buns—each one dotted with red or green or blue, which told him which were stuffed with pork or sesame and sugar, or green chives—had long since cooled.

It was early summer. The air was fresh and cool. Light rains turned the mountains green and in the gardens the cherry blossoms had gone, but the buds on the trees were opening fresh, pale-green leaves. This was his favorite time of year, but he was too anxious to enjoy it.

Sir Te heard voices and prepared himself. He saw the shadows approaching the round moon gate, and then the figures appeared. Shulien in conversation with Silent Wolf, then Snow Vase, following behind at a distance. Snow Vase's hair was combed back, her head was bent, and there was a sadness about her, Sir Te thought, which made her even lovelier than before.

Shulien and Silent Wolf bowed, and Sir Te bowed back and gestured to where a table had been set for tea.

It was a stone table, with stone stools in the morning shade of the bamboo. The tall stalks were bright green with the fresh leaves, long and slender like almonds, or arrowheads. They fluttered gently in the early summer breeze. They had an odd way of twisting in the wind, and the light that fell through them was green with leaf-life, yellow with sun.

Snow Vase watched the patterns on the floor at her feet.

"Tea?" Sir Te asked. She started, and looked up.

Sir Te held an ugly little pot in his hand. It had a fat body and thick handle and a little curved spout. He filled it with pale green spirals: the first bud and leaf twisted together, scented with flowers.

"Jasmine," he said. "Picked this spring."

He poured the first soaking away into the slats of his tea tray. "This washes the leaves," he said, "and releases the perfumes."

Snow Vase gave a noncommittal smile.

Sir Te smiled tolerantly back. "You are not a tea-drinker?"

"I drink," she said.

Sir Te lifted the lid of the pot. A string, beaded with jade and pearls, connected the handle and the lid. It allowed the top to be lifted off without falling and breaking. He smelled the tea inside and offered it to Snow Vase to smell.

Snow Vase watched Sir Te carefully. The duke's son was so content with little rituals like tea-making, or calligraphy, or admiring the moon from his bamboo gardens. When she'd arrived she had thought him pitiful, contemptible and weak.

But now she was not as sure as she had been. Now, she saw peacefulness and gentleness and humility as well. Things worth fighting for, she thought. Perhaps more worth fighting for than fame or glory.

Sir Te filled a white porcelain jug with the first brew, refilled the pot, and after a slightly longer infusion he added that to the jug as well. One by one he filled their cups, and offered them, two-handed, to his guests.

First he served Silent Wolf, then Shulien and finally Snow Vase.

She smiled as she took the cup, and the fragrance was shockingly clear and fresh.

Each of them sipped. There were murmurs of appreciation. Snow Vase felt Sir Te watching her, and her cheeks colored.

"It is good," she said.

Sir Te seemed satisfied. He refilled the kettle with spring water, and set it back on the coals.

"So," he said. "Here we are to discuss what to do with the sword. My father was a martial man, but I am not. You have all fought and sacrificed for us. It is my turn. I have spoken to my family, and they are all agreed. We shall look after this thing. We will do what is necessary."

Snow Vase watched him speak. She saw that his hand was trembling. He is as scared as a mouse, she thought.

"Sir Te," Shulien said. "You have done much. But you are not the man to guard the Green Destiny."

Sir Te's mouth opened. Shulien put up her hand. "You are not your father," she said.

Sir Te stammered, and he hung his head. Shulien watched him for a moment. Her eyes were gentle, and when she spoke her words were soft. "It is nothing to be ashamed of. Sir Te, each man has a different road to travel. The road is set according to each man's nature. Unhappiness comes when a man tries to follow the road that is not destined for him. Your road is not the Iron Way. You should not feel ashamed of this. What are we for, if not to protect men like you? Your pleasures are gentle. Tea, gardens, growing things. These are the spheres within which you excel."

Sir Te seemed deeply ashamed.

Shulien reached out to him. "Sir Te," she said. "Let us take the

Green Destiny. There is no shame here for you. Only honor that you stood up against Hades Dai, when no one else would help us."

Sir Te looked up. He took in a deep breath and sighed. "I am not my father," he said.

"And he is not you," Shulien told him. "You have skills he could not dream of. I saw his efforts to grow chrysanthemums."

The comment brought a brief smile to Sir Te's face. "You're right, he was not much of a gardener. When I was young I wanted so much to be like him. He trained me, but I could see in the way he looked at me that he was disappointed. It is hard on a father not to have the kind of son he wanted."

"And it is hard on the son whose father sees disappointment in him." It was Snow Vase who spoke, and her words seemed to have more effect than Shulien's.

He took in a deep breath. "So you will take the Green Destiny."

The three fighters nodded.

"And my family will not be troubled anymore?"

"No," Shulien assured him.

Sir Te looked up. "Thank heavens," he said. The kettle had boiled. He took it off the coals and set it aside to cool a little. Boiling water was too hot for jasmine tea. It needed a more delicate temperature. He refilled their cups, sipped his tea, and savored the flavor.

"How is Wei-fang?" he asked.

Snow Vase bowed her head. "I think he will live."

"And the others?"

"Flying Blade will live. We have burned offerings for the others. Their ghosts will dine well."

Sir Te smiled sadly. "So many have died, and it always seems the sadder when they are young. I am cheered to hear Flying

Blade will live. And this Wei-fang. That is very heartening. He is a good man, is he not?"

His tone seemed uncertain, and he looked to Shulien and she smiled and nodded. "Yes. He was misled for a while, but his heart is good."

Snow Vase looked at her. She had never heard her teacher speak so positively of Wei-fang before. "I am glad you think so," she said.

Shulien smiled. "Well. Much happens in the world that we wish we could control, but cannot. I would have had things differently, but now that the battle is fought, and won, perhaps it was all meant to be."

Snow Vase nodded. A gentle breeze carried the note of the midday bell. She sipped her cup, and refused a refill. "I will go and see Wei-fang," she said, and stood and bowed.

Sir Te watched her go, and when she had slipped through the moon gate the three of them exchanged looks. "I never had a daughter, but if I had I would wish her to be as beautiful as Snow Vase." There was a long pause. "It is not easy being young. I feel for her." He poured another round of tea. "You know," he said, as they raised their cups to one another, "some men yearn to recapture their youth. I would not be young again for any coin."

Shulien half smiled. "No?" she said.

"No," Sir Te said. "When I was young I had so many things to do. Now I am gray, I have a wife and children, and I see what I have done with my life and I am content. I thank you for your words. I think perhaps I have been traveling the right road for me. I see my sons, my wife, my gardens, and I am content."

"That is a good feeling to have," Shulien said, and felt a deep sadness within her, because she could not say the same. Sir Te looked at her, and she tried to smile, and almost succeeded.

"To the quiet life," she said, and they all drained their cups.

剑

The afternoon shadows were lengthening when Wei-fang woke.

He sat up, and winced.

"Where are we?"

"You are safe, and healing, and your enemy is dead."

"Flying Blade?"

"Will live."

"And the others. I tried to help Thunder Fist ..."

She hushed him, and moved to slip a cushion behind his back. "They fell valiantly."

He sighed, winced once more and fell back onto the pillows.

"How do you feel?" she said.

"I've felt better."

"Can you move your arm?"

Wei-fang wiggled his fingers. It was clear that that was the limit of his ability.

"Do you think you will be able to fight again?" she said.

Wei-fang pursed his lips. "I don't know if I want to fight again."

She looked at him. "No?"

"No," he said. "I used to think that fighting was the supreme art. The most glorious thing a man could do. But now I have fought with the greatest, and I know I will never be as great as them."

"Why not?"

"I am not like Hades Dai or Silent Wolf or Shulien," he said.

"No?"

She sat on the edge of the bed. He reached out a hand and found hers and held it. He smiled and looked down at the hand that was bandaged and held in a sling. "I only have one hand," he said.

"And what would you do if that hand were free?"

"I would touch your cheek," he said. Snow Vase's cheeks colored a little. They were like the flowers of the magnolia, which blush to pink at their base.

The two of them sat in silence for a while.

"Look at Shulien," he said. "Silent Wolf comes sniffing and she gathers in her skirts and sits with her knees together as if she is a nun. And he cannot bring himself to say to her what he feels."

Snow Vase smiled. There was a wicked light in her eyes, as if she had seen the same thing too.

"So you want to be a scholar like your father?"

"Heavens no," Wei-fang said. His face was ashen. He looked about the room and swallowed. "No. I had a long time to think. Before the battle. Let me tell you. When I was growing up, I found an old teacher and he was kind to me, and I loved to go and visit him. He had no sons, so I was like a child to him. He taught me his skills. I wish he had lived longer, or that I had been more disciplined. But my mother forbade me from visiting him, and when I had the courage to go myself, he had died.

"I did not belong to my family. They were oil and I was water. We did not mix. When we sat at meals I could not bear to hear their conversation. They drove me mad. My father was only interested in the Buddha, and poor people and how much suffering he had alleviated. My mother . . . my mother cared about who was marrying who, how many grandchildren her friends had, and when I was going to produce grandchildren for her to spoil.

"I could not bear it. I was a warrior. I wanted a different life. I wanted freedom, adventure. I wanted a life worthy of living. I wanted to see the world. And so I fled. My mother had found me a wife and I fled from her like a coward. I was not proud of it, but I would have gone mad if I'd stayed. It was desperation.

"And then I was alone, and I wandered. I was lost. There was no one like me, I thought as I passed through villages and towns and saw families sitting around their evening tables, happily chatting and eating."

Snow Vase squeezed his good hand as he talked.

"Then I found Iron Crow. I think he was a good man. At the start. Hades Dai had a power over men. Iron Crow feared him, and his fear undid him. It undid me too. I feared having my head added to the pile. And for once I was not alone, and loneliness was what I feared more than anything."

"And now?" she said.

Wei-fang swallowed and laughed, and shook his head. "I still fear it."

They looked at one another.

"But now I understand what loneliness is."

"Really?"

He nodded.

"I found you," he said. "How could I be alone when you are in the world?"

She did not blush, but looked at him and held his gaze. After a long pause she leaned forward and put his hand to her cheek. "It is not cold," she said.

He cupped her face in his good hand.

"No. It is warm. And soft, and tender."

Snow Vase kissed his palm and looked at him. He was hers, she thought, and leaned forward and kissed him. But she thought of Shulien, and what she had always said about love, and stood up abruptly.

Wei-fang did not know what he had done to cause this.

"I think I should leave,' she said.

He watched her with a strange sense of loss. There was a light within her face, like a candle flame that shone on those around her and gave them warmth and a deep yellow glow. As she moved across the room it seemed the darkness pressed in around him and he longed for her touch.

Snow Vase hesitated at the door and looked back. He thought for a moment that she would pause, but with a last fleeting glimpse, such as a startled deer in the dappled forest shadows might give, she stepped out of his sight, and he took in a deep sigh, put his hand to his head, and closed his eyes.

剑

Snow Vase was pensive that night; even when they had finished sparring, and she had acquitted herself very well indeed; Shulien had spoken to her kindly. "Very good."

"Thank you, teacher."

Snow Vase bowed, sheathed her sword, and walked inside without anymore conversation. She hung her sword on the peg on her wall, and sat down.

Shulien followed her in.

"How should a warrior live?" Snow Vase said suddenly.

Shulien sat down opposite her. "How do you mean?"

"I mean: what code should a warrior live by?"

Shulien sat back. "A warrior should be hard and disciplined and stern and honest."

"Should they deny themselves pleasure?"

"Why?"

Snow Vase did not answer. "You never married."

"No," Shulien said.

"Why not?"

Shulien stopped.

"You say you loved him. Why didn't you marry Mubai?"

Shulien took in a deep breath. "We did not marry," she said, speaking slowly, "because of honor."

"Really?"

The question had an odd effect on her teacher. Shulien clenched her jaw hard, and it seemed to take a great effort to speak. "Yes," she said. The word came out like a strangled gasp. "But I would never have been as fine a warrior. If you want to be a great warrior, then you must do as I have done. Love is a distraction."

Snow Vase looked at Shulien. Children and students knew their elders ways' much better than their elders knew theirs. Snow Vase had spent more time than anyone with Shulien. Her teacher gave off an appearance of calm, like still lake-water, dappled with the reflections of trees and clouds. But there was much hidden under that calm.

"Really?" she repeated.

Shulien paused, and shook her head. "I don't know," she said.

There was a knock on the door. Both women turned to look. Silent Wolf stepped inside. He nodded to Snow Vase first, then pulled a stool out and sat down.

"So," he said.

Shulien looked at him. "So?"

"What shall we do with the sword?"

"We?"

He laughed. "Yes. We."

"Mubai entrusted this sword to Duke Te," she said. "I helped him in this. It is I who should decide what happens to the sword."

Silent Wolf held her gaze for a long time. "I think you are wrong," he said. "It is a matter too serious for any single person to deal with. *We* all helped save it from Hades Dai. I think that means *we* all have a voice in what should happen with the Green Destiny."

Shulien looked from one to the other. "I do not agree," she said. Silent Wolf was staring at her.

"You were not the only one close to Mubai," he said. "I knew him in a way you did not. I was his oath brother. You were never his wife."

Shulien looked stung by these words. She turned away. "I will think on this," she said. The silence deepened. At last she said, "I will listen to your words. But I will decide."

Silent Wolf and Snow Vase looked from one to the other. There was a brief moment and she took it. "If we are to discuss this, then I think we should ask Wei-fang what he thinks as well," Snow Vase said. She spoke carefully. "His fate is closely bound to that of the sword. He carried the sword against our foe."

Her words had weight. The air felt heavy. The silence stretched. Shulien's frown deepened, but at last Silent Wolf nodded. "I think you speak right," he said. "Shulien. We should go to Wei-fang's room, and there we can decide what will happen with the sword."

"I decide," Shulien said. When she turned back to them her face was hard.

"Let us talk first," Silent Wolf said.

30

Wei-fang spent an uncomfortable night. He could not lie on his right side without his shoulder aching, and the wound was itching terribly but he could not scratch it through the bandages. It was three hours after dawn when Sir Te's doctor came. He was a tall, gangly man, whose robes seemed too large for him. He wore heavy glasses with frames of bronze and lenses of ground crystal. He peered over these as he picked up Wei-fang's wrist, placed middle, index and ring finger on it and took the three pulses at the same time, each one representing the heart, the liver and the kidney.

"Hmm!" he said as he let the wrist go. Wei-fang was not sure if this was a good sign or not.

"Let me see," he said as he started peeling away the dark-stained bandages from around his shoulder and under his arm.

"It itches," Wei-fang said.

"Hmm," the doctor said. He was clearly uninterested in the opinions of the patient. His skin had a thick look to it, and his cheeks were deeply pitted with acne scars or the ruin of childhood pox. But his eyes were bright and sharp, and made Wei-fang think of the house rat that sits in the corner and watches and waits. He unwrapped the bandages, carefully peeled the poultice off. The ground-up medicines had formed a damp dark cake which came away with the dressing. Wei-fang looked down. The skin was stained dark and around the wound was pale and puckered. The doctor bent to it, sniffed it and then put his fingers to either side of the wound. Wei-fang gritted his teeth as the doctor squeezed. He held back his groan as pus oozed out, pale and green and with red mixed in as well.

The second time the doctor squeezed Wei-fang looked away and ground out a moan.

The third time seemed unnecessary. Wei-fang stared at the doctor, who was staring at the wound over the top of his glasses.

"Good," the doctor said at last. He dabbed the wound. The pus and blood had stopped. A clear liquid leaked out. The doctor dabbed it away and spoke to the wound, not to Wei-fang.

"Good," he said. "Good."

"It is looking better?"

The doctor glanced at him over the top of his glasses. "Yes," he said. "Much better. The poison is slowly working its way out."

"Is that good?"

"Yes," the doctor said. "Of course."

Wei-fang lay back as the doctor prepared another poultice, sprinkled it with wine, and then cupped it onto his chest and bound it tightly.

"Itching is good," he said. "It is a sign of healing."

He tied the bandages tight, then smiled briefly. "You should eat eggs," he said. "I will speak to Sir Te."

As the doctor gathered up his things Wei-fang flexed his hand into a fist, and the exertion and pain brought sweat to his forehead, which gleamed yellow in the candlelight. His look brightened when Snow Vase stepped inside, but then Shulien and Silent Wolf followed. Their faces were serious.

Shulien was the first to sit down, then Snow Vase and Silent Wolf.

"What?" Wei-fang said.

"We have matters to discuss with you," Shulien said.

Wei-fang looked at their eyes, and saw no hint of what this was about. He looked to Snow Vase, and her gaze was hard to read.

They waited for the doctor to leave, and then Wei-fang saw that Silent Wolf had brought Green Destiny in with him. He set it down on the bed at Wei-fang's feet.

Wei-fang wanted to reach out and touch it. So much had rested on this sword. He had suffered and risked so much for it. It lay innocent as a kitten.

"We need to discuss what we should do with the Green Destiny. It cannot stay here, that is clear," Silent Wolf said. "Sir Te is not his father, and he is not the one to defend this blade and to keep it from the hands of evil. Snow Vase said that you have a right to help decide, as you helped to keep the sword safe." Wei-fang felt strangely responsible now. Strangely mature, sitting like a judge over the future of the Green Destiny. "So," Silent Wolf said. "What shall we do with it?"

Wei-fang felt like all their eyes were on him. "Why don't you take it?" he said.

Silent Wolf looked at the others.

"I think it should be hidden," Shulien said. "I will take it. I will be the guardian. I will disappear and the sword shall go with me."

"But what happens when you die?" Snow Vase said.

"When death is coming, the secret of the sword shall die with me."

Snow Vase shook her head. "Shulien," she said, "I think what we have seen is that the Green Destiny cannot be hidden. That has been tried. It will always draw men to it, and men like Hades Dai will find a way to uncover its location. We cannot break the

sword. We cannot destroy it. It is a sword. That is its nature—
why should we try to go against it?"

"Because it is too dangerous," Shulien said.

"No. It is a sword. No more, no less. I say that we accept it for
what it is."

"So what should we do with it?"

"The power of the Green Destiny lies in the hand that wields
it. The only way of ensuring that the Green Destiny does no evil
is by putting the sword in the hand of one who shall not do evil."

"Who?" Shulien said. "Silent Wolf? You?"

"I say that Silent Wolf should take it," Wei-fang said.

Silent Wolf shook his head.

Snow Vase shook her head in exasperation. "No."

Shulien stood up. "Then who?"

Snow Vase looked at each of them. "Do you remember what
Genghis Khan told his sons? How each of them was an arrow
shaft, easily broken. But when they all stood together, like a
sheath of arrows, then they were unbreakable. Teacher, you think
in ones. You think this is your strength, but I think it has
brought you failure. It has brought you sadness. And it will not
serve the sword."

She saw the look on Shulien's face and spoke quickly. "Why
don't we all take the sword? We four. Together we will be far
stronger than alone. We shall uphold the Code of the Iron Way.
We shall bear the memory of Mubai and Jiaolong. We shall be
as one, and if one of us should be lost, then the others will be
there to carry the memory of the lost one along."

Wei-fang watched Snow Vase in awe and astonishment. The
wisdoms of Silent Wolf and Shulien had failed. They fought
alone. They lived alone. There was a different way.

He felt a thrill as he listened to Snow Vase's words. He could
see it. The four of them, riding into the red glow of legend.

"No," Shulien said. She took the sword and stood up. "No," she said again, more determined this time.

Silent Wolf and the others exchanged glances as Shulien nodded to each of them and walked out.

剑

Snow Vase looked hurt by her teacher's refusal. Silent Wolf stood up and walked to the door, but he did not follow Shulien.

"I liked your idea," Wei-fang said.

"Thank you," she said.

"Silent Wolf," Wei-fang called out. "What do you think?"

Silent Wolf turned and smiled. "I don't know," he said. "Look at me. When I was young I knew exactly what to do, but age has made me wise. I see many solutions, and none of them seem right."

The room grew silent.

"I will talk to her," Silent Wolf said after a while, and walked out.

剑

"How are you?" Snow Vase asked.

"I'm getting better, apparently," Wei-fang said. "The doctor comes twice a day to press and prod. I think he squeezes until he makes me curse. I should just curse when he comes through the door now. Then perhaps he'll leave me alone."

"I should let you rest," she said.

He nodded, but he was disappointed as she went out.

Snow Vase needed to clear her head.

She was angry at Shulien. It was clear to her that her teacher was wrong. She had made the wrong decisions, Snow Vase was sure. She had relied too much on honor, seen virtue in abstinence; mistaken loneliness for virtue.

Snow Vase walked through the palace, barely seeing the people she passed. There were servants, wives, concubines, sons, grandsons. It was full of life and vitality. One generation passed on as new ones were being born. It was so different to the household she had grown up in, which was detached, quiet, excluding.

Her mother had never seen the point of family. She had almost resented her daughter and Snow Vase wasn't sure why. Was it because she was adopted? Was it because she was family, and had claims upon Jiaolong? Was it because her mother loved her, but had spent so long alone that attachment was too hard?

She stopped suddenly. It was the fourth month and the sun was warm, the birds were singing clearly.

The world was bursting with life and opportunity. Snow Vase savored the earth's rich, damp smell. She felt balanced, suspended, poised. So many possibilities stretched before her. The boundaries of her future were still unset, uncertain. She looked out and did not see walls or barriers or hidden places, but wide open plains, vast steppes and deserts, snow-capped mountains.

She turned around and walked quickly back toward Weifang's yard.

She found him standing in the doorway. He wore a simple gown, a jacket thrown over his shoulders, his arm in a sling. He was leaning against the doorpost, looking out on the day. The trees had a light green light around them, as the first buds were growing.

剑

"I thought you were resting," Snow Vase said.

"I am," he said. "Smelling the earth. Seeing the world. These things bring healing."

She walked toward him. It was good to see him standing in the daylight. Color was returning to his skin. She stopped before him, put up a hand to his cheek, and then kissed him.

His lips were soft, his stubble prickled her cheek, she pressed her lips to his, and then let his head go.

He looked at her. "Well," he said.

"What?"

"You surprised me."

"Really?"

"Yes."

She put her hand up and pulled him down again, and this time he put his good arm around her shoulders and pulled her close. He kissed her lips, inhaled the smell of her, and as he did so her lips parted.

They stood kissing for a long time, pressing their bodies against each other.

She pulled away.

"We should go inside," she said.

He took her hand, shut the door behind her, and still kissing, they moved, slow step by slow step toward the bed.

At the bed they stopped. His hand slid down her back. She was young and firm and beautiful. One of her hands was around his neck, the other held his back. She tugged at his jacket, pulling it off his shoulders.

"Does it hurt?" she said, meaning his arm.

"No," he breathed, as his jacket fell to the floor.

She started unbuttoning his gown as they kept kissing, then

she took his hand and put it inside her gown, onto her breast, and she heard him groan.

"I thought Shulien said a great warrior should not take lovers," he said.

She whispered back at him, "I do not think I want to be a great warrior."

Layer by layer they stripped each other naked. In the world around them swallows were making their nests, the first cicadas were beginning to call out, and high overhead honking geese were returning north in wide vees. But they were oblivious as she lay back on the bed, and opened her legs, and he lay down between them.

31

Shulien had been pacing the floor like a chained leopard. Silent Wolf had taken his time, but now he sat on her bed, legs drawn up and folded under him. The Green Destiny lay on the bed next to him. He had not spoken a word since he had come into the room, but she could tell what he was thinking.

She continued to pace back and forth. She was going to wear a hole into the carpet at this rate, and still she felt chained. She did not know why he was here, staring at her.

"You cannot tell me what to do. You have no power over me. We may have been betrothed, but we were never married," she said. She turned and glared at him, but he was not looking at her, but at the sword. "Stop looking at the damned sword," she said. "I am talking to you!"

He looked up at her. His eyes were hard and dark and unfathomable. She wanted a sign from him, but he was as flat as the reflection in the mirrored water.

"Why did you come here?" she said.

"You needed help."

"I did not."

"You would have died in the woods if I had not come."

There was a pause. "I might have escaped. You never gave me

the chance." There was another pause. She walked slower now. At last she stopped. "You think I am wrong."

He tilted his head slightly. He irritated her so much she could hardly contain herself. Mubai would not have behaved like this, she thought, and the answer came quick. *But he is dead.* And another, sharper voice hissed: *And when he was alive you would not marry him.*

She bit back recriminations.

"How can we trust them?" she said.

Silent Wolf looked back down again at the sword, but this time he spoke. "There is little certain for any of us on the Iron Way," he said. "What we think is solid, crumbles; what we think is weak grows strong. That is what we learned as children. What is strong is weak, what is soft is strong. It is the fundamental truth of fighting." He paused for what seemed an age to Shulien. She could feel her irritation rising. "But I think you ask the wrong questions, and in doing so find the wrong answers."

She sat down. "What do you mean?"

"The question is not can we trust them, but why shouldn't we trust them."

"Good," she said. "Then I have the answer to that. We should not trust them because they stole the sword."

"And why did they steal the sword?"

"To kill Hades Dai."

"A good reason, don't you think?"

"But they failed."

"Is failure a sin? You failed to save Mubai. I failed to kill Hades Dai twenty years before. We all fail, but perhaps we should not be judged by what we have tried to do and not succeeded at, but by the things we have set out to do. They failed to kill Hades Dai, but they succeeded in stealing it from us, and Hades Dai never got the sword."

"But *we* had to be there," she said.

"Is that what you are angry about?"

She looked at him, and felt something hard and knotted within her open, like an old nut, and the seed fall out. "Maybe," she said, but her voice had softened.

She came and sat down on the bed near him. Green Destiny lay between them. She put out a hand and touched it, almost like touching a friend's arm. She had lived in fear that she would be called back to protect Green Destiny, and her fears had come true, and here she was, having passed through her fears, like a curtain, finding daylight on the other side.

What was it you were frightened of? she asked herself.

Was it not being dragged out of retirement and isolation?

She knew the answer. It was living without Mubai all this time but still having to sort out the problems he left behind. No, she thought, and paused to let the true answer come to her. She feared loss. She feared letting others get as close as Mubai had been, and losing them as she had lost him.

Silent Wolf looked at Shulien as she touched the sword with her fingers and ran them gently along the snakeskin sheath. The scales were worn almost smooth with age, especially where it had rubbed as men carried it on their backs. Since the day it had been forged. Hundreds of years. A thousand and more years.

"Do you want to know what I think?" he said.

Shulien looked up and he saw that her eyes were wet with tears.

"We have tried to hide this thing, and we have failed. The Green Destiny is older than all of us. It has great powers, if used for good. It should be taken out into the world to battle evil and ignorance and fear. It should be borne by great warriors. Just think what you or I, or Mubai even, could have done in the last twenty years with that sword. I tell you this because I know what it is to be hidden. I know what it is to disappear from the world, and even though I thought I was doing good, I achieved nothing. You and Mubai did not marry. I was not there to save Mubai, as I would have been. We were oath brothers, remember. We were as close as reeds in a basket. I wept when I heard that he had died. That you had let him die when I left him to your care."

Shulien looked imploringly at the man she had once been betrothed to.

"I know those words hurt," he said. "But it was how I felt. Sometimes we feel things that are not justified. That is what is happening here, with you, with Snow Vase and with Wei-fang."

Shulien looked down. "So we give it to them?"

"No. I did not say that."

"Then what?"

"How good is Snow Vase?"

"She is very good."

"Better than you?"

"Not yet, but soon, perhaps."

"And Wei-fang?"

Shulien frowned. "He is untrained. He is wild. He is undisciplined."

"Do you think he can be trained?"

Shulien considered. "He seems like he would make a good student."

"Then why don't we take the sword and ride out with them? They can be our pupils."

Shulien puffed out her cheeks. "Really?"

"What better way of teaching them?"

Shulien sat for a long time, trying to think of reasons why they should not do what Silent Wolf had suggested.

But all she could think of were reasons to support him.

At last she turned to him, and said, "I agree."

"Good."

"Shall we go and tell them?"

剑

Silent Wolf and Shulien walked side by side toward the courtyard where Wei-fang was resting. The early summer sun was bright, and they passed two servants carrying Sir Te's caged songbirds on the end of long poles to the bamboo garden. They stared at the two warriors with wide-eyed admiration, and stood well to the side to let them pass.

It was a short walk to Wei-fang's courtyard. The gates were ajar; Shulien pushed the door open and stepped over the threshold.

Silent Wolf came with her. They walked up toward the central hall. It was three steps up to the doorway. The door windows had not yet had their winter paper removed; this would not be done until the full heat of summer had come, but there were many tears and holes and through these came an unmistakable sound.

Shulien stopped and looked at Silent Wolf. She lifted a fist to knock on the door, but he reached out and caught it, and put his finger to his lips: shhh!

"They're in bed together," she whispered.

He pulled her back down the steps.

"They're sleeping together," she said again as he bundled her out of the gate and let it close behind them.

"He is bedding my student," she said, once they were safely on the other side of the wall.

"I think she is bedding him back," he said.

Shulien paused. She did not know where to start. "Why are you smiling?" she said.

"Maybe we should come back later."

"You still want to ride with them?"

"Why not?"

"Because!" she said. "Did you hear them?"

Silent Wolf laughed. "Do not be so angry," he said. "It sounded to me like they were having fun."

剑

It was evening before Snow Vase pushed Wei-fang back.

"I can't," she said. "I'm a little sore."

He looked upset, but she lay and kissed his mouth. "You can't be ready again,"

"I can," he said.

She laughed again. "Save it for later," she said.

Wei-fang yawned and stretched, and stood up. He was broad-chested, slender-hipped and his long body was smooth and tanned and honed. His buttocks were full and firm and dimpled. She loved the silhouette of him as he strode toward the papered windows.

He pulled the door open, and an angle of sunlight fell through the door, illuminating his flanks with a thin golden light.

Even with the arm in a sling, there was a lean beauty about him. She drank the sight of him in. He had been kind and gentle too, and hard when he needed.

She moved over to where he stood and put her arms around him, and felt him, skin to skin. She had never held anyone so close. Had never been so close, had never shared so much, had never opened herself to another soul. Had never surrendered without a fight.

Together they looked out into their courtyard. It was little changed from when they had stood there earlier that day. The cherry tree still stood, the gate was shut, the shadows had lengthened as the sun westered. The world was little changed, but they had done so irrevocably.

Snow Vase did not feel alone anymore. She carried his seed within her, and she pressed her naked body close to his. What more could she want? she thought, and kissed him again.

"I'm hungry," she said. "Should we ask for our dinner to be brought here?"

He squeezed her with his good arm. "Yes," he said.

剑

Shulien waited for Snow Vase to come back to her room.

She was ready with stern looks, disapproving airs, but Snow Vase did not come. The shadows lengthened, the sun set, and the darkness deepened.

Why am I always waiting for others? Shulien asked herself, and decided not to sit at home. She may as well have been a concubine for all the waiting for others she did, she thought.

She walked to Silent Wolf's hall, but his yard was dark, his room was empty.

She went to Sir Te's courtyard, and heard Sir Te's wife singing. She fancied herself an opera singer. She doubted that Silent Wolf was enjoying an evening of Sir Te's wife's musical talents.

So where could he be? she wondered.

She went back to her own courtyard, and her lone lamp burned in her room.

She checked Silent Wolf's hall again, and at last she walked to Wei-fang's hall.

As she approached she could hear laughter. There was a particular note to the sound. She stopped. It had been a long time since she had heard joy. The joy of people sitting together: talking, drinking, laughing.

She came closer. She walked silently, as if she were stalking an enemy.

There was silence and then laughter again. Wei-fang's voice was unmistakable. Snow Vase was there as well, but there was a third voice too.

Shulien stood at the gate and peered through the crack.

How silly she was, a voice in her head told her, standing alone in the dark, peering through a crack at another's evening party. She pushed the gate open and stepped inside.

Silent Wolf, Wei-fang and Snow Vase were sitting around a table. The doors of their hall were thrown back, and a pair of yellow lanterns hung from the beams. They threw a gentle yellow candlelight on all their faces as they stopped and looked up, and saw her and smiled.

Snow Vase was the first to stand. "Teacher," she said. "Come! Sit! Join us."

All of Shulien's prurience fell from her. She found herself smiling and nodding.

"Thank you," she said. "I will."

EPILOGUE

Sir Te sat in a magnificent gown of thick red silk, embroidered with flowers, as he presided over a great feast for the four warriors, and afterwards, his wife sang for them the concubine's soliloquy from the opera *Ba Wang Bie Ji*.

The four fighters had all been provided with clothes appropriate for the occasion. Silent Wolf wore a long black gown. Shulien was dressed in a modest dress of deep gray wool. The younger fighters were dressed in brighter colors: Wei-fang looked smart in a cream suit of the finest cotton, with slippers sown by Sir Te's wife herself, while Snow Vase wore a red jacket with high collars, a little rouge on her pale cheeks, and in her piled black hair her mother's pin with the blue grasshopper crouched at the end.

When the soliloquy ended Wei-fang showed his appreciation by engaging the lady in conversation. "Very fine," he said, and went on at some length, covering the key points of the song, and noting how well Sir Te's wife had managed.

By the end the hostess's plump cheeks were red and she waved her hands in a modest gesture. "No, no," she said. "Too kind. Really!"

Snow Vase watched Wei-fang charm the sir's wife, and lifted her sleeves to hide her smile.

At last they got down to business.

"So you are leaving?" Sir Te said.

He looked at each of the fighters in turn, and they all bowed.

"And Shulien tells me that you are determined to go together. With the sword."

"That is right," Snow Vase said. "We shall all take the sword. How long our paths shall remain entwined we cannot say, but we have all resolved to set out together. If I had my choice, I would say that the first place we will go to is the West Lotus Temple. There are ghosts there that I think we all have to put to rest."

She looked at Wei-fang and caught his eye.

At the same time Shulien and Silent Wolf exchanged looks as well. Release dragons back into the sea, the proverb went, let tigers go back to the mountains.

剑

Next morning, dawn was just breaking when Old Horse pushed the stable gates open. The drum tower struck the first hour of the day.

The gates of the Forbidden City, Tiananmen, and the three great gates in the south walls of the city, the three in the west, the three in the east, and the two in the north were thrown open for the daily business of the great city again. Ministers and scholars hurried into the Forbidden City to petition the Emperor. Scholars, merchants, farmers, traders and warriors passed into and out of the city, and as the first of the morning traffic began to thicken, Shulien, Silent Wolf, Snow Vase and Wei-fang rode side by side through the streets. Sir Te had left them with kind words, offering a warm welcome should they ever return, and he gave them all gifts such as they could take with them, as well as much silver, in the shape of ingots, as they could carry safely.

"Sometimes silver smooths the path for travelers," he said, "even for those who are as fearless as yourselves."

They were dressed in their plain travel clothes as they passed through the west gate just before a long camel caravan entered.

The guards did not know them, who they were, or what they had done. But they stopped and watched the four horsemen canter off, the morning sun rising behind them.

One of them carried a sword on his back, the hilt of which flashed green in the sunlight.

They slowly diminished in size as the distance between them lengthened, and then when the guards looked up, the four horsemen had dropped out of sight, and only the memory of their faces, their air of confidence, remained.

剑

As they paused Shulien looked out onto the vast green land that stretched out before them. It was a new world she was riding into, she thought. A new future, where much was unsure.

The past was behind her, like a city that a traveler lingers in for a while, and then leaves behind. Before them was West Lotus Temple, and a chance to make peace with Jiaolong, and her ghost.

She thought of the young girl who had come to Duke Te's house all those years ago, with Jade Fox. They had bound their lives and deaths to Green Destiny. The sword gathered lives and great tales to it. Shulien wondered how her story would end.

She had once wanted nothing more than to disappear from the world and memory, but she had been found and remembered, and now she wondered why she had abandoned the world when there were still many springs to enjoy, many summers to savor, the last autumn she would see: glorious in its skirts of orange and yellow; and the last gentle silence of winter.

Silent Wolf rode beside her, jacket thrown loosely over his shoulders. She was comforted by his presence. She did not need to turn to see him, she knew he was watching her. She turned and saw Snow Vase and Wei-fang sharing a joke. There was a tender beauty in Snow Vase's eyes as she gazed up at her lover's face as he talked.

Her student had taught her much, Shulien thought.

Snow Vase had found a different path. She was neither like Shulien, nor like Jiaolong. Perhaps the Iron Way would lead her where she wished.

Joy was rare, Shulien thought, but perhaps Snow Vase and Wei-fang had found it together. She hoped so. The road narrowed, and Snow Vase and Wei-fang's horses took the lead, and Shulien and Silent Wolf's horses fell in behind.

The sun was still rising at their backs. Noon was not far off. Now, that morning, sunset still seemed a long way away.

Justin Hill has lived and worked in China since 1992. His novel *The Drink and Dream Teahouse*, a portrait of small-town China, won the Geoffrey Faber Memorial Prize and a Betty Trask Award and was a Washington Post Book of the Year in 2001. It was banned within the People's Republic of China.

Hill's translations of Chinese poetry have been published in *Modern Poetry in Translation*, *Asian Literary Review*, and *Asian Cha*. His work on the poems of Tang Dynasty poetess Yu Xuanji led to her reimagined life in the novel *Passing Under Heaven*, which was shortlisted for the Encore Award and awarded the 2006 Somerset Maugham Award.

The *Independent on Sunday* listed Hill as one of its Top Twenty Young British writers. He currently lives in Hong Kong and is an assistant professor at the City University of Hong Kong, where he teaches creative writing. Learn more at www.justinhillauthor.com.

"Justin Hill knows China inside out. Every sentence is filled with knowledge, affection and a poignant sense of loss."
—*Washington Post*

Wang Dulu is considered one of the four greatest *wuxia* (literally "martial hero") writers of modern China. His writing is known for its fresh, complex renderings of women and warriors. He reconceived the archetypes of the genre, moving beyond formulaic chivalry and romance, and his original voice and enduring legacy have thrilled writers, readers, and audiences around the world.

Wang was born into a poor Manchu Banner family in Beijing in 1909. When Wang was twelve, his father passed away. As the eldest son, he then had to leave school to support his family. While working as a newspaper editor, Wang began to write martial arts romances. But he was not interested in writing about bloody and ruthless killings; instead, he focused on his characters' development—their emotions, friendships, alliances, and passions. Wang had great sympathy for women who suffered cruel oppression by Chinese society and its feudal system, and his novels featured many strong female characters who battled alongside and against the men. Most of his stories featured tragic endings. Another unique characteristic of Wang's work is that in many of his novels he described vivid and detailed Beijing culture, especially bannermen's lives.

Like Dickens and Dumas, Wang's tales were originally serialized in newspapers and were hugely popular. Many of his writings were bound together as novels, the best known of which, *Crouching Tiger, Hidden Dragon* (part of his five-part epic series known as the *Crane-Iron Pentalogy*), was adapted by Ang Lee for his Academy Award–winning film in 2000. *Crouching Tiger, Hidden Dragon: Sword of Destiny* by Justin Hill is based primarily on *Iron Knight, Silver Vase*, the fifth and final book of the *Crane Iron* series.

From 1938 to 1949 Wang published dozens of books. In 1949 he retired from writing and became a high school

Chinese teacher. Though his works remained popular with Chinese communities overseas, they were not available in mainland China until the 1980s, when they were republished with the help of his widow, Li Danquan, and many friends. No official English-language translations of his novels exist, but they are immensely popular in his homeland.

Wang lived through many periods of political upheaval, including Mao Zedong's Cultural Revolution, when Wang, his wife, and many writers, teachers, and students were deployed to the countryside. He died in 1977 and was survived by his wife and two children.